THE HIDEAWAY L

Hi...
Martin Cole—
R...
T...
Ariana

Hidden Agenda
Alejandro Delgado—Eve Blackwell—Matthew Sterling
Christopher Delgado
Sara Sterling

Vows
Joshua Kirkland—Vanessa Blanchard
Emily
Michael

Heaven Sent
David Cole—Serena Morris
Gabriel
Alexandra
Ana and Jason

Harvest Moon
Oscar Spencer—Regina Cole—Aaron Spencer
Clayborne
Eden

Just Before Dawn
Salem Lassiter—Sara Sterling
Isaiah
Eve and Nona

Private Passions
Christopher Delgado—Emily Kirkland
Alejandro II
Esperanza
Mateo

No Compromise
Michael Kirkland—Jolene Walker
Reresa
Joshua

Homecoming
Tyler Cole—Dana Nichols
Martin II

Other books by Rochelle Alers

HOMECOMING

Rochelle Alers

ARABESQUE

★BET

BOOKS™

BET Publications, LLC
http://www.bet.com
http://www.arabesquebooks.com

Do not forget to do good and be generous, for with such sacrifices God is well pleased.

Hebrews 13:16

Prologue

The sound of voices raised in anger forced Dana Nichols to pull the handmade quilt over her head. However, it still did not muffle the hateful, virulent words her mother and father hurled at each other.

Before turning out the lamp on the bedside table, Dana did what she'd done for the past three months: she prayed—prayed for the shouting and accusations to stop and that her parents would soon settle their differences.

She loved her mother and father, wanting the three of them to live like a normal family. However, despite her tender years, she knew they would never be a normal family again. Not as long as Mommy continued to do the things Daddy said she did with other men.

"Stop lying to me, Alicia!" Harry Nichols's accusation bounced off the walls in the room across from his daughter's. "How can you still do it now that I have proof? Don't you have any shame?"

"Do what, Harry?" Alicia countered, her voice lowering seductively.

"Tramp around."

"Are you calling me a tramp? Are you calling the mother of your child a tramp?" Her tone indicated her husband had wounded her deeply.

"You should be ashamed to call yourself a mother."

"How . . . how dare you!"

"I dare, Alicia. I dare because I love Dana. I'm the one who's concerned about her well-being, not you."

"I'm concerned about her, too."

"Stop lying to me and yourself. I can't believe you've come home with another man's scent between your legs. At least you could've taken a bath before coming to my bed. But that doesn't matter anymore. I've had enough of the lies and your sordid behavior."

Ten-year-old Dana hadn't known what sordid meant until she'd looked it up in the dictionary. What was it her mother was doing that was so dirty and filthy? What had her father meant about another man's scent on her mother's legs?

Alicia Sutton-Nichols's seductive voice punctuated the swollen silence that ensued. "Are you threatening me, Dr. Nichols?"

"No, I'm not." Harry's voice was soft, calmer. "I'm going to divorce you, Alicia, and give you everything you've ever wanted since the first time you set out to seduce me. You can have this house and every stick of furniture in it. I'm also going to give you enough money to take you into old age. But what I will not give you is my daughter."

Alicia laughed, the sound maniacal. "No, I know you've gone and lost your mind, Harry Nichols. Do you actually think I'm going to hand my child over to you like a sack of groceries you've paid for?"

"You don't have a choice," he countered. "You have the morals of an alley cat in heat and the reputation of a fifty-cent whore, so no judge within fifty miles of Hillsboro will ever award you custody of Dana. You're unfit—as a wife *and* a mother."

The sound of flesh hitting flesh resounded in the room like the crack of a rifle. "You sneaky, conniving bastard. I'll never let you take my child from me."

"You've never been more wrong in your life, Alicia." Harry's voice was dangerously soft and ominous. "And if you fight me for Dana, I swear I will destroy you."

Dana burrowed deeper under the quilt, crying softly as her favorite psalm spilled from her trembling lips. "The Lord is my shepherd, I shall not want. He makest me to lie down in green pastures. He leadest me beside still waters . . ." The remaining verses whispered inside her head.

She finished the prayer, then repeated it over and over, unaware of the moisture soaking the pillow beneath her head.

Heavy footsteps were muffled in the thick pile of carpeting running the length of the hallway outside the bedrooms, the footsteps fading as Harry descended the staircase. The next sound was the slam of a solid door, followed by a car's engine merging with the cacophony of nocturnal life serenading the Mississippi countryside.

Uncovering her head, she lay motionless, listening to the sound of her own heart pumping wildly in her chest. The fighting had stopped; it had ended—at least for now.

Wiping the back of her hand over her moist cheeks, she closed her eyes in the protective darkness of her bedroom. It took a while, but she was finally able to fall asleep.

Dana stirred once before the sun rose to herald the beginning of a new day. Another sound had disturbed her restless slumber. It was the rhythmic slamming of a shutter against the side of the house. A rising breeze meant cooler weather and hopefully a break in the heat wave that had held Mississippi and the Deep South in its brutal grip for more than six weeks. Daddy had promised her he was going to get a carpenter in to repair the broken shutter, but so far he hadn't.

Rolling over, she pressed her nose into her pillow, waiting for sleep to claim her again. She did not have to wait long. Within minutes she had forgotten the sound of her parents' angry voices as soft snores escaped her parted lips.

What Dana Nichols did not know was that it would be the last night she would ever sleep under a roof with Harry *and* Alicia Nichols.

One

The day dawned as it had for the past ten weeks—early morning temperatures in the low eighties, a brilliant cloudless sky, and a continuing drought.

The earth that had been rich Mississippi Delta topsoil was bone-dry; water in small brooks and streams had evaporated, revealing their cracked beds, and the once-green shoots from spring plantings lay on the parched ground in seared repose.

The populace of the region looked to the heavens and prayed. The citizenry of Hillsboro, Mississippi, was no exception. They, too, prayed for rain, but for the first time in more than two months they had something else to talk about other than the weather.

The gossip had begun with Johnnie Mack, the undertaker, who told Reverend Wingate, the pastor of Mt. Nebo Baptist Church, who in turn informed Deacon Enright that Dr. Harry and Alicia Nichols's daughter Dana had returned to Hillsboro to bury her maternal grandmother.

Two decades ago Georgia Sutton had taken her granddaughter north to live with her sister following the tragic deaths of Dana's parents. Even now, twenty-two years later, longtime residents still whispered about how Harry Nichols had murdered his young beautiful wife, and hours after he'd claimed he'd discovered her

lifeless body, had set fire to his home to cover up the
evidence of his heinous transgression. He'd been
found guilty of the crime and sentenced to a term of
life in prison. Harry's scandalous criminal act was com-
pounded when he subsequently took his own life. His
suicide had coincided with his daughter's eleventh
birthday.

A stooped-shouldered figure stood off to the side in
Hillsboro's colored-only cemetery, waiting. Eugene Payton watched Dana Nichols as she stood at a freshly
covered grave, head bowed, hands clasping a single
red rose, and her lips moving silently.

He and Dana were not alone in the cemetery. A few
of Hillsboro's curious, non-believers, and gossipmong-
ers had come with the pretense of placing flowers or
saying prayers at the graves of their deceased family
members.

Eugene was certain many were as shocked he was
when he saw Dana Alicia Nichols for the first time in
more than twenty years. Her resemblance to her late
mother was uncanny. Only those who had viewed Alicia
up close would've noticed the minute difference in the
two women: Dana had a tiny mole high on her right
cheekbone.

Not only did Dana look exactly like her murdered
mother, but she had also inherited the woman's sultry
voice. The only difference was their speech patterns.
Alicia had spoken with the slow cadence that had come
from spending all of her life in the Deep South, while
Dana had the flatter, more nasal inflection of upstate
New York.

Despite his age and declining eyesight, he'd recognized her immediately when she came through the arrival gate at the Greenville Municipal Airport. She

hadn't flown to Mississippi with a carry-on and garments bag, but with a large Pullman case and two other smaller pieces of luggage. As soon as he spied her coming toward him, Eugene knew Dana hadn't come back to Hillsboro, Mississippi, to stay a week. She had come stay a while. She subsequently told him that she planned to remain in Hillsboro as long as it took for her to discover the truth behind her parents' long-ago murder/suicide and at last clear her family's name.

Dana finished all of the prayers she'd been taught as a child. She opened her eyes behind the lenses of her sunglasses. Her grandmother would've been proud that she hadn't forgotten the prayers she had taught her. It wasn't that Georgia Sutton was an overtly religious woman, because she wasn't. She'd informed her granddaughter, however, that she was a spiritual person.

Georgia had stopped attending services at Hillsboro's Mt. Nebo Baptist Church, because the church elders had debated for two days whether they would grant Georgia permission to have Alicia's funeral at the church, which had prompted the older woman to have a graveside-only observance. Generations of Hillsboro Suttons had attended the historic church, but the tradition had ended with Georgia. She preferred staying home Sunday mornings, listening to church services on her radio, or viewing them on television. No one ever heard her speak a disparaging word about Mt. Nebo or its pastor. It was as if she'd forgotten their existence.

Bending at the knees, Dana placed the single rose on Georgia Rose Sutton's grave. Georgia's name had been carved into a headstone years before, but now a recent date had been added. Arrangements were made before Dana was born that Georgia would be buried in the same plot as her husband.

"Take care, Grandma," she whispered. "Tell Mama, Daddy, and Grandpa I said hello."

Three red roses lay on an adjacent plot with the names of Alicia and Harry Nichols carved into a pale pink limestone headstone. Dana had placed one rose for her mother and one for her father on the grave. The third flower had come from a stranger. Every day of every year since the week following Alicia's burial, the cemetery's caretaker had placed a single flower on the grave. Sworn to secrecy, the man had never divulged who had paid him to place the flower on the controversial woman's tombstone. The ritual was halted once—when Harry was buried in the same plot as his murdered wife—but resumed a month later.

Dana turned and smiled at Eugene Payton. The retired attorney had been more than gracious to her since her return. He'd offered the hospitality of his spacious home, but she'd declined, preferring instead to stay at the small house that had belonged to her grandparents.

Closing the distance between them, she curved her arm through his, as much for comfort as to support the older man, accompanying him out of the cemetery to where he'd parked his car.

"I want to thank you for everything, Mr. Payton."

He patted her hand in a comforting gesture. "There's no need to thank me, child. Your grandmother was my friend, and I promised her I would take care of you if anything happened to her."

Dana covered his hand with hers. "And you've kept your promise."

She stole a look at his profile. His once fair skin now resembled yellowed parchment. A profusion of age spots added more color to his angular face. The epitome of an aging Southern black gentleman, Eugene still wore a collar, tie, and hat regardless of the temperature. Today it was a light blue seersucker suit, tie, white shirt, and a soft Panama straw hat. He had affected the style of turning down the brim on his hat, which afforded him a rakish look that hadn't faded despite his age.

He gave Dana a comforting smile. "I'll give you a few days for yourself, then I'll call and come over to meet with you. There is the matter of your grandmother's last will and testament and a few other legal documents that will require your signature."

Nodding, she smiled. "Thank you."

Lately, it was as if they were the only two words in her vocabulary. She was glad to have a few days to herself. Since the fateful telephone call, she hadn't had more than four hours of uninterrupted sleep. Within hours, she'd informed the owner of the two-family house where she rented an apartment that she had to leave for Mississippi. She'd paid her rent four months in advance, while forwarding her mail and telephone calls to her grandmother's address and number. She'd requested and was granted an emergency leave from her employer at the *Carrollton Chronicle,* a weekly with a total circulation of less than twelve hundred. The *Chronicle* had earned a place in publishing annals when it won a Pulitzer for its exposé of abuses at a foster home for adolescent girls in nearby Utica.

The abuses were as shocking as those involved—several employees at the state-funded facility were related to elected officials in the New York State Senate and Assembly. Dana had gone undercover as a counselor with a detective from the Utica Police Department's Sex Crimes Unit, and for seven months gathered enough evidence to send several involved to jail for lengthy sentences. The ripple effect was felt in Albany after three elected officials had resigned under a cloud of suspicion.

Dana was promoted to associate editor and given a generous salary increase. But she had left the *Chronicle* and everything familiar behind to return to Mississippi.

She had left Hillsboro at the age of eleven, returning for the first time at thirty-three, and now with the death of her grandmother, there was nothing left connecting her to her place of birth except rumors of scandal, adultery, murder, arson, and suicide.

The set of her delicate jaw and the look of determination in her amber-colored eyes were something many in Hillsboro would have been familiar with. It was the same look Alicia Sutton had employed once she had set out to seduce the man she wanted to marry and father her children.

Dr. Tyler Cole had caught snippets of gossip about a family named Nichols from his patients at the Hillsboro Women's Health Clinic. He had relocated to Mississippi as a Johns Hopkins University Medical-College-trained obstetrician-gynecologist to participate in a government-sponsored research study targeting infant-mortality rates.

The United States Department of Health and Human Services had documented and identified Hillsboro, Mississippi, as having one of the highest rates in the country. He'd accepted the assignment to offer quality prenatal care to below-poverty-level women with the proviso that he live in Hillsboro for five years. It would be the first time since he'd become a doctor that he would spend more than three consecutive years in one city. At forty-one years of age, he was ready to put down roots and call a place home.

Home.

A slow smile deepened matching dimples in his sun-tanned cheeks. He hadn't called a city or state home in twenty-three years—not since he'd left Fort Lauderdale, Florida, at eighteen for premed studies. He'd become a nomad, moving from city to city whenever he was recruited for a new study. His name and celebrated reputation had become synonymous with medical research.

However, it wasn't smal- town gossip that garnered his attention, but pregnant women receiving adequate prenatal care as a requisite to delivering a health baby.

The hot morning sun beat down on Tyler's exposed arms, as he berated himself for taking the early morning walk. A layer of moisture coated his exposed flesh. He was Southern-born and bred, having grown up in central Florida, but never in his life had he ever experienced the intense heat holding the inhabitants of the Delta hostage in a savage grip from which there appeared no immediate escape.

What he'd seen of Hillsboro, he liked. It was small, its inhabitants were friendly, and the pace was slow enough to lend it a laid-back ambiance. What he liked most was that it was wholly Southern in character, because his Southern roots ran deep: he had relatives whose families had been native Floridians for four generations.

The house he'd commissioned an architectural firm to design was now complete. It was reminiscent of an historic Mississippi mansion. A pillared front, low-pitched roof, recessed entry, and intricate railings identified the structure as true Southern-style Greek Revival.

He'd moved to Hillsboro last August, and it was now the first week in June and he'd lived in his house for two weeks. The contracting crew had put the final touches on painting the exterior a week before, while the landscaper had completed the gardens his older sister, Regina Spencer, had designed for him.

Tyler had been anxious to move in because he'd been living in a tiny one-bedroom cottage behind a bed-and-breakfast for nine months. Several times a week he took his breakfast at the B&B, but had made it a practice to prepare his own dinner in the cottage's tiny utility kitchen. After working an average of ten hours a day, six days a week, he coveted his privacy.

Coming over a slight rise now, he spied the two-story plantation house gleaming whitely in the brilliant sun. Slowing his pace, he made his way across a path of rose-pink bricks laid out in a herringbone pattern. Taking long strides, he mounted three steps to a solid oak door painted a distinctive sapphire blue that matched the shutters framing the windows. Wiping his feet on a mat, he unlocked the front door at the same time the cell phone clipped to the waistband of his jeans chimed softly.

A slight frown lined his smooth forehead. The only time his phone rang that early was when his service called him. And that usually meant a summons to the county hospital for the delivery of a baby.

Slipping the phone off his waist, he stared at the numbers showing on the display, his frown fading. The area code and number were familiar. Pressing the TALK button, he said softly, "Yes?"

A husky feminine voice came through the earpiece. "Have you deleted hello from your vocabulary?"

"Of course not, Mom. What do I owe the honor of hearing your mellifluous voice so early in the morning?" It was five A.M. Central Time. He could always identify his mother's sultry voice.

"I just hung up with Arianna. She and Silah have decided to move to the States."

Tyler smiled. His youngest sister had finally married

her live-in Moroccan-born dress-designer boyfriend earlier in the year.

"When?"

"She says she wants her baby born on American soil."

His smile was dazzling. "She's pregnant?"

"Yes. She found out last week. At thirty-seven, she's a little anxious about the baby."

"Even though she's now in the high-risk category, she shouldn't worry too much."

"That's what I told her," Parris Cole said. "But I didn't try to dissuade her from coming back home. Just for once I'd like one of my grandchildren to be born in the United States." Her eldest daughter, Regina Cole Spencer, lived in Bahia, Brazil, and although Regina's son and daughter had elected to come to the States for their higher education, Parris still had not gotten to see them grow up.

"Have they decided where they're going to live?"

"I've offered them the house in Fort Lauderdale. Your father couldn't understand why I refused to let him sell that house until now. Arianna was ecstatic when I told her she could have the property."

Martin and Parris Cole had relocated to West Palm Beach, where they'd taken up permanent residence at the Cole family ancestral estate to care for Martin's 101–year-old mother.

"At least she's coming home to something familiar."

Tyler loved the house where he'd grown up with his two sisters. The sprawling beachfront property was airy, always filled with brilliant Florida sunshine, and exquisitely decorated by Parris Simmons-Cole. He'd lost count of the number of times he'd begun his day with a swim in the Atlantic Ocean. An Olympic gold medal winner, Arianna Cole-Kadir had preferred swimming in the ocean to the family's pool.

"You're right, Tyler," Parris continued. "After Arianna and Silah are settled in, I'm going to throw a little something to welcome her home."

"Let me know when it is, Mom, and I'll be there. It's going to be exciting to have another new baby in the family."

Parris's smoky laugh floated through the earpiece. "At least for your father and me. It's been twenty years since we've had a grandchild. Speaking of grandchildren, have you found that special someone, Tyler?"

His smile faded. "No, Mother."

"Don't you dare *Mother* me, Tyler Simmons Cole. I don't intend to go to my grave worrying about you spending the rest of your life as a lonely old man."

"I'm not old," he countered, his soft voice hardening slightly. *And I'm not lonely,* he added silently.

"You're forty-one, Tyler. It's time you settled down."

He rolled his eyes, even though he knew his mother couldn't see him. It was always the same argument. His mother wanted him married.

"Dad was forty when he married you," Tyler said.

"Your father and I had had a child when we married. And if circumstances had been different, we would've married ten years before. We had an excuse. What's yours?"

"I don't have one and I don't intend to make up one. When I find that special woman, then I'll gladly give up my bachelor status."

Parris emitted a delicate snort. "You'll find her."

"Do you want to make a bet?" he teased.

"Yes. I get to name your firstborn."

"You're on." His smile was back in place.

Even if his mother wagered one-half her personal wealth, she still would probably come up a loser. Unlike his sisters, he did not want to marry. He loved medicine, finding it a jealous mistress. He wasn't a monk, but there also hadn't been a lot of women in his past. Most of them had realized that even though they were willing to compete with another woman, there was no way they could compete with his profession. But *if* he did find that special woman, then he would be forced to reassess his priorities. Promising his mother he would call her more often, Tyler ended the call.

Stepping into the expansive entryway, he stared up at the recently hung light fixture as lit filtered golden light onto the parquet floor, which was laid out in the same herringbone design as the path leading up to the house. Smiling, he removed his sunglasses. His interior-designer mother's taste was impeccable. Parris had selected the light fixtures, patterns for the wallpaper, window treatments, rugs, and most of the furnishings.

Once he'd notified his family that he was going to build his first home, his mother and sister had conferred with each other long-distance, offering their professional services to the confirmed bachelor. He'd agreed with all their suggestions and recommendations. His sole focus was offering pregnant women adequate prenatal care, not decorating.

A mechanical engineer had divided the house into four heating and cooling zones, each regulated by separate controls. Even the detached three-suite guest house claimed its own system.

The four-bedroom, six-bath main house, set on thirty acres, claimed more space than one person needed, but Tyler looked forward to hosting several holiday celebrations for his sisters, niece, nephew, in-laws, and countless cousins.

Closing the door, he gloried in the cool air sweeping over his face and body, temporarily forgetting the bet he'd just made with his mother.

TWO

Dana spied the road sign pointing the way to Hillsboro's business district, and smiled. She hadn't bothered to turn on the air-conditioning in her grandmother's car despite the sultry heat. She breathed in a lungful of hot air. What she had remembered most about her place of birth was the smell. Hillsboro had a scent all its own, and she hadn't yet figured out whether it was the sap from the pine trees or the Mississippi River. Whatever it was, it evoked a feeling of nostalgia in her for the first time since her return.

After sleeping twelve consecutive hours, she'd awakened alert and refreshed for the first time in days. Eugene Payton had yet to call her, and for that she was grateful. She'd been numbed by the news of her grandmother's unexpected death from a massive heart attack. It had happened a day before Georgia was scheduled to leave Mississippi for New York for their scheduled summer reunion. And for the first time in more than two decades, Georgia Sutton would not spend the months of June, July, and August with her granddaughter.

Within minutes, downtown Hillsboro came into view. The storefronts that had lined two square blocks had undergone a transformation. The two blocks had expanded to four as fast-food restaurants now competed with an eating establishment that had catered to generations.

Shops with new facades, awnings, and attractive window displays silently advertised the latest fashions, fads, and household gadgets. The movie theater had become a duplex, showing two movies simultaneously; the tiny, crowded hardware store had disappeared, replaced by a Home Depot, and the small functional supermarket had expanded to an impressive Publix superstore.

Tiny, sleepy Hillsboro had joined the twenty-first century, claiming Staples, Barnes and Noble, Eckerd's, and Target.

Making a right turn into an area behind a row of stores, she maneuvered a space at the rear of Smithy's Family Diner. Anyone who'd lived in Hillsboro could be counted on to eat at Smithy's at least once during their lifetime, and Dana had lost count of the number of breakfasts, dinners, ice cream sodas, and banana splits she'd been served at the family-style restaurant.

She and her girlfriends had crowded into booths in the rear on late Saturday afternoons, after they'd left the movie house. They'd devoured monstrous ice cream concoctions as they waited for their parents or older siblings to drive them home.

Dana had always asked her father to come for her, because he did not scold her about the girls she'd befriended. It was Alicia Nichols who'd lectured her that, as a Nichols, she should not consort with riffraff, that she was better than the people who lived across the railroad tracks.

And what had confused Dana, even though she'd never verbalized it, was that her mother had grown up across the tracks, and her grandmother still lived across the tracks.

Georgia Sutton had reprimanded Alicia, claiming

she was being too hard on Dana; that she was over-compensating, that the people she'd grown up with were decent, hardworking, and God-fearing folks. Alicia never argued with her mother, but nothing Georgia said to Alicia could make her change her opinion of those she deemed beneath her.

Turning off the engine to the ten-year-old Chevy Lumina, Dana opened the door and stepped out of the car. She hadn't taken more than two steps when she noticed a man blocking her way.

He extended a grimy palm. "You got money for coffee?"

Eyes narrowing, she stared at the dirty young man. The odor emanating from his unwashed body in the stifling heat nearly gagged her. He was several inches taller than she was, but she doubted whether he outweighed her. A filthy white T-shirt and ragged jeans hung off his emaciated frame. His long dreaded hair was littered with lint and particles of leaves and twigs. Dark eyes, in an equally dark face, glittered wildly. Each time he exhaled, she caught a whiff of his malodorous breath.

"You got a quarter?" His voice was louder, stronger, as his hands curled into tight fists.

It wasn't the first time Dana had been approached by a panhandler, but it was the first time she'd felt threatened by one. She debated whether to open her purse and give him some money, or try to escape him.

"Are you bothering the lady, Leon?"

Dana let out her breath in an audible sigh when she heard a soft, drawling male voice behind her.

The panhandler's aggressive stance dissipated within seconds. Lowering his head, he mumbled, "No, sir. I want coffee."

"Didn't I tell you not to bother the ladies?" the soft

voice continued. "That if you want coffee you should come and see me?"

"Yes, sir."

"I want you to go back home, take a shower, put on clean clothes, and then come see me."

Leon shook his head, his gaze shifting between Dana, who hadn't moved, and the tall man standing behind her.

"She your lady?"

"Yes, Leon, she's my lady. Now will you please do as I ask?"

"I . . . I don't know."

"Go home, Leon." The soft voice had taken on a sharp edge of authority.

The disturbed man's eyelids blinked rapidly. "You want Leon go home and then come back?"

"Yes, Leon. Then come back and see me."

Leon dropped his head, turned, and shuffled slowly through a walkway between two stores. It was only after he'd disappeared from sight that Dana turned and looked up at her rescuer, her breath halting momentarily before starting up again.

The man staring down at her was literally and figuratively tall, dark, and handsome—almost beautiful, and never had she ever attributed that adjective to any man. His close-cropped hair was a shimmering black and liberally feathered with gray. She leisurely studied his face, feature by feature. His smooth deeply tanned olive coloring and high cheekbones made him look exotic. Sweeping black silky eyebrows curved over a pair of large glossy dark eyes. A thin nose and full sensual mouth completed his startling, arresting face.

"Thank . . . thank you, Mr. . . ." she stuttered, recovering her voice. It had come out in a breathless sigh.

"Cole, Tyler Cole."

It was Tyler's turn to stare at the woman who looked as good from the front as she did from the back. His obsidian gaze lingered on her face. And what an exquisite face it was: delicate chin, full, lush mouth, a pert nose, and then there were her eyes—eyes that were large, oval, and a clear warm brown with glints of gold that reminded him of tortoise-shell. The light brown, gold-streaked hair swept up off her slender neck was a perfect match for her eyes.

His lazy, penetrating gaze caressed the outline of her slender body under the sleeveless white cotton blouse she'd paired with a slim black skirt, ending at her knees, and black leather sandals. He forced himself not to gawk at the perfection of her bare legs and slender feet. As a man who had lost count of the number of women he'd examined since becoming a doctor, Tyler Cole was stunned by the beauty of the strange woman in front of him.

She smiled, extending her right hand. "Dana Nichols."

A slow smile crinkled Tyler's eyes as he flashed his trademark dimples, displaying a set of perfectly aligned white teeth. His parents had spent a small fortune in orthodontic care to correct an overbite from a thumb-sucking habit he'd developed from birth. It wasn't until he'd entered the third grade that he had come to the realization that sucking his thumb was for babies.

He arched an expressive raven eyebrow, taking her hand in his, cradling it gently. Her palm was soft and cool. He glanced down at her fingers. The nails were polished a pale pink—an attractive contrast to her tanned golden skin. So, he thought, she was the one who had tongues wagging faster than a hummingbird flapping its wings.

"I'm sorry if Leon frightened you," he said.

"I don't think he frightened me as much as he startled me," Dana said, extracting her hand from Tyler Cole's loose grip. "When I got out of my car, I didn't expect to see him standing in front of me."

"He's been warned about asking women for money."

She anchored the strap to her purse over her shoulder. "Is he a relative of yours?"

Tyler smiled again. "No, he isn't."

"Thank you again, Mr. Cole."

He nodded. "You're welcome, Ms. Nichols."

Tyler watched Dana walk from the parking lot, and then followed her. It wasn't until he reached the front door to Smithy's that he realized they were going to the same restaurant.

Reaching over her head, he held the door open. She smiled up at him. "You can really thank me by sharing breakfast, Ms. Nichols."

Tyler had no idea why he'd asked Dana to have breakfast with him, but the words were out and he could not retract them.

Dana's smile widened. "Okay. But only if I treat," she added quickly.

"No."

Dana stared at the tall man towering over her by more than half a foot. She was five-six, and estimated he had to be at least six-three. The top of her head reached his shoulder.

A slight frown appeared between her golden eyes. "No?"

"I can't permit you to pay."

She walked into Smithy's, glancing at Tyler over her shoulder. "Hasn't a woman ever paid for a meal for you?"

He held her gaze. "No."

"Well, Mr. Cole, this is going to be the first time."

She didn't intend to owe anyone in Hillsboro anything—not even for a morsel of food.

"Only if the next one is on me," Tyler insisted.

She went completely still. Is that the way it had been
with her mother? When she'd asked her grandmother
about her mother, Georgia had always said that Alicia
had only to smile at a man and they would flock to
her like bees to honey. Dana may have looked like her
mother, but she wasn't in Hillsboro to attract men. She
was there to investigate a murder.

"Look, Mr. Cole—"

"Tyler," he corrected.

"Tyler?"

"Yes, Dana?"

"I've come to Smithy's to eat breakfast, not debate
social etiquette or protocol."

She hadn't eaten in nearly twenty-four hours. She'd
prepared an omelet, a slice of toast, and a cup of coffee
for herself after she'd returned from burying her
grandmother. After cleaning up the kitchen, she'd
spent most of the afternoon on the screened-in back
porch dozing, before retreating to the bedroom where
she'd had slept as a child and falling into a deep sleep
that had lasted for hours. She'd awakened several
hours before sunrise, disoriented. Lying in bed and
waiting for the sun to rise, she'd mentally planned
what she needed to do. Dana had one priority—reac-
quaint herself with Hillsboro, Mississippi.

Clamping his jaw in frustration, Tyler reached for
her hand, leading her over to a table in a corner set
with place settings for two and a couple of heavy cafe-
teria-style white mugs turned upside down on cloth
napkins. Dana Nichols was the first woman he'd ever
met that made him want to know more about her with
only a single glance. And wanting to know her had
nothing to do with the whispers floating around town.

Even though it wasn't quite eight, many of the tables were occupied. Some had a single diner, while others held as many as six. The distinctive aroma of brewing coffee, broiling bacon, and frying eggs wafted in the air circulated by the whirling blades of ceiling fans.

Laughter had faded as several middle-aged men stared at Dana, their mouths gaping, when she'd walked into Smithy's with Tyler Cole. If Alicia had still been alive, she would've been fifty-three, close enough to the ages of the men exhibiting stunned gazes. There was no doubt they knew who Dana was, because she was an exact replica of her late mother. It was as if Harry Nichols had had no part in her conception.

Tyler seated Dana before taking a chair opposite her. She compressed her lips, staring straight ahead. "Are you all right?" His voice was filled with genuine concern.

She forced a brittle smile. "Of course." Dana knew she'd lied. She wasn't all right, wouldn't be until she uncovered the truth and cleared her family's name.

A full-figured waitress with a net covering her salt and pepper hair sauntered over to the table, glaring at Dana under her lashes. She slapped two plastic covered menus on the Formica-topped table, grunting under her breath. "I'll be back directly with coffee and to take your orders." She flashed Tyler a practiced smile, and then walked away with an exaggerated roll of her generous hips.

"Her disposition hasn't changed much in twenty years," Dana said in a quiet tone.

"You know Cheryl?"

"I remember Miss Cheryl from a long time ago."

"How long have you been away?"

She studied the backs of her hands. "A long time. Twenty-two years." Her head came up, and she met

Tyler's direct stare. "How long have you lived in Hillsboro?"

"Ten months."

The beginnings of a smile tipped the corners of her mouth. "You're a newcomer. I suppose you've heard the gossip about me coming back?"

"I admit I've heard your name, but hadn't paid much attention to what has been said."

"So, you don't listen to gossip?"

He leaned closer. "I don't have time for gossip."

Resting her chin on her hand, she offered him a warm smile. "Good for you." He returned her smile. The gesture contained enough eroticism to make her hold her breath for several seconds.

She continued to stare at Tyler, her journalistic instincts kicking into high gear. He was new to Hillsboro, which meant he hadn't known her family. In other words, he would be unbiased. And if she gained his confidence, there was always the possibility that he could become an ally.

"How does your family like Hillsboro?" she asked.

He regarded her for several seconds. "If you're talking about a wife and children, I have none. Personally, I happen to like it. It's very different from some of the other places I've lived."

Knowing he was single would make it easier for her, because she was prepared to smile, flirt, and do anything short of using her body or bribing someone to get what she wanted.

"How so?" she asked.

"It's small, and everyone seems to look out for one another." Hillsboro's last census had listed the population at 3,320 residents. "Of course, it's not exempt from the social ills of the country at large, but on a smaller scale. What about you? Why have you come back?"

"It's my home." She knew her response was ambiguous, and because she didn't know Tyler Cole, she wasn't ready to bare her soul. Once she began her investigation, he and everyone else in Hillsboro would know the reason why she'd elected to extend her stay.

"Where was home before you decided to move back?" he asked.

"A little town in upstate New York not far from the Adirondack Mountains."

"You don't sound like New York."

She laughed softly. "What I don't sound like is downstate New York. I've been told that I still have a trace of a Southern drawl."

Tyler angled his head. "Only when you say certain words."

A smile trembled over her lips. "No one would ever *not* take you for a Southerner," she teased. His soft drawling voice clearly identified him as a son of the South.

His smile matched hers. "I'm one down to the marrow in my bones."

"You don't sound like a Mississippian."

"Florida."

She lifted an eyebrow, the fingertips of her right hand tracing the design on the handle of a knife at one of the place settings. "So, you're a Gator."

"The Heat, Magic, Marlins, Dolphins, Devil Rays, the Orange Bowl, Florida Citrus Bowl, the Panthers, and Tampa Bay Lightning."

"You sound like a serious sports fan."

Placing a large, well-groomed hand over his heart, he crooned, "I'm not ashamed to admit that I'm addicted." Although he hadn't lived in his home state for two decades, he still followed Florida's sports teams.

Dana glanced at his broad shoulders under a sand-washed silk short-sleeved shirt in a blue-gray shade. He had tucked the shirt into a pair of khakis. His tanned arms, corded with natural muscle, appeared even darker because of the profusion of black hair covering them.

"Have you ever played ball?" she asked.

"Only a little pickup B-ball with my cousins."

"How tall are you?"

"Six-four."

"Why did you move to Hillsboro?" she asked, continuing with her questioning.

Tyler wasn't given the opportunity to answer her question. Cheryl reappeared, carrying a carafe of coffee. Turning over the mugs on the table, she filled them with streaming black coffee.

Picking up one, Cheryl placed it in front of Dana. The cup touched the handle of a spoon, tipping over and spilling hot liquid over the back of Dana's left hand. Tyler moved quickly, pulling Dana from her chair as the coffee ran over the side of the table and onto the floor.

"I'm so sorry!" Cheryl gasped, her eyes wide with fright.

"Get me a plastic bag filled with ice. Now, woman!" Tyler shouted at Cheryl as she stood rooted to the spot, her mouth gaping. Within seconds she turned, racing toward the kitchen.

Dana clutched her injured hand to her chest, while biting down on her lower lip to keep from moaning aloud. Her fingers were on fire. Tyler eased her down to the chair he'd vacated. The talk in Smithy's stopped, all of the diners leaving their seats and crowding around trying to see what had happened.

Tyler reached for her wrist, pulling her hand gently away from her breasts. "Let me see it, Dana." Extending her injured hand, she stared at his lowered head as he cradled her palm in his larger one. Red splotches dotted her fingers and her wrist. There was no doubt it would blister if she didn't cool down the outer layer of her skin.

Cheryl returned with a plastic bag filled with ice cubes, thrusting it at Tyler. He released Dana's hand, and then pressed the bag to her scalded flesh.

"You need to keep it on for about twenty minutes."

She did as he ordered, and within seconds the burning subsided. "That feels better."

Leaning closer, Tyler pressed his mouth close to her ear. "I'm going out to my truck to get something to put on it."

Dana stared at the face only inches from hers, noting several tiny lines around the large expressive eyes for the first time. Despite his graying hair, Tyler Cole's clean-shaven face was virtually unlined.

A flicker of awareness dilated his pupils as he continued to stare at her. It was a look she recognized. It was desire.

Closing her eyes against the intense black orbs burning her face, she nodded. When she opened her eyes, Tyler was gone and most of the other diners had retreated to their tables. Only Cheryl remained, her hands clasped together and her expression mirroring her anguish.

"I'm so sorry, Dana."

She offered the waitress a comforting smile. "It's all right, Miss Cheryl. It was an accident. Please go take care of your other customers."

Cheryl hesitated. "Are you sure you're going to be okay?"

"I'm not going to sue you or Smithy's." There was a hint of laughter in her voice.

Cheryl's net-covered head bobbed up and down. "Thank you." She walked away, her step heavier, gait slower. The usual babble at Smithy's had returned to its normal level.

Dana alternated holding the bag of ice against her injured hand and removing it briefly when she felt numbness.

"I thought I told you to keep it on your hand."

Dana's head came up and she saw Tyler standing over her, frowning. She hadn't registered his silent approach. How had she missed it when the scent of his distinctive aftershave floated around her? The fragrance was a sensual masculine blend of spices.

"It's freezing my skin," she said.

Pulling up another chair from a nearby table, Tyler sat, placing a black leather bag on the floor next to his feet. It wasn't until he leaned over and unsnapped the bag that Dana went completely still, her eyes widening in recognition. The bag was an updated version of the one her father had carried with him whenever he made a house call. The bag could always be found on a small table in the office adjoining the large house that was home to Dr. Harry Nichols and his family. The house and the office had been owned and occupied by several generations of Dr. Nicholses, going back to the turn of the century.

"You're a doctor." It came out like more of an accusation than a question.

Tyler flashed a quick smile. "Yes, I am."

Closing her eyes, she recited:

"You do solemnly swear, each man, by whatever he holds most scared:
"That you will be loyal to the Profession of Medicine and just and generous to its members.
"That you will lead your lives and practice your art in uprightness and honor.
"That into whatsoever house you shall enter, it shall be

*for the good of the sick to the utmost of your power, you
holding yourself far aloof from wrong, from corruption,
from the tempting of others to vice.*

*"That you will exercise your art solely for the cure of
your patient, and will give no drug, perform no operation, for criminal purpose, even if solicited, far less suggested.*

*"That whatsoever you shall see or hear of the lives of
men which is not fitting to be spoken, you will keep
inviolably secret.*

*"These things do you swear. Let each man bow the head
in sign of acquiescence.*

*"And now, if you will be true to this, your oath, may
prosperity and good repute be ever yours, the opposite,
if you shall prove yourselves forsworn."*

Tyler stared at her, stunned. "You know the Hippo-
cratic Oath?"

"I'd memorized it by the time I turned eight on a
dare from my father. He, my grandfather, and great-
grandfather were doctors."

He wanted to tell her that they had something in
common. His brother-in-law was a doctor, and his
nephew was in medical school.

Reaching for her hand, he examined it again. Most
of the redness had faded. "Keep the ice on it for another five minutes. The secret to fast burn healing is
to cool down your outer layer as quickly as possible."

"Do you think it's going to blister?"

"I don't believe it will. I'm going to apply a soothing
salve called Silvadene and cover it with nonstick gauze.
Burns hurt if they are allowed to dry out. Keeping
them moist will speed recovery and reduce scarring."

Dana watched as Tyler pulled on a pair of latex
gloves; he applied the salve and then wrapped her

hand with the gauze. His touch was soft, almost featherlike. It was obvious he was a gentle doctor.

"Can I use aloe vera?" Her grandmother's back porch was crowded with a profusion of green and flowering plants, including an aloe vera plant.

"The Silvadene works as well or better than a processed aloe vera gel."

"My grandmother always used the sap from an aloe vera plant whenever she burned herself cooking."

"Aloe soothes burns by inhibiting the body's pain-producing chemical bradykinin. The gel also cuts down on the formation of thromboxane, another natural chemical that keeps wounds from healing. I'm a proponent of homeopathic and alternative medicine, but only when a patient isn't at risk for a more serious illness or ailment."

Tyler cut a length of tape with a pair of scissors, securing the gauze around Dana's tiny forearm. He hadn't realized the fragility of her slender body until he'd dressed her hand.

Holding up her hand, Dana examined Tyler's handiwork, smiling. "Thank you, Dr. Cole. You can bill me for services rendered."

"I should send the bill to the owners of Smithy's." Removing the gloves, he placed them, the gauze, and the scissors in the black leather bag, securing the lock. "We did come in here to eat, didn't we?"

"Yes, we did." She was surprised her stomach wasn't rumbling loudly.

"What do you want?"

"What I haven't had a very long time: eggs, grits, biscuits, and bacon. I think I'll pass on the coffee."

Tyler winked at her. "Don't run away. I'll go put our orders in."

Dana stared at his retreating back, silently admiring his broad shoulders and trim waist. Dr. Tyler Cole was hazardous to a woman's nervous system: the timbre of his soft, mellifluous voice was X-rated, his face XX-rated, and his tall, lean muscular body XXX-rated.

She was still staring at Tyler when he returned, a smile deepening the dimples in his lean cheeks. Closing her eyes briefly, she thought, *I forgot to add charming.* The man was in fact very, very charming.

"Come," he said softly. "Let's move to another table." Curving an arm around her waist, he led her over to a nearby table, seating her. He lingered over her head, inhaling the subtle fragrance clinging to her skin. He'd found the perfume as alluring as its wearer.

Sitting, he studied the face of the woman sharing his table. The words his mother had said to him whispered to him in vivid clarity: *Speaking of grandchildren, have you found that special someone? I don't intend to go to my grave worrying about you spending the rest of your life as a lonely old man.*

But he had to ask himself, did he want a woman? There were occasions when he physically *needed* a woman. But need and want were very different.

A look of determination shimmered in his near-black eyes. There was one woman in Hillsboro that did intrigue him—Dana Nichols. And he'd concluded it just wasn't her face. He had dated a quite a few beautiful women before, women who'd made their living because of their faces and bodies. But there was something about Dana that was different—very, very different from the other women.

A teenage boy had mopped up the spilt coffee and then cleaned off the first table and chairs when Cheryl returned, carrying a tray with Tyler and Dana's breakfast selections. Working quickly and efficiently, she carefully set the plates on the second table.

"I'll be back with your coffee, Dr. Cole."

Dana stared at the appealing presentation on her plate, hesitating. How was she going to eat with her hand and fingers wrapped in gauze?

Tyler, noting her hesitation, said, "What's the matter?"

Her gaze shifted from the plate in front of her to meet the questioning gaze of her dining partner. "I'm left-handed."

Rising to his feet, Tyler shifted his chair, sitting on Dana's right before he reversed their plates. His breakfast—a bowl of wheat flakes, a glass of milk, and sliced fruit—could be eaten later. Picking up a forkful of grits and eggs, he turned to face Dana, cupping his free hand under her chin.

"Open up."

She opened her mouth, stunned that she was going to be fed her breakfast. As their eyes met, she felt a shock run through her. Something sensual flared through his intense entrancement, and she knew within an instant that becoming attracted to Tyler Cole would be perilous—to *her.*

He projected a virility she could not ignore—a hypnotic virility that pulled her in despite her silent protests.

Tyler stared at Dana's mouth as she chewed and swallowed her food. He was unable to pull his gaze away. She had the sexiest mouth of any woman he'd ever seen, and he wondered if it would taste as good as it looked. There was enough petulance in her lower lip to give her the appearance of sulking.

He hadn't decided what he liked more—her mouth or her eyes. Meanwhile, both had him entranced like a motionless deer staring into a car's headlights.

"I'm finished," Dana said after taking several bites of a strip of crisp bacon.

The fork he held was poised in midair. "You hardly ate anything."

"I'm full," she lied smoothly. How could she eat with him staring at her like she was dessert? "Please eat your breakfast." She broke off a small piece of her biscuit with her right hand, placing it in her mouth.

Turning his attention to the cereal, milk, and fruit, Tyler poured half a glass of milk on his wheat flakes, picked up a spoon, and began eating. He'd finished the bowl of cereal, drunk the milk, and was finishing up his fruit when another waitress came over and placed a mug of steaming black coffee on the table in front of him.

Tyler took a sip of the strong brew, savoring the rich taste and warmth spreading throughout his chest. Drinking black coffee was a habit he couldn't seem to break. It had begun in medical school. Most nights he'd slept an average of three to four hours while fortifying himself with gallons of caffeine-laced coffee. He'd promised himself over and over that he would stop, but so far he hadn't been successful.

His obsessions were strong and uncompromising—medicine and his enthusiasm for sports. What he did not want to acknowledge was his surprising attraction for Dana Nichols. Something about her had pulled him in, refusing to let him go. The very air around her seemed electrified, intensifying emotions he did not want to feel. What frightened him most was the realization that what he was beginning to feel for Dana was similar to what he'd felt when he walked into a lecture hall his first day at medical school. It was frightening and exciting.

Three

Tyler paid for breakfast against Dana's protests. "You can pay the next time," he said, compromising. He led her out of Smithy's and to the parking lot behind the diner. "I have some samples of Silvadene in my office. I'll bring them to you later."

Dana smiled up at him. "I owe you for Leon and tending to my hand."

Bending gracefully from the waist, he placed a hand over his heart. "Sir Black Knight at your service, milady."

She laughed, the soft sound floating and lingering in the sultry air. "I thought the black knight was always the villain."

Straightening, Tyler winked at her. "Not in the modern versions." He waited until she opened the door to her car. "I'll see you later."

Dana glanced at him over her shoulder. "But you don't know where I live."

His expression changed, becoming solemn. "Hillsboro is a very small town. I'm certain I'll find your house without getting lost." What he didn't tell her was that her grandmother had come to the Hillsboro Women's Heath Clinic for a health fair four months before she succumbed to a massive heart attack. Georgia Sutton's medical records contained not only her health history, but also her personal information. One glance in the chart would give Tyler the information he needed to find Dana.

She nodded, and then slipped in behind the wheel. Seconds later, she started up the car and backed out of the parking space as Dr. Tyler Cole stood in the same spot, fingers resting on his slim hips.

Only after Dana's car had disappeared from his line of vision did he retreat to his own vehicle to drive the short distance to the clinic where he'd become the medical director.

Tyler walked into the Hillsboro Women's Health Clinic at nine-twenty, smiling at the office manager seated at a desk behind a Plexiglas partition. "Good morning, Miss Lincoln."

The efficient middle-aged woman's head came up quickly. Her normally pleasant expression was set into a frown. "You wouldn't think it was such a good morning if you know what I know."

His smiled vanished. "What is it I should know?"

"Vesta called and left a message on the voice mail that she's not coming in today."

Tyler's face was a mask of stone. How could he run an efficient clinic if his support staff did not show up as scheduled? "What's her excuse *this* time?"

"She says she hung out last night and was feeling poorly this morning."

A muscle twitched in his cheek. "Please call Miss Richards and inform her there's no need for her to get up today, tomorrow, the next day, or the day after. Write a check for what we owe her, and kindly include a note indicating I'm terminating her employment. Then, call the employment agency in Greenville and inform them that we need a receptionist with a medical background."

Expecting Miss Lincoln to follow his directive without question, Tyler turned on his heels and made his way down a corridor to his office. The solid slam of the door was the only indication of his rising temper. He'd issued the order with the same soft comforting tone he always used with his patients.

Imogene Lincoln hadn't expected Dr. Cole to fire the young woman. Vesta was a single mother with two preschool children. She needed her job and the money. And Imogene had felt personally responsible for Vesta, because she'd recommended her as the clinic's receptionist.

What Imogene wanted to do was plea with Dr. Cole not to fire the trifling girl, but changed her mind. This was one time she would not enable her. Cousin or not, Vesta had to face up to her responsibilities or fail as a mother.

Picking up the telephone, she dialed her aunt's number, asking for Vesta. It took all of a minute to tell her that she'd been fired and could expect a check for a week's pay. Imogene hung up at the same time her cousin's wrenching sobs came through the earpiece.

Biting down on her lip, she completed the task of pulling patient charts. It was going to be a long day. Dr. Cole was scheduled to see eight patients.

The front door opened again. It was the nurse, followed by the first patient of the day.

Tyler ripped off his latex gloves. It had taken all of his self-control not to lose his temper when he'd examined a very pregnant young woman. She'd tried concealing the bruises on her upper arms after he'd opened the examining gown to monitor her unborn child's heartbeat. He had completed the examination, his touch impersonal and his expression one of pained tolerance.

He swung his angry gaze to his nurse's startled one. "Please help Mrs. Connelly get dressed, then I'll see her in my office." Picking up the chart, he stalked out of the examining room.

The nurse curved an arm under the patient's shoulders, assisting her to sit upright. She saw tears fill the woman's eyes and flow down her pale cheeks. Mrs. Connelly knew what awaited her once she entered Dr. Cole's private office. It wasn't as if she hadn't been warned.

Tyler sat behind his desk, entering notes in Miranda Connelly's chart. His dark sun-browned face was set in a vicious expression that did not bode well for his patient. His head came up and he saw her paused in the doorway.

Rising to his feet, he beckoned her to enter. "Please, come in," he said gently.

She was rooted to the spot, and he came around the desk to take her arm and seat her on the chair in front of the desk. Instead of retaking his seat, Tyler sat next to Miranda, holding her cold pale fingers within his larger, warm grasp.

He stared at her bowed head. "I told you the last time I examined you, if I saw new bruises, exactly what I was going to do."

Miranda shook her head and a thick wave of light brown hair fell over her forehead, obscuring her vision. "No, Dr. Cole. Please don't."

Tyler leaned closer. "I'm mandated by law to report what I suspect is domestic abuse. And your husband has been abusing you. If you don't care about yourself, then you should about your unborn child."

"Chuck's not really abusing me," she mumbled.

His eyes glittered wildly with repressed rage. "You're six months pregnant, and I've also documented vaginal tearing because your husband has been raping you, and you say he's not abusing you."

Miranda glanced up. Blotches of red color dotted her cheeks. "He's a little rough because I don't want him to touch me. I told you before I don't feel nothin' now that I'm carrying this baby. I was the same way with the last two."

Tyler took a deep breath before exhaling audibly. "Mrs. Connelly, it's normal for some women to experience a decrease in sexual desire during their confinement. And just because they do, it's not an excuse for their husbands to rape them."

He wanted to tell his misguided patient that it was probably her husband's ignorance and arrogance that had contributed to her miscarrying her last child.

Reaching out, Miranda captured Tyler's free hand, her nails biting into his flesh. "Please don't call the sheriff." Her blue eyes filled with unshed tears. "I want you to talk to him, Dr. Cole. I know he'll listen to you. He wants this baby as much as I do, especially since it's a boy. I . . . I'll make certain he comes with me for my next appointment." Ultrasound images had indicated the Connellys were expecting their first boy.

Easing his hand from her punishing grip, Tyler shook his head. He couldn't afford to wait a month. "I need to talk to him *now.*" He'd stressed the last word.

"But . . . but that's not possible. He has to put in two weeks in advance for a day off."

"Where does he work?"

"He's over at the bottling factory in Calico."

Tyler glanced down at the gold watch with a genuine alligator band on his left wrist. The timepiece had been

a gift from his parents when he had graduated medical
school.

"What time does he get off from work?"

"Tonight's his late night. He doesn't get home until
after nine."

The seconds ticked off as Tyler stared at Miranda.
"I'm going to see your husband today. I'll talk to him,
but if I don't get his cooperation, then I'm going to
the sheriff. All of my medical findings have been documented in your chart, so there's no way he's going to
lie out of this. And if you don't carry this baby to term,
then I'll personally make certain he spends time in jail
for manslaughter. The unborn have rights, too."

A trembling smile parted Miranda's lips. "Thank
you, Dr. Cole."

He smiled for the first time since viewing her
bruised body. "Thank me only after you deliver a beautiful healthy son." She bobbed her head as she stood
up, Tyler rising with her. "Miss Lincoln will give you
an appointment for a month from now. I want you to
continue to chart all of the changes you notice about
your body in your journal. I also want you to see the
nutritionist before you leave today. She will set up a
specialized menu for you with the recommended por-
tions. You'll need three or four snacks in addition to
your regular meals. Of course, your meals need to be
smaller to offset the snacks.

"And I don't want chips and sodas. Cut-up fresh
vegetables and fruits are the required snacks. Peanut
butter—regular or reduced-calorie, pretzels—preferably unsalted, and plain popcorn are also good
choices. Low-fat cheese and cottage cheese will provide
the additional calcium you need."

"One thing I try do is eat healthy," Miranda boasted
proudly.

Tyler flashed his dimpled smile. "That's what I want to hear."

A smile lit up her brilliant blue eyes. "I'll see you next month." She reached up to hug him, but quickly lowered her arms, blushing. "Thank you for everything, Dr. Cole."

He nodded. "You're welcome, Mrs. Connelly."

Waiting until she left his office, Tyler sat down behind the desk, running a hand over his face in a weary gesture. The women who attended the Hillsboro clinic presented not only a myriad of health problems, but also social and economic ones.

Many had given birth to their first child while still in their teens, which meant at least half hadn't completed high school. More than seventy-five percent were single mothers, living below the national poverty level. They came to him undernourished, malnourished, and five had been diagnosed with STD's.

Since his arrival, he'd increased staff and developed a curriculum offering classes in nutrition, prenatal care, and family planning. He'd been hired to treat women's health needs, not offer moral advice, and he'd refused to take sides in pro-life or pro-choice issues. But he'd taken an oath to save lives, not take them; therefore, in all the years since becoming a doctor, he'd never performed an abortion.

The sound of the intercom garnered his attention. He pressed a button on a small console. "Yes?"

"You have two cancellations." Miss Lincoln's voice came clearly through the speaker. "Cassie Maynard's mother called to say that Cassie went down to Jackson for the week and because she was having contractions the hospital there admitted her.

"Mr. Timmons called for his wife. He claims she prefers coming in Saturday morning. I told him we were booked up for Saturday, and would get back to him."

"Call him back and tell him I have to see his wife today. If she can't make it this morning, then we'll fit her in before closing. Her last urine sample showed traces of albumin."

"Okay, Doc."

Depressing the button, Tyler stood up and removed his white lab coat. Two cancellations meant he had almost three hours for himself. The clinic usually opened at nine, closed between the hours of noon and two, then reopened until six. Tuesdays and Thursdays were the late nights when they remained open until eight. Friday and Saturday they saw patients from nine to two.

Reaching for the keys to his sport utility vehicle, he switched on a pager and cell phone, attaching them to the waistband of his slacks, and left his office. He met Miss Lincoln as she locked the front door and turned over the sign indicating the hour when the clinic would reopen.

"Going out, Doc?"

"Yes. You can page me if there's an emergency." He didn't tell the office manager he planned to drive to Calico to talk to Miranda Connelly's husband.

Miss Lincoln opened the door, and then closed it behind his departing figure.

Tyler waited in a private office at Calico Bottling for Charles Connelly to arrive, taking furtive glances at his watch. He'd driven to the large beverage plant with the image of Dana Nichols's haunting beauty swirling around in his head. He hadn't realized he'd been speeding until he heard the siren and saw flashing blue and white lights. A deputy had recognized him as he approached his truck, and had waved him on.

Closing his eyes, he recalled his mother's words.

You're forty, Tyler. It's time you settled down. What Parris Simmons Cole did not know was that he'd never come close to settling down. He did not need a wife—not when he was already married—to medicine.

However, he had to admit that he'd found Dana very attractive. She wasn't tall, but he couldn't say she was short either. He estimated she stood about five-five or six—almost ten inches shorter than his own impressive height. What he'd found unsettling was that he normally was drawn to taller women—those who had reached the requisite height for high-fashion modeling.

What the woman in his private thoughts lacked in stature she more than compensated for with her face. Dana's lush mouth, cute button nose, and shimmering gold eyes were indelibly imprinted on his brain.

The sound of a door opening shattered his daydreams as Charles Connelly walked into the small space with a confident swagger. He was young, probably no older than twenty-five, medium height, and heavily muscled. It was obvious he lifted weights.

Charles wiped his right hand down the front of his cotton shirt before extending it. "Dr. Cole," he said with a quick nod of his head. "Is something wrong with Mandy's baby?"

Tyler deliberately ignored the proffered hand, crossing dark brown arms over his chest. He glared down at Miranda Connelly's husband, wishing for the first time in his life he wasn't a doctor, because he truly wanted to hurt the man.

"Sit down, Mr. Connelly." The four words, though spoken quietly, had the same effect as someone screaming at the top of their lungs.

The man's eyes misted. Chuck, as Miranda had called him, complied, backpedaling and sitting on a straight-back chair. All of his bravado seemed to dissipate as his shoulders slumped noticeably.

Pulling over a matching chair, Tyler sat down facing him. He glared at Charles, increasing his uneasiness. "I'm here because I need to discuss something with you. And I don't intend to talk about this ever again, because the next time you see me it will be a courtroom."

Vertical lines appeared between a pair of vivid blue eyes. "What the hell are you talking about?" He'd recovered some of his cheekiness.

"Your wife, Mr. Connelly. She came to the clinic this morning for her scheduled monthly checkup. This is the second time I've noticed bruises on her arms. She also has vaginal trauma. In other words, you've been physically abusing your wife. You are *raping* her!" He spat out the word.

A rush of blood darkened Chuck's face. He exhaled, his nostrils flaring. "She won't let me touch her."

"Then don't touch her," Tyler retorted.

Chuck leaned forward. "A man has needs. And that's what a wife is for."

Tyler struggled to control his temper. "*Real* men don't rape their wives."

A vein bulged in Chuck's forehead. "A husband can't rape his own wife."

"That's not what I've documented in your wife's medical chart. It's not only Miranda's health that's being compromised, but you've put her baby at risk." His large, penetrating dark eyes narrowed slightly. "If she comes to the clinic next month with one bruise— even a single smudge, then I'm going to file a report with the sheriff to have you arrested for assault and endangering the viability of the unborn."

Chuck jumped up, his chair crashing to the floor,

but Tyler was quicker as his right hand shot out, grabbing the man's throat.

Charles Connelly realized he had underestimated the soft-spoken doctor as he felt the power in the fist holding him fast. Why hadn't he noticed Dr. Cole stood a full head taller than he was? That his arms were corded with natural muscle that had not come from pumping iron. Surely the doctor would follow through on his threat to have him arrested. He'd worked hard to get to where he was as a plant foreman; he had married his high school sweetheart, and now looked forward to fathering a son who would carry on his name.

"Swing at me, Connelly," Tyler taunted as he tightened his grip. "Hit *me* and you'll find out what pain truly is, because right now I feel the *need* to punish you for taking a woman against her will."

Charles Connelly may have been a swaggering sexist, but he was not a fool. He'd wanted a son ever since Mandy told him she was pregnant with their first child. He wanted to be the kind of father his own father never was or could be. His father was as mean as a junkyard dog with a sore paw whenever he drank. And he had been cruel and unfeeling to his wife and children when sober.

No, Charles did not want to spend time in jail, away from his wife and children. He didn't want his son to grow up knowing that his father wasn't there to witness his birth because he'd been imprisoned for hurting his mother.

Gasping, he tried escaping his captor. "I'm sorry, Dr. Cole," he whispered hoarsely. "I don't mean to hurt Mandy. I love her."

Tyler let go of his throat. His eyebrows were down together in an angry scowl. "Please sit down again, Mr. Connelly. We have to talk about your wife and her physical condition." Chuck picked up the chair, sat down, and stared at his hands sandwiched between his knees.

It took less than ten minutes for Dr. Tyler Cole to explain to Charles Connelly what to expect during his wife's confinement. He also extracted a promise from his patient's husband that he would come to the clinic with Miranda for her next visit. He walked out of the office at the Calico Bottling Company, leaving Chuck staring at a pair of broad shoulders under a blue-gray silk shirt.

"I'm losing it," Tyler whispered to himself after he'd retrieved his vehicle from the visitors' parking lot. He'd never touched another human being, except to comfort and heal. He sat, staring out the windshield, unable to believe how he'd acted so unprofessionally. It was the first time he'd let his emotions override his training.

He turned the key in the ignition, then ran his left hand over his face, trying to fathom why he'd threatened to hit Charles Connelly. And he doubted whether the short, muscular man would've permitted him to beat him without attempting to defend himself. Tyler shuddered to think of what could've transpired, imagining the *Hillsboro Herald's* headlines: LOCAL DOC DUKES IT OUT WITH PATIENT'S HUBBY.

He'd studied and worked too hard to jeopardize his reputation with a scandal. Perhaps, he thought, he'd stayed in research too long, missing so much of the give-and-take of a doctor-patient relationship.

Perhaps, just perhaps, his mother had been right when she'd said he'd become too involved in his work. The last time he'd visited with Parris Cole, they'd sat for hours talking about what he truly wanted for himself; she'd asked how he wanted to be remembered after he no longer practiced medicine, and he'd been mute, unable to answer her query.

And now he had to ask himself the same question. What would he have if he didn't have a medical career? He had more money than he could spend in his lifetime, and stood to inherit five times that amount whenever his parents passed away.

He had the money, the family name, and nothing else. He was a Cole—a member of the wealthiest African-American family in the United States—but that did not change the fact there was no special woman in his life, no children to carry on his name or his genes. Even his marriage-shy younger sister had committed to her longtime live-in boyfriend, and now looked forward to starting her own family.

At this time in his life he didn't want a wife, even though there was one woman in Hillsboro that did intrigue him: Dana Nichols. A woman he wanted and needed to know more about.

Tyler smiled. His mother would be shocked if she knew his thoughts, because for the first time in his life Tyler Simmons Cole felt the pull of a woman—a stranger with a lush mouth and hypnotic golden eyes.

Four

A stately grandfather clock in the corner of the living room chimed the half hour. It was seven-thirty. Dana had turned off all of the lights in the house to offset the buildup of heat, lit several candles, and switched on overhead fans on the porch, in the living and dining rooms, and in the kitchen. A pair of oil candles in hurricane chimneys on the fireplace mantel provided enough light for her to study a quartet of photographs.

There was one of her grandparents on their wedding day. Another wedding picture with a similar pose with Harry and Alicia Nichols was positioned next to it. The third one was of Harry, Alicia, and their newborn daughter. Their smiles mirrored a happier time in their young lives.

Dana peered at the last photo—a black and white one of her mother, seeing her own face staring back at her as she examined the image of an adolescent Alicia Sutton behind the glass of a decorative silver-plated frame. The picture had been taken the day of her mother's high school graduation.

She wondered what had Alicia been thinking the moment the shutter captured her image. Her head was angled for optimum sensuality, a half smile curving her pouting mouth. The smile matched half-lowered eyelids that screamed blatant seduction. There was no doubt a man had taken her mother's picture.

Alicia's expression was one Dana remembered whenever her mother sought a special favor from Harry Nichols. All Alicia had to do was lower her voice, rub her body against Harry's like a graceful cat, and the soft-spoken family doctor melted like a pat of butter on a heated griddle. Dana had been too young at the time to understand the dynamics of staged seduction, but she hadn't been too young to know that whenever Alicia acted this way, Dr. Harry Nichols could never deny his wife anything she'd asked for.

Although Dana had come back to Hillsboro to clear her family's name, she loathed having to reopen her father's murder trial. Her grandmother had not permitted her to discuss the murder investigation, or visit the courtroom during her father's trial. Georgia also had ignored her pleas to visit Harry in jail while he'd awaited trial.

The presiding judge had denied Harry's attorney's request for bail, declaring he was a possible flight risk. Bailed denied, Harry languished in jail for more than three months before he took his own life, an hour before he was to be transported to a state prison for a term of life in prison without the possibility of parole.

Dana had come to dislike her father for his selfishness as much as she'd loved him for his gentleness. The day she celebrated her eleventh birthday, Dr. Harry Nichols had changed his daughter's life forever. She'd lost her mother, her father, and been wrested from all that was familiar. Georgia had hastily packed a bag, purchased two tickets, boarded a train, and brought Dana to live with a relative in upstate New York.

It had taken a long time, but after years of therapy, Dana had finally forgiven her father for making her an orphan. On the other hand, every man she met still became Harry—someone she couldn't trust, because she always believed he would desert her when she needed him most.

The doorbell rang, shattering her reverie. The only other sound in the house was the dulcet voice of Billie Holiday singing her jazz classic "Strange Fruit." Dana had sent Georgia the five-set CD anthology, "Ken Burns Jazz—The Story of America's Music," for Christmas because she knew how much her grandmother loved jazz.

Walking down a narrow hall, she acrossed the living room, she made her way through an entryway to the front door. The late Georgia Sutton had been proud of her house. The two-story structure was immaculate and tastefully furnished. It contained three bedrooms, a large modern kitchen, living and dining rooms, and a spacious screened-in back porch.

Georgia had always paid someone to cut the grass in the front and rear of her property after her husband died, but personally maintained her flower and vegetable gardens. Dana remembered eating fruits and vegetables from her grandmother's garden all year long.

The outer door stood open to catch any breeze for the house, and was protected from intruders by a locked screen door. Standing on the other side of the screen was Tyler Cole. He'd exchanged his silk shirt, khakis, and loafers for a stark-white T-shirt, faded jeans, and a pair of jogging shoes.

Seeing him again sent Dana's pulse racing along her nerve endings. She stared mutely, shocks of surprise and awareness tearing through her scantily clad body.

Tyler held up a small black leather case. "I brought the salve for your hand."

Dana unlatched the door, pushing it open to permit

him entry. The heat of his body intensified the fragrance of his cologne, the perfect complement to his body's natural masculine scent.

Tyler felt his stomach muscles contract. He hadn't expected to see so much of Dana's silken flesh displayed, a pair of white shorts riding low on her slim hips and the matching skimpy tank top bearing her flat midriff. Turning, he stared at the perfection of her legs: firm thighs, curvy calves, and slender ankles. However, it was her high firm breasts under the top that captured his rapt attention. She wasn't wearing a bra, and he forced his gaze not to linger on the outline of the prominent nipples showing through the cotton fabric. His stare was bold, blatant, and when she turned to face him, Tyler was certain she could see the smoldering flame in his eyes.

Dana's heart pounded an erratic rhythm as she felt the heat from Tyler's gaze on her face. They stood less than a foot apart, their chests rising and falling in unison, and for the first in a long time she felt a strange shiver of desire settle in her center.

It had been six years since she'd been in a relationship with a man. She'd thought herself in love for the first time in her life; her perfect world had been shattered when Galvin Seely ended their affair abruptly, telling her he was moving to California to reunite with an old girlfriend. The unresolved issue of her inability to trust a man had again reared its ugly head, and she'd sworn she would never put her faith in another man as long as she lived.

At that moment she wanted Tyler gone. She did not want to feel what she was feeling. Clearing her throat and pretending not to be affected by his devastating virility, she smiled, holding out her uninjured hand.

"I'll take the salve now, thank you."

Tyler lifted an eyebrow and, if possible, his eyes darkened. "Let me look at your hand first."

Her arm dropped to her side. "It's okay."

Reaching out, he cupped her elbow. "I'll let you know if it's okay after I examine it."

He wasn't going to make it easy for her. Did he know what he was doing to her? That he turned her on just by looking at her? She didn't want to be attracted to a man, especially Dr. Tyler Cole, because she did not need or want any distractions. It would take her months to go over and analyze newspaper articles, as well as the court transcripts of her father's trial. Then there would be interviews with her father's attorney, the jurors, the prosecutors, the fire marshal, the coroner, and the technicians who'd gone over the crime scene. She even planned to study the report documenting her father's suicide. Even though the case was more than twenty years old, she prayed some of people involved in the investigation and subsequent trial would still be alive.

Instead of asking Tyler to leave, she said, "We can sit out on the back porch." She led the way across the living room and to the back of the house, his hand still cupping her elbow. She wanted to scream at him not to touch her, but didn't, suffering his closeness.

Tyler followed Dana to the screened-in porch, admiring the profusion of flowering and potted plants. White and pistachio green wicker tables and chairs were covered with plush green-and-white chintz cushions and tablecloths, inviting one to come and stay a while.

And he wanted to stay for a long time. He wanted to stay long enough to discover exactly what it was about Dana Nichols that had him thinking about her when he least expected.

He'd found her beautiful, but so were a few other

women with whom he'd been involved; however, there was something about Dana—something intangible that drew him to her to the point he was helpless to resist the pull of her lush mouth, golden eyes, and sultry voice.

"We can sit here."

Her voice pulled him from his reverie. "After you," he said, pulling out one of the chairs at a round glass-topped table. He seated Dana and then shifted a matching chair, sitting down on her left.

Shivering despite the oppressive heat that seemed to linger long after the sun set, Dana forced herself not to look away from Tyler's perfect symmetrical features. There was nothing about his face to denote that he was anything other than male, but his classically handsome features had a blatant sensuality she'd never encountered before.

She placed her left hand on the table as Tyler unzipped the black bag, withdrawing a pair of bandage scissors. Quickly, expertly, he removed the gauze, staring intently at the back of her hand.

"How does it look?"

His head came up and he smiled at her. "Good."

"Can you leave the gauze off?"

He shook his head. "No. It should be covered for another day."

"It handicaps me."

"How?"

"I can't eat or dress myself properly. How am I going to effectively comb my hair or brush my teeth?"

He went completely still. "You haven't eaten anything since this morning?"

"How can I cook with only one hand?"

Tyler glared at her, frowning. "How do you expect to survive if you don't eat? I'm going to dress your hand, then I'm going to take you out to dinner."

"I'm not going out with you."

"Why not?"

"Because I can't go out dressed like this."

His frown vanished, a slow grin taking its place. He lifted his curving eyebrows. "I happen to like what you're wearing. If you want, I can help you change your clothes," he added as her delicate jaw dropped.

Dana was relieved that lengthening shadows hid the flush in her cheeks, and she was angry with herself for being embarrassed. "Thanks, but no, thanks."

"This is no time for you to be modest, Dana. I've seen so many female bodies over the years that I've lost count."

At that moment, she did not care that he was a doctor, because she was unable to separate the man from his profession.

Tyler opened a tube of Silvadene, gently applying the salve to the tender flesh on the back of Dana's hand. Then he withdrew a roll of nonstick gauze and wound it around her hand and fingers. Only her fingertips were visible. It had taken him less than five minutes to complete his ministrations.

"If you don't want to go out, then you can come home with me. I'll cook something for you." She opened her mouth to refuse him, but he held up his hand. "Enough, Dana." His voice was soft and firm at the same time. "Go put some shoes on. I'll wait for you outside."

He left the tube of Silvadene on the table, repacked the case, rose to his feet, and walked away, leaving Dana to glare at his broad shoulders under the white T-shirt.

She sat, arms crossed under her breasts as fury nearly choked her. She was not one of his nurses that he could intimidate just by glaring at her. If he'd asked her politely, she would comply with his request because she was hungry. However, she did not take orders from any man!

And as if her stomach could read her thoughts, it rumbled loudly. Dana had barely eaten her breakfast, and she'd drunk water most of the day, because she hadn't been able to move the fingers on her left hand to manipulate them enough to even open a can of tuna. The day she'd arrived in Hillsboro, she'd cleaned out her grandmother's refrigerator of leftovers, planning to restock it once she settled in. Well, she had settled in and she was temporarily handicapped. It had taken her more than twenty minutes to change her clothes. Her stomach rumbled again, and she knew she was just being stubborn. She stood up at the same time Tyler reappeared.

"I'm coming," she snapped angrily.

"I just came back to see if you needed my help." His voice was soft and comforting.

Her defiance dissipated quickly. Since she'd met Tyler Cole earlier that morning, all he had done was help her. She was hungry. and he'd offered to feed her. And she knew if she didn't put some food into her stomach, in another hour she would wind up with a pounding headache.

Tilting her chin, she smiled up at him through her lashes, unaware of the seductiveness of the gesture. "Will you do something for me?"

His gaze lingered on her parted lips. "What?"

"Please turn off stereo and put out the candles while I get my shoes."

"Sure."

She followed Tyler back into the house, mounting the staircase to the second floor while he retreated to the living room. Walking into her bedroom, she stared down at her toes. They were covered with a light film of dust. She couldn't go out with dirty feet, even if no one saw her other than Tyler.

Making her way to the bathroom, she sat on the side of the tub and turned on the faucet, letting warm water wash over her feet. Reaching for a towel on a nearby bar, she blotted away the water, using her right hand.

Tyler was leaning against the bumper of his truck when she finally closed the outer door, locking it behind her. Four young girls were in the middle of the street, jumping Double Dutch as several others waited their turn. A smile touched her lips. When she was younger, she'd also played in the street, jumping Double Dutch and playing various other games that had been passed down through generations. All of her friends had been black girls, while the girls now jumping rope were black, white, and Mexican-American. At one time Hillsboro had had an all-black population. But that had changed along with everything else. A car manufacturing plant had set up production in Hillsboro two years before, bringing newcomers to the region while adding longtime residents for their workforce. Hillsboro was now representative of the many ethnic and racial groups in most towns and cities in America.

Tyler opened the passenger-side door for Dana, his hands going around her waist as he lifted her effortlessly onto the leather seat. Winking at her, he closed the door, rounded the black BMW X5, and took his seat behind the wheel. He turned the key in the ignition and cool air flowed from the vents, washing over her moist face.

Leaning over, Tyler pulled Dana's seat belt over her chest, his fingers grazing her breasts. He heard the soft exhalation of air escape her parted lips at the same time he swallowed back a groan.

"I'm sorry," he mumbled under his breath.

Dana nodded, turning her head and staring out the window. She did not look at Tyler again until he turned down a narrow, paved, unlit road, coming to a stop in front of a three-car garage behind a magnificent Greek-Revival structure.

The two-story plantation-style structure rose from the earth like a two-tiered wedding cake on a forest-green tablecloth. Though most of the land in and around Hillsboro was brown and dry from the continuing drought, Tyler's property was like an oasis in the desert. The magnificent house had been built on a section of land realtors and developers considered prime property. Tyler's house was only two miles west of where she'd lived with her parents.

Most of the Delta's topography was flat and monotonous, with the exception of prime locations. These sites were usually higher in elevation, offering panoramas overlooking the Mississippi River, and there had been times when Dana could detect the distinctive scent of the muddy river before a change in the weather. It had become her barometer.

Strategically placed floodlights illuminated the path leading up to the house, and sensor lights brightened and dimmed whenever an object entered or left the range of sensitive beams.

"Don't move," Tyler said in a quiet voice. "I'll help you down."

Dana sat motionless, trying to still the runaway pounding of her heart. Sitting in Tyler's truck two miles from where she'd spent the first ten years of her life, while staring at a structure that closely resembled the house that had become home to several generations of her family caused a momentary rush of uneasiness.

You're home, a silent voice whispered in her head.

And for the first time since she stepped off the plane at the Greenville Municipal Airport, she felt as if she had truly come home.

But, she wondered, could she live permanently in Hillsboro when she'd made a life for herself in Carrollton? She'd set up an apartment that had become her sanctuary, and had a promising career as an investigative reporter for a small but celebrated publication.

The only object linking her with her past was her grandmother's house and its contents. And it wouldn't be until after Eugene Payton disclosed the contents of Georgia's will that she would know what she would be able to do or not do with the property.

The passenger-side door opened, and Tyler reached in and unsnapped her seat belt, this time taking care not to touch her chest. Seconds later she found herself in his arms, his fingers tightening around her waist as he held her effortlessly, her feet dangling several inches off the ground. Her arms circled his neck as she attempted to maintain her balance. This time her chest touched his, her breasts pressed against the solid wall of his chest.

Her head, level with Tyler's, eased forward until she felt the whisper of his moist breath sweep over her mouth. "Please, put me down," she said.

Dana did not recognize her own voice as a riot of apprehension swept away the aloofness she had always been able maintain with most men. Only because she'd allowed it had Galvin been able to slip under the protective barrier she'd set up to keep all men out of her bed and her life. She'd waited until she was twenty-four to offer him her virginity, when the pull of desire and passion had been too great to ignore.

Tyler stared at Dana, gorging on her beauty. "Not yet." Wrapping an arm around her waist, he tightened his hold on her body. He hadn't known her twenty-four hours, yet he wanted her—in his life and in his bed!

Dana smothered a groan. She was certain Tyler could feel her breasts swelling against him at the same time her sensitive nipples hardened like tiny pebbles. Passion pounded the blood through her chest and head, roaring like a waterfall.

Helpless to resist his blatant virility, she eased her head down to his shoulder as she closed her eyes and breathed in his essence. She did not know why, but being held by Tyler communicated a sense of protectiveness. It was the first time in twenty years that a man made her feel completely protected. Tightening her hold on his neck, smiling, she breathed a kiss under his ear.

"Isn't it unethical for a doctor to compromise his patient, Dr. Cole?"

Tyler laughed softly, the sound rumbling in his wide, deep chest. "Who said anything about you being my patient?"

"I'd assumed I was your patient because you did make a house call."

"You assumed wrong, Miss Nichols. If I'd come to your house as your doctor, then it would not have been your hand I would've looked at."

Her head came up and she stared directly at Tyler. It was difficult to see his expression in the encroaching darkness. The setting sun had turned the sky orange-red as lengthening shadows heralded the advent of nightfall.

"What's your specialty?"

"Gynecology and obstetrics." Dana's mouth formed a perfect O, and Tyler dissolved in a paroxysm of laughter. He loosened his grip, but did not release her as she slid down the length of his body, leaving a swathe of heat racing from chest to groin.

Dana's eyes widened as she felt the hardening of Tyler's flesh pressing against her thigh. They did not move or speak as the silence between them loomed like a heavy fog.

She held her breath for several seconds, and then let it out slowly. If Tyler Cole was playing a game, then she wanted no part of it, because she had to keep reminding herself why she'd come back to Hillsboro. And it was not to become involved with a man.

A smile trembled over her lips. "I think you'd better feed me before I faint on you."

Tyler blinked as if he'd just come out of a trance. "Come."

Turning, he led her around the garages to the house, blatantly aware that she would become the first woman, other than his mother and sister, to come under his roof.

Five

Tyler unlocked the front door, walked into the entryway, stood to one side, and watched Dana seemingly float into the space. It was the first time he'd noticed her graceful, fluid body language.

Tilting her head, she glanced up at the chandelier illuminating the entryway like a rising sun. Waning daylight shimmered off the glass over the arched transom with weblike tracery surrounding the sapphire-blue paneled door. The door's rich hue and brass hardware gave the entrance a traditional tone that offset the Chippendale furnishings. A mahogany credenza, flanked by matching chairs, and a wall mirror facing a curving staircase invoked elegant sophistication rather than extravagance.

Tasteful and elegant—the two words hinted what little she'd seen of Dr. Tyler Cole's property. The two words could also be attributed to Tyler, but Dana knew she could add a third adjective—sexy.

Closing the door, Tyler reached for Dana's uninjured hand, cradling it gently, leading her past empty spaces that would become a formal living and dining room, to an oversized kitchen with an adjoining breakfast room, at the far end of the house. The ceiling in the kitchen and breakfast room, reaching one and a half stories, was constructed with skylights that brought the outside in; the eerie glow of an emerging half-moon lit up the space like a spotlight. He turned a dimmer switch, creating a festival of light from recessed fixtures under cabinets and strategically placed wall scones that resembled gaslights from another century. The eclectic mix of modern, Victorian Revival, Art Deco, and a new American style was not only attention-grabbing, but also visually satisfying.

"Your home is beautiful, Tyler." Dana took a deep breath. Everything smelled new.

"Thank you. It's only partially furnished. I'm still awaiting the arrival of furniture for more than half the rooms."

"How long have you lived here?"

"Two weeks."

She smiled up at him. "This section of Hillsboro was vacant land when I lived here."

Tyler regarded her intently. "The builder broke ground and laid the foundation last October. I would come by every other day to watch the progress, and it wasn't until February that it began to resemble the architect's rendering." His home was a classic depiction of a few of the old mansions in the region.

"Come sit," he said, leading her to the breakfast room and seating her on a chair with a pale woven fabric that was a stark contrast to a decorative wrought-iron frame reminiscent of the grillwork seen in the French Quarter in New Orleans.

He hunkered down, his head level with hers. "Do you have an allergy to shellfish?"

Dana resisted the urge to trace the outline of his expressive eyebrows. They were arched over his eyes like the drawings she'd done as a child of a bird's outstretched wings. She noted that the slight stubble on Tyler's chin and jaw made his face appear not only darker, but also rakish. He'd called himself the Black Knight, and that he was.

"No." The single word floated from her lips as a whisper.

He smiled, the minute lines deepening around his penetrating eyes. "If that's the case, then I'll prepare a dish of farfalle with arugula pesto and shrimp. The pieces will be small enough for you to pick up with a fork even if you have to use your right hand." Straightening, he winked down at her. "I'll be right back after I wash my hands."

"May I watch you cook?"

"Of course." He pulled back her chair, and she stood up. He gave her a sidelong glance. "Can you cook?"

Wrinkling her pert nose, she said, "A little."

Dana had told him a half-truth. She could cook and very, very well. The great-aunt who had raised her had worked as a cook at an elegant country inn that also doubled as a bed-and-breakfast. Once her aunt felt Dana was old enough to work at a stove, she would take her with her on weekends. Aunt Fanny taught her to make bread and sweetbreads from scratch, before she graduated to decorating cakes and roasting prime cuts of meats to a succulent tenderness.

Dana excelled in the preparation of sauces and gravies, changing the taste and consistency of traditional ones whenever she experimented with different herbs and spices. Her specialty had become presentation. If it wasn't eye-appealing, then she did not serve it.

Yes, I cook very well, she longed to tell Tyler. And if she'd had the opportunity to prepare a meal for him in the ultramodern stainless steel and ebony kitchen, she probably would shock him with her culinary expertise.

She was certain one reason Galvin had dated her for two years was because he couldn't get enough of her cooking. There were occasions when she'd demanded he take her out to a restaurant or she would stop seeing him. But he'd turned the tables on her because, in the end, he'd ended their relationship. What had surprised Dana most was that she hadn't dwelt on his deception. He'd validated what she had already known: She could not trust a man.

The other reason was their compatibility in bed. She hadn't known she was capable of intense passion until she shared her bed and body with Galvin, and she wanted to rationalize that her attraction to Tyler Cole was because she'd missed not only the passion, but also the personal intimacy, between a man and a woman.

Dana sat on a high stool at a cooking island, drinking a glass of orange juice, while she watched Tyler put fresh argali, toasted pine nuts, garlic, freshly grated parmigiana-reggiano cheese, and measured amounts of extra-virgin olive oil into a food processor, while a pot filled with bowtie-shaped pasta cooked on the stove. A platter of large grilled shrimp, covered with several paper towels, sat on a nearby butcher-block table. The warmed arugula pesto and shrimp would be added to the al dente farfalle, and topped with more grated cheese.

She was grateful she hadn't boasted about her cooking prowess because there was no doubt Tyler was more than familiar with the inner workings of a kitchen. A variety of pots and pans hung from overhead hooks. A specialized unit for storing and cooling wine stood alongside a walk-in freezer. A state-of-the-art refrigerator/freezer, a built-in dishwasher, a compactor, a microwave oven, a dual-level oven, and double stainless-steel sinks at the cooking island provided maximum convenience for him to cook for two or twenty-two.

Tyler poured the pesto into a saucepan, adjusting the flame so it could simmer. The tantalizing aroma of grilled shrimp and garlic wafted in the climate-controlled air. Lifting an eyebrow, he smiled as Dana slipped off the stool to stand beside him.

"Will you share a glass of wine with me?" he asked. She nodded, returning his smile. "What would you like?" She stared at him through her lashes, her moist lips slightly parted.

Don't look at me like that! he wanted to scream at her. Her seductive glance made him hot; it turned him on so much he was helpless to control the quiet storm brewing in his groin. He had to get away from her, even if it was only for a few minutes, or embarrass himself.

The Delta was experiencing a drought and Dr. Tyler Cole was also experiencing a drought—a sexual drought. It had been months since he'd slept with a woman, and since relocating to Hillsboro he hadn't looked at or lusted after any woman—not until now.

He'd celebrated his forty-first birthday May twelfth, joining those who claimed middle-age status, and he wondered whether he truly wanted to spend the rest of his life alone. Did he want his DNA to end with him, or continue for another generation?

Meeting Dana Nichols had him off balance; just her presence had him thinking about his priorities. Interacting with her helped him to recognize something he'd denied for years—he was lonely.

"White, please," she said.

Tyler walked to where he'd stored his wine, took out a chilled bottle of Chardonnay, placing it on the table in the breakfast room. Working quickly, he set the table with china, silver, and a pair crystal wine glasses and water goblets. Returning to the cooking island, he checked on the pesto and pasta.

Ten minutes later, he and Dana sat down to eat, while the distinctive voice of Sade filled the space after he'd turned on a stereo unit built into one of the overhead cabinets.

Dana felt awkward, but she managed to feed herself. Several times a farfalle or a shrimp slipped from her fork, eliciting an encouraging smile from her dining partner. The entrée was delicious.

"Who taught you to cook?" she asked.

Tyler took a sip of wine. "My father. All of the males in my family are mandated to go through what we call culinary survival training. We were raised not to depend on a woman if we wanted to eat."

She raised the goblet filled with sparkling water and a slice of lemon, saluting him. "It appears you've graduated summa cum laude."

He smiled, the gesture as intimate as a kiss. "Thank you, milady."

They continued to eat and drink, both content to listen to the distinctive haunting words of "Sweetest Taboo."

Putting aside his fork and resting his elbows on the table, Tyler laced his fingers together, staring at Dana as she slowly and methodically speared a shrimp and brought the fork to her mouth.

"Have you come back to Hillsboro to stay?" he asked.

She placed her fork next to her plate, and then touched her napkin to the corners of her mouth. "Stay how?" Her voice was calmer than she actually felt.

His lids lowered as he studied her impassive expression. "Live here permanently."

She shook her head. Several wisps of hair had escaped the twist she'd pinned up earlier that morning,

gold-streaked strands brushing a bared shoulder with
the motion. "I don't know, Tyler. I've taken a four-
month leave from my job to settle my grandmother's
estate. After I can take care all of the legal matters,
I'm going back to New York."

What she didn't say was that settling her grandmother's estate would become a simple task when compared to her investigating her parents' murder/suicide.

Four months, Tyler mused. Was that enough time to
get to know Dana well enough to reevaluate his own
future? Did he want her to become a part of his life
and his future? The questions attacked him while he
refused to acknowledge that Dana could possibly have
a boyfriend or fiancé waiting for her back in New York.

"What do you do for a living?" he asked.

She gave him a direct stare. "I'm a journalist."

"Newspaper?"

"Yes."

"Which one?"

"The *Carrollton Chronicle.* It has a very small circulation."

"How small?" Tyler asked.

"About twelve hundred subscribers."

"That's equal to Hillsboro's *Herald.*"

Dana was more than familiar with her hometown
weekly, remembering how most of the adults had
waited for Thursday evening to read the headlines,
then devour each word from the front page to the last.
The publisher of the *Herald* had continued a century-
old tradition of publishing a periodical with a distinct
hometown flavor. The black-owned newspaper had
been as essential to Hillsboro for reporting the local
news as *The New York Times* was to New York City, major
U.S. cities, and world capitals.

"Is it still owned by the Davis family?"

Tyler shook his head. "No. Someone named Ryan

Vance is the current publisher and editor in chief. The word is that he bought it from the Davises last month. It was said the current generation of Davises saw no future in newspaper publishing and put the *Herald* up for sale."

Dana stared down at the slice of lemon floating in the glass of water. So many things had changed in Hillsboro during her exile, and she wondered for the first time how difficult would it be for her to glean the information she needed about what had become Hillsboro's most celebrated murder.

Tracing the rim of the goblet with a forefinger, she looked up. Tyler sat motionless, staring across the table at her. "Why did you move to Hillsboro?" she asked. It was the same question she'd put to him before the waitress at Smithy's burned her hand.

"I was recruited by the federal government for a research study."

Tyler related the statistics on infant-mortality rates in Hillsboro in relation to the national average. She listened intently as he gave her an overview of the number of research projects he'd been involved with since becoming a doctor.

"I made a visit to Hillsboro before I decided to head the project, to see the facility where I'd be working, and was horrified with the conditions. Most of the medical equipment was antiquated, and the physical condition of the facility was definitely not conducive for adequate medical treatment. I told the surgeon general I would assume responsibility for the study, but only if the Department of Health and Human Services doubled their original appropriation to cover the cost of renovating the site and purchasing updated equipment. It took four months of haggling before they agreed.

"I increased the staff to include a nutritionist, X-ray

technician, and a part-time social worker. Renovations were completed in January, bringing the site up to code, and the Hillsboro's Women's Health Clinic can boast that it has some of the most sophisticated, state-of-the art medical equipment in the state of Mississippi."

Dana was impressed with his obvious confidence. There was no doubt his experience in medical research had earned the attention of the U.S. surgeon general.

"What's the time frame for your study?"

"Five years."

"What are you going to do once it ends?"

Tyler paused, his eyes caressing the sensual beauty of the delicate woman sharing his space. "I plan to stay in Hillsboro."

"And do what?"

Angling his head, he lowered his lashes, smiling. "I'll become a small-town family doctor."

He had planned his future carefully. The detached guest house adjacent to the three-car garage would become his office. He wouldn't have built a home in Hillsboro if he hadn't planned on putting down roots in the Delta.

It had taken more than twenty years, but he now had a place he called home.

I'll become a small-town doctor. His statement set off an alarm in Dana's head. She was sitting under the roof of a man, a doctor to whom she'd felt an intense attraction. Had it been the same with her mother? Had Alicia seen Harry and decided she wanted the small-town doctor?

Stirring uneasily in the chair, she moved to stand, and Tyler came to his feet, rounding the table and pulling out her chair. "I think I'd better be getting home. Thank you for everything. I owe you," she added softly.

And you will pay, Dana Nichols, Tyler mused. And he

would make certain she would enjoy what he had in store for her.

Curving an arm around her waist, he pulled her close to his side. "I'll come by tomorrow and look at your hand again."

She nodded, praying she would be able to wash and dress herself without too much difficulty. "I can't wait to get this dressing off."

Tyler led Dana to his truck, and ten minutes later escorted her through her front door. They stood in the entryway staring at each other. A lamp on a drop-leaf provided enough light to see Tyler's impassive expression. When he didn't smile, he looked like an entirely different person. There was an air of seriousness about him that silently communicated that Dr. Tyler Cole was a very private person. She also felt he could be dangerous when crossed.

"You should name your home," she said in a quiet tone. "All grand houses in Mississippi have names like St. Charles, Black Acre, or The Oaks."

Tyler wanted to tell her that antebellum plantations were also identified by their names—magnificent mansions and thousands of acres of cotton, sugar cane, rice, or tobacco built, planted, and maintained by his enslaved ancestors. He was a Southerner living in the South, but what he did not want was to be reminded of the South's infamous, sinful past wherein fortunes were made on the backs of those kidnapped, raped, and tortured because their captors deemed them chattel.

He shook his head. "I'd rather not. To do so would remind me of a period in our history when we were in bondage."

She nodded slowly. "I understand."

And Dana did understand. Her home had been called Raven's Crest because her father had inherited

the house and its title from *his* father, who in turned
had inherited it from *his* father. The original structure
had belonged to a slaveholder. The former owner, one
of the last surviving widows of a Confederate officer
in the region, had sold Raven's Crest to Dr. Silas
Nichols to pay off back taxes and creditors. The elderly
woman had taken the money Silas had given her and
moved with an unmarried daughter to Louisiana.

Taking a step, Tyler leaned over and kissed Dana's
cheek. "Good night."

She shivered despite the lingering heat. She knew
her house would feel like a sauna when compared to
Tyler's climate-controlled one. "Good night."

Waiting until she'd closed and locked the door behind her, he walked back to his truck and drove back
his own empty house.

And for the first time since relocating to Hillsboro,
Dr. Tyler Simmons Cole did not want to go to bed—
alone.

Six

Dana woke up feeling as if she'd just closed her eyes. After Tyler drove her back home, she'd sat out on the porch on a swing rocker, staring out into the darkened countryside. The heat, the smell of the parched earth, the intermittent croaking of frogs, and the incessant chirping of crickets had lulled her into a hypnotic trance as she recalled the happier times she'd shared with her parents and widowed grandmother.

She hadn't remembered her grandfather, who'd been killed in an accident the year she turned two. Daniel Sutton, who had worked for the railroad as a track worker, lost his life after a coupling between two freight cars broke loose, crushing him to death. The railroad compensated Georgia Sutton for her husband's death, but grieving the loss of her first and only love, she vowed she would never remarry or take up with another man. Waiting a year, the socially acceptable time limit for mourning the loss of a spouse, men began calling on what most considered a handsome widow woman. Dana remembered her grandmother glaring at the men standing on her doorstep, before sending them away with a curt reply that she did not want to be bothered.

Dana had also recalled the Sunday dinners with her grandmother. After church services concluded, Alicia and Georgia would retreat to the kitchen, where they'd prepare enough food to last until the next Sunday dinner. It was only during the winter months that the two women cooked every day. Turning on the stove and ovens had helped to filter warmth throughout the house.

She could count the times Alicia cooked in her own kitchen: Thanksgiving, Christmas, and Easter. She only used the kitchen at Raven's Crest for major family holidays.

Dana had sat up thinking about her family because she did not want to think about Tyler Cole. Seeing him was visually shocking, and interacting with him had short-circuited her nervous system. He was a man who was certain to become an enticing distraction. And she did not need any distractions—especially from someone who looked like him.

She'd finally left the porch to go to bed, and as soon as her head touched her pillow she'd begun dreaming—dreaming about a tall man with sun-browned olive skin, large penetrating black eyes, and a voice soft and sensual enough to send shivers up and down her spine every time he opened his mouth to speak.

If you're talking about a wife and children, I have none. His statement was branded in her mind. He was a bachelor, yet he had built a home with enough space for a large family. He may not have had a wife, but that did not mean there wasn't a woman to whom Tyler had pledged his life and his future. It was after three when Dana finally fell asleep, shutting out the haunting image of the man who unknowingly had snared her in a web of desire.

Bright sunlight poured through the sheers at the tall windows. It was going to be another day without rain. Rolling over, she sat up, her bare feet dangling over the side of a four-poster mahogany bed standing more than a foot off the floor. Her toes touched a matching stool as she climbed down. The bare wood floor was warm under the soles of her feet.

It was imperative she go to the supermarket to stock the refrigerator and pantry. But first she had to find a plastic covering for her gauze-covered hand before showering.

It took more than an hour for Dana to brush her teeth, shower, and dress herself.

Wearing a loose-fitting light blue, flowered-sprigged Laura Ashley dress and a pair of pale-blue leather mules, she descended the staircase. The telephone rang as she walked into the kitchen. Quickening her pace, she picked up the receiver to a wall phone before the second ring.

"Hello."

"Hello, long-lost friend."

Vertical lines formed between Dana's eyes. She did not recognize the female voice.

"Dana?" The woman's voice came through the earpiece after a prolonged silence.

"I'm sorry, but you seem to have the advantage. I don't recognize your voice."

"Remember when we pricked our fingers and became blood sisters?"

"Lily Mitchell!" Dana's smile was dazzling. Lily had been her very best friend. They'd been practically inseparable.

"You got the first name right. I've been Lily Clark for several years now."

"Don't tell me you married Billy." Lily had had a crush on Billy Clark since the fourth grade.

"I sure did. I just got back from a week-long anniversary cruise, and the first thing I hear from Billy's mother is that you'd come back to Hillsboro."

Dana was certain every tongue in Hillsboro was wag-

ging about her return. "I came back to bury my grandmother and settle her estate."

"I'm sorry to hear about your grandmother, Dana."

"Thanks."

"Are you going to be home later?"

Dana glanced up at the clock over the sink. It was
eight-forty-five. "How much later?" she asked Lily.

"Around five or six."

"Yes."

"Then I'll come by. I have something to show you."

Dana smiled even though Lily could not see her.
Out of all of the girls in their group, Lily had been
the prankster.

"I'll be here," Dana said.

She ended the call, a warm smile softening her features. Reuniting with her childhood friend evoked a
time when she'd believed she lived in a perfect world.
But the disintegration of her fairy-tale existence coincided with the breakup of her parents' marriage.

Their constant bickering had had her fleeing to her
room for sanctuary. It was there she'd covered her
head with a pillow, or hidden in a closet, to shut out
the sound of their arguing. She hadn't wanted her
mother and father to separate or divorce; however,
there were several occasions when she wished they'd
had. Anything was better than them screaming at each
other while hurling accusations like falling meteorites.

She had witnessed friends and classmates whose parents had split up, always believing that if parents really
thought of the pain it would cause their children, they
would try to work out the differences in order to save
their marriage.

And it wasn't until Dana was older that she realized
her parents' marriage couldn't be saved. Alicia Sutton-
Nichols was an adulteress, and she hadn't bothered to
hide her infidelity from her husband whenever she re-

turned home without washing away the evidence of her indiscretions.

Knowing her mother had slept around was always a deciding factor for her whenever she was faced with the decision of whether she would have an intimate relationship with a man. She'd always agonized whether she'd inherited Alicia's proclivity for promiscuity. However, she'd been faithful to Galvin, belaying the fear that she would not be able to maintain a monogamous union.

After she and Galvin parted, Dana purposely rejected any man who expressed an interest in her, while embarking on a pattern of eating dinner at restaurants, going to the movies, and attending social gatherings without an escort.

During the summer months of June, July, and August, she always decreased the number of hours she worked at the newspaper because she wanted to spend extra time with Georgia Sutton. They usually shared long weekends visiting the Canadian provinces of Ontario and Quebec. They'd hold hands and talk about anything and everything—except Hillsboro. It was if that topic had become taboo. Now, she'd ended a twenty-two-year exile to return to Hillsboro and a house filled with memories of another time in her family's past, and what made her return even more poignant was that this would become the first Hillsboro summer she would not have her grandmother to confide in.

Pushing the memories of her family's past to the farthest recesses of her mind, she slipped the car key off a magnetic hook affixed to the door of the refrigerator. A smile softened her mouth when she remembered the vow she and Lily had made one afternoon on the Mitchells' front porch: Lily would grow up and marry William Clark, while Dana would become Mrs.

Ross Wilson, Jr. Billy and Ross were three years their senior, which made them older, exciting, and somewhat dangerous to the prepubescent girls.

She was still smiling when she walked out of the kitchen, locked up the house, started up the car, backed out of the driveway, heading in the direction of the downtown business district.

Tyler maneuvered into the driveway, parking behind Dana's Chevy, refusing to acknowledge he was acting like a lovesick fool. He wasn't in love with Dana Nichols, didn't know her, but he had admitted to himself that he was drawn to her in a way he had never been attracted to another woman—not even the first woman who'd shared his bed.

Whereas he'd always been two to three years ahead of his peers intellectually, the reverse was the case when it came to sex. While most of his friends had experienced their first sexual encounter when still in high school, he'd waited until his first year in college. His on-again, off-again affair with a fellow college student taught him what self-control meant. Once he'd discovered his libido was stronger than he'd ever expected it to be, he'd learned to control his sex drive with meditation. It usually worked for him—until now.

There was something about Dana Nichols: her eyes, voice, smile, the way she stared up at him, and her slender compact body that meditating could not neutralize. He'd taken two icy-cold showers, but to no avail. If he hadn't been so disturbed by his instant attraction to Dana, he would've thought he was going through a premature midlife crisis. Although forty-one, he found himself more randy than he'd been as an adolescent.

Turning off the engine, he reached over and picked

up the small leather case and a large white shopping bag off the passenger-side seat. Opening the door to his vehicle, he stepped out into the smothering heat. A few clouds dotted a blistering white sky. Meteorologists were watching the weather carefully, because there were sightings of several twisters in Arkansas, Tennessee, and Oklahoma. The bone-dry Delta region needed rain, not tornados.

"Good afternoon, Dr. Cole. I hope Dana's not feeling poorly."

Tyler turned, nodding to the elderly woman standing on the steps of the neighboring house with a broom in one hand as he made his way to Dana's front door.

"Good afternoon, Miss Janie." He offered her a friendly smile.

He had no intention of replying to Miss Janie's query about Dana's health. She'd probably heard about the accident at Smithy's within minutes of its occurrence. And it was apparent the elderly woman had come out of her house when she saw him drive up, curious why he would be making a visit to her recently deceased neighbor's house in the middle of the afternoon. He had lived in Hillsboro long enough to know that Janie Stewart was an incurable gossip.

"Let me know if she needs my help," the older woman continued as Tyler rang the bell.

"I will, Miss Janie."

Within minutes of his ringing the bell, Dana came to the door. She looked different today. Her hair was loose, parted off-center, the blunt-cut ends grazing her shoulders. His gaze was fixed on the shimmering gold strands threaded through the light brown ones. At first he thought she'd artificially lightened her hair, but upon closer inspection he realized the gold highlights were natural. The pale-blue dress with tiny purple flowers was flattering to her body, and he wondered how long it had taken her to dress and style her hair.

Smiling at her stunned expression, he said, "I've come to examine your hand and share lunch." He held up the large white shopping bag.

Dana stood on the other side of the screen door, staring numbly at Tyler. She hadn't expected to see him in the middle of the afternoon. She was glad he'd come because she was frustrated by her temporary handicap. Before entering Publix, she'd stopped at a fast-food restaurant's drive-through window and ordered a greasy, sodium-filled concoction that impersonated a breakfast fajita. She'd opted for orange juice to relieve her dry throat instead of a container of coffee. Since the accident at Smithy's, she'd avoided hot beverages.

"Please open the door, Dana, before Miss Janie begins the second round of her inquisition," Tyler whispered softly.

Unlatching the door, she pushed it open. "What are you doing here so early?"

Waiting until she'd closed and locked the door behind him, Tyler stared at her upturned face, his expression impassive. "Can't I even get a 'good afternoon,' Miss Nichols?"

Pinpoints of heat dotted her cheeks. She'd forgotten her manners. She flashed a demure smile. "Good afternoon, Dr. Cole."

He nodded, smiling. "Good afternoon, Miss Dana. To answer your question as to why I'm here so early—the clinic closes at two on Fridays."

Dana lifted an eyebrow. "I don't want you to neglect your patients just to come and see me."

Tyler wanted to tell her he'd never put a woman before his patients—that patients were more important than any personal assignation. "Have you forgotten I think of you as one of my patients?" he said instead.

Dana smiled again, the expression lighting up her face and her eyes. "You make house calls and feed your patients. I'm really impressed."

He bowed slightly from the waist. "Thank you. Playing the small-town doctor is a new experience for me. I want you to let me know when I'm not getting it right."

But everything about Tyler is so right, she mused. From the top of his graying curly hair to the soles of his expensively shod feet, from his soft sensual deep voice to his gentle bedside manner, Dr. Tyler Cole was perfect.

"I'm certain you'll do just fine," she said. "Come, we can sit out on the back porch. It's the coolest place in the house right now." Every ceiling fan in the house was working tirelessly to dispel the buildup of heat.

Tyler followed Dana through the living room, his gaze sweeping around the space and cataloguing its contents. The interior of Georgia Sutton's house was larger than it had appeared from the outside—its furnishings harkening back to another era. He wanted to linger and examine the stately towering grandfather clock softly chiming the half hour.

Owning a home for the first time had surprisingly elicited a new interest in home furnishings. His mother, with his approval, had selected and ordered all of the furnishings for the main house, but had left him with the responsibility of deciding what he wanted for the three-suite guest house.

Large books and catalogues with differing architectual styles, home furnishings, and antiques were stacked on a table in his sitting room, and he had yet to glance at them. There was no pressure for him to complete the guest house because his cousin Michael

Kirkland had informed his relatives that he and his wife Jolene had offered to open their Georgetown home for this year's Thanksgiving gathering.

Jolene Kirkland had called him at the clinic, informing him she was pregnant again, and her second child's due date was Christmas Day. Michael and Jolene's daughter would celebrate her first birthday next week. He had already mailed off a gift for Teresa April Kirkland. Not only was the black-haired, green-eyed delicate little girl his second cousin, but also his goddaughter. He was son, brother, uncle, and with the birth of Teresa Kirkland, had become a godfather for the second time.

He'd delivered Teresa along with nearly a dozen other second and third cousins. He'd become the family obstetrician, and his brother-in-law Aaron Spencer the family pediatrician. The dizzying rush of delivering a healthy child was something Tyler never wanted to get used to. Holding a trembling mucus-and-blood-covered infant while waiting to hear the first cry, filling its tiny lungs with precious oxygen, was equivalent to a rush associated with free fall. It was heart-stopping, breathtaking, and exhilarating.

Now that he'd become responsible for the health clinic, he realized interacting one-on-one with patients had taken precedence over medical research. He had wanted to become like his brother-in-law once he decided to focus on medical research. Aaron had the perfected a balance of seeing patients and heading a Brazilian-based research institute at the São Tomé Instituto de Médico Pesquisa. But that was before Tyler settled in Hillsboro.

He liked the daily interaction with his patients, the small-town ambience of the region where he'd built a home and planned to spend the rest of his life, and he was beginning to like Dana Nichols—much more than he wanted to. He hadn't openly pursued or come onto her because he'd assumed the responsibility of treating her burn. But their pseudo-doctor-patient relationship would end within minutes, and he planned for another to begin—one where they would meet each other on equal footing as man and woman.

Stepping out onto the porch, Tyler was able to appreciate the inviting beauty of the space in the bright daylight. The round table, attractively draped in a white chintz tablecloth dotted with varying shades of green leaves, and surrounded by the white and pasticho-green wicker chairs, would be equally suited for sharing breakfast, lunch, or dinner. A wicker desk set under a window held several books and magazines. A thick cushion covered with the same chintz fabric as the tablecloth rested on the seat of a straight-back wicker chair. He thought of the conservatory at the rear of his own home. As soon as the furniture and plants for the space were delivered, he planned to spend most of his time there. Meanwhile, he wanted to spend all of his free time with Dana on her porch.

Pulling out a chair at the table, he seated Dana, and then sat down on her left. Opening his case, he put on a pair of latex gloves, withdrew a pair of bandage scissors, and removed the gauze bandage from her hand. Cradling her hand, he examined it. It looked smaller and even more delicate resting on his much larger one. There was no sign of blistering or redness.

Smiling, he glanced at her enchanting profile. "It looks very good." His thumb grazed the skin on the back of her hand. "Does that hurt?"

Dana shook her head. "It's just a little sensitive to the touch."

"Remember to put the ointment on it several times a day to keep the skin from drying out."

She smiled. "It can remain uncovered?" There was obvious apprehension in her query.

He applied a light layer of Silvadene to her hand, removed his gloves, and dropped them into the case. "Yes. It should heal completely with any scarring."

Dana stared at Tyler staring at her from under her lashes, sensing an immediate change in him. He seemed to be waiting—for what, she did not know. "How much do I owe you, Dr. Cole?"

He came closer without actually moving, his chest rising and falling in a deep even breathing. "A date."

Dana's breathing halted, and then started up again. The pulse in her throat beat an erratic rhythm. "A date?" she repeated, her sultry voice lowering an octave.

He leaned closer, and his moist breath swept over her mouth as his heated gaze lingered on her parted lips. "Yes, Dana, a date. I'd like you to share dinner with me at a restaurant of my choice. However, if you're committed to another man, then I'll withdraw my request."

Dana's defenses began to subside as she stared at the hopeful expression on Tyler's face. Despite the confidence he exuded, there was also a vulnerability he was unable to conceal. Had he also experienced a failed relationship? Had a woman he loved left him or vice versa?

Don't do it, an inner voice whispered. Every fiber in her body warned her not to accept his invitation for a dinner date, warned her to tell Tyler Cole that she did not and could not see him again, but knew she had to get past Galvin's deception. Besides, Tyler only wanted to take her out to eat, not enter into a relationship.

"When?" she asked, ignoring the shiver of apprehension snaking up her spine.

His mercurial black eyes lovingly caressed her beautiful face. "Are you committed to someone, Dana?" He had to know because he'd never come onto another man's wife or girlfriend.

Her expression was impassive. "No, Tyler, I'm not committed to anyone." And she wasn't, hadn't been even when she had been involved with Galvin.

Tyler smiled, the dimples in his chiseled cheeks winking attractively at her. "How about tomorrow night?" She nodded, lifting an eyebrow. "If it's all right with you, I'll pick you up at seven-thirty."

"Seven-thirty is fine." A slight frown furrowed her smooth forehead at the same time she dropped her gaze. "Why are you asking me out when there are hundreds of other women in Hillsboro who I'm certain would love to share dinner with you?"

He gave her a long, penetrating look. "Because it's you I want to share dinner with me, Dana Nichols, and not some other woman. Does that answer your question?"

She glanced up at him, the pupils in her golden eyes darkening with a rising awareness of who Tyler Cole was and what he represented. He was X-rated and dangerous—dangerous to her emotional well-being, dangerous to the wall she'd erected around herself—because she couldn't afford to be distracted by romantic notions once she set out to clear her family's name, and dangerous because of her distrust of men. A calmness she hadn't known she possessed settled in her chest, and she knew in an instant that she had turned a corner in her life. She could go out with a man and remain completely detached.

"I'm only going to commit to one date with you." The words were spoken with a quiet determination she was certain he understood implicitly.

She fixed her gaze on the shape of his mouth, visually admiring its firm upper and fuller lower lip. She felt as if his black eyes could look inside her, seeing what she sought valiantly to protect: her heart. Her initial attraction to Tyler was strong, much stronger that it had been with Galvin, and in the end Galvin had validated what she'd come to acknowledge as a child—every man she loved eventually left her. Six years ago she'd sworn she would never permit herself to become involved with another man, commit to a future with him, or bear his child.

Tyler nodded. "If that's the case, then we'll begin with one." His voice was soft, filled with quiet assurance. And it was in that instant that Tyler Cole revealed much of who he was.

He'd grown up privileged, getting most of whatever he'd wanted. He'd decided on a career in medicine, and given his intelligence and family resources, there was never a doubt he would not fulfill his goal to become a doctor. He did not have to concern himself about applying for student loans to pay tuition or purchase books. The money had been available for anything and everything he needed.

At twenty-five, he had come into a five-million-dollar trust fund. ColeDiz International, Ltd., a privately held family-owned conglomerate, operated coffee and banana plantations in Belize, Mexico, Jamaica, and Puerto Rico. They also owned vacation and private properties throughout the Caribbean.

Several months before his thirty-fifth birthday, his grandfather, Samuel Claridge Cole, died, and the distribution of the Cole patriarch's wealth afforded him more than five times that amount. He paid for all or any of his purchases with a single signature on the bottom of a check. An aunt managed his portfolio, sending him quarterly statements, which he usually glanced at before filing away with several other financial documents.

Tyler had decided to go into research because of remarkable breakthroughs in modern medicine. It had never been his goal to become a surgeon, performing operations to advance his reputation or earning thousands of dollars from each surgical procedure.

Since living and working in Hillsboro, meeting and interacting with Dana Nichols, Tyler knew exactly who he was and what he wanted. And at that moment he wanted Dana. He wanted her with the same passion he'd experienced when he realized he wanted to become a doctor.

"One it is," she confirmed.

Her consent gave him the opening he needed as he touched his mouth to hers, savoring the soft sweetness of her lips. She moaned softly as he deepened the kiss. Her left hand came up, her fingertips grazing the stubble of an emerging beard on his cheek. Fighting the dynamic virility he exuded, she failed profoundly, losing herself in the passionate kiss.

It had been too long since she'd been kissed, too long since she gloried in the natural masculine scent of a man's body mingling with his sensual fragrance of aftershave and cologne. Too long since she'd felt the flames of desire feather over her body, igniting a fire in the center of her being. Pulling back, she dropped her hand but not her gaze.

Tyler smiled at her, his expression mirroring supreme masculine satisfaction. "Are you ready for lunch?"

She returned his smile, her body throbbing with banked desire. "Yes."

Dana was ready to share a meal with Tyler, but more than that, she was ready for him now that he'd revealed how he felt about her. One thing she knew, and that was that she wasn't immune to his charm, but at thirty-three she'd come to know herself quite well. She was focused, controlled, and determined. She had proven that when she'd gone undercover at the girls' group home. There had been a few times when she'd thought her actual identity had been compromised; however, quick thinking and an even quicker tongue had extricated her from what would've become a life-threatening situation.

Tyler withdrew two large plastic containers from the shopping bag. Both were filled with a Caesar salad with strips of grilled chicken. Smaller plastic cups with the accompanying dressing followed. He emptied the bag when he placed a large bottle of Perrier on the table along with another container of assorted melon slices.

Dana pushed back her chair, rising to her feet. "I have to get plates, silverware, and glasses."

Tyler rose with her. "I'll help you."

Together they retreated to the kitchen, each lost in their private thoughts and unaware of the invisible thread binding them tightly together.

Seven

Tyler had consumed half of his salad when the cell phone attached to the waistband of his slacks chimed softly. He picked up the tiny instrument, pressed a button, recognizing the number and knowing his lunch date with Dana had just ended.

"Dr. Cole," he said softly, identifying himself. He listened intently to the professional-sounding voice. One of his patients had gone into labor; the attending doctor was concerned because the baby's head still had not entered the birth canal. "Make certain she's comfortable, and let her know I'm on my way." Ending the call, he stood up. "I'm sorry, Dana, but I have to leave."

She smiled up at him. "There's no need to apologize."

Bending slightly, he wound his fingers through her unbound hair, while brushing his mouth over hers. "I'll be back later," he crooned against her moist parted lips. Tasting her mouth sent a back draft of incendiary heat roaring through his groin.

Dana held his gaze, admiring the smoothness of his dark skin, the silken black eyebrows arching over a pair of large penetrating eyes, and the delicate line of his thin nose and firm masculine mouth.

"There's no need for you to come back."

"But I *want* to come back." What Tyler wanted to

tell Dana was that he *needed* to come back, *needed* to see her, again and again, until he uncovered why she and not some other woman had touched something so deep within his psyche that he feared losing control of his emotions. He wanted to know why he'd waited forty-one years to meet a woman who unknowingly elicited a pull that exceeded his obsession with medicine.

Dana forced herself to look away. Staring into the deep dark depths of Tyler's fathomless obsidian gaze was perilous. Just a look, a single glance from him, sent her hormones out of kilter. She'd tried ignoring the heaviness settling in her breasts, tightening her nipples until they were hard as pebbles, and the sudden rush of wetness between her legs. It had been so long since she'd lain with a man that she had almost forgotten the pleasurable sensations that always left her with an amazing sense of completeness.

"Please go, Tyler, and take care of your patient."

He hesitated, seemingly committing everything about her face to memory, then turned on his heels and walked back into the house. Dana sat motionless, staring at the profusion of vibrant purple flowers spilling over the clay pot of a hanging fuchsia.

Tyler rushing off to see a patient reminded her of her father. Had Alicia strayed because Harry hadn't given her the attention she craved? Had Harry's patients become more important than his wife and child?

Dana remembered her mother's frustration because Harry hadn't been there for his daughter's milestones: her first piano recital, sixth-birthday party, and when she'd gone to Jackson to compete in the statewide spelling bee.

Why had everyone in Hillsboro blamed Alicia and not Harry for her infidelity? Had anyone, other than Dana, overheard Alicia accuse Harry of "carrying on" with several of his female patients?

Closing her eyes, she tried recalling the virulent accusations whenever her parents verbally attacked each other. There was the name-calling, the threats, and the constant bickering that had never failed to set her nerves on edge. Alicia and Harry's arguments had escalated until she could not remember when they hadn't fought.

She sat sipping the chilled Perrier until she heard the telephone. Pushing to her feet, she rushed to the kitchen to answer the call before the answering machine activated itself.

Picking up the receiver, she greeted the caller with a friendly hello, sobering when she heard Eugene Payton's voice. "Yes, Mr. Payton. Thank you. Good-bye." She hung up, her hand trembling.

The call had lasted less than twenty seconds. Eugene Payton had set up an appointment to see her Monday morning. And at that time, the contents of Georgia Rose Sutton's last will and testament would be revealed to her.

With the reading of the will, the past would meet the present, while at the same time impacting on her future. Exhaling, Dana closed her eyes; there was no doubt Monday's events would stay with her for a long time; she was certain the conditions of he grandmother's will would change her and her life forever. Not to mention that she'd committed to date a man socially for the first time in six years—a man she'd found herself attracted to despite her resolve not to fall under his sensual spell.

Dana opened her eyes, mentally dismissing the image of Tyler. Now that she had use of both hands, she would begin the task of sorting through her grandmother's possessions to see what she would keep, give away, or discard.

Turning on her heels, she returned to the porch.

First, she would clear the table, and then change out of her dress into something more suitable for cleaning. She'd planned to begin with the upstairs closets.

Dana had showered, moisturized her body with a perfumed lotion, and pulled a cotton sundress over her head as the doorbell chimed throughout the house. Quickening her step, she made it down the staircase to the front door.

It had taken her more than two hours to go through one closet, the first of four, excluding two others where her grandmother had stored stacks of tissue-wrapped tablecloths and heirloom linens. There was a time when Georgia had supported herself as a skilled seamstress, making everything from her own clothes to household accessories.

A brilliant smile lit up her eyes when she saw a face from her childhood. Lily Mitchell-Clark had grown up to become an extremely attractive woman. She was tall, slender, and her naturally curly hair was stylishly cut, framing a rounded face from which sparkled large dark laughing eyes. Dana's gaze shifted from Lily's smiling face to the small child in her arms. The tiny rosebud mouth was open and relaxed in sleep.

Unlatching the door, Dana pushed it open. Curving an arm around Lily's shoulders, Dana pressed her cheek to Lily's. "Please come in and rest yourself."

Lily stepped into the entryway, her smile still in place. "How would you like to hold your namesake?"

Dana went completely still, her arms falling limply at her sides, her gaze fusing with Lily's amused one. It had been more than two decades, but it was apparent that her best friend hadn't forgotten her.

"You named your baby after me?"

"I call her Dana even though her name is Danella."

"Give her to me, please." Dana held out her arms as Lily laid the delicately formed baby girl in her embrace. "How old is she?"

"Fourteen months."

Danella Clark was a beautiful child, inheriting her mother's hair and features and her father's burnished-gold coloring. Lowering her head, Dana pressed a kiss to the silken curls covering a perfectly rounded pate.

"She's adorable, Lily."

Curving an arm around Dana's waist, Lily hugged her. She wanted to tell Dana *she* was beautiful. Just like her mother had been. Lily always thought that Alicia Nichols was the most beautiful woman in all of Hillsboro. At least that was what all of the men used to say, much to the chagrin of their wives and girlfriends. Whenever Alicia walked into Mt. Nebo Baptist Church with her husband and daughter, all heads turned in their direction. Alicia always took advantage of any situation where she'd become the center of attraction. She'd slow her pace, smiling and nodding like a celebrity, until she was seated on a pew where prior Nichols generations had sat and worshipped.

What Lily hadn't understood was Dana's unwillingness to acknowledge her own budding beauty. Even when everyone had remarked about her resemblance to her stunning-looking mother, Dana always denied the claim. It was as if she'd been ashamed of her looks.

"Come, let's sit on the porch," Dana urged, leading the way across the living room. "Have you had dinner?" she asked, glancing at Lily over her shoulder.

"I just came from Billy's mother's house. I ate so much I can hardly move. The woman's idea of a snack is a four-course dinner."

Sitting on a slider love seat, one leg tucked under her body, Dana cradled Danella Clark to her breasts. The baby stirred, her tiny mouth making sucking sounds, but did not wake up. Holding the little girl close to her heart, and inhaling the clean scent exclusive to babies, evoked a foreign emotion of longing in Dana—a longing for her own child.

She sat motionless, not knowing who or what had stirred her maternal instincts. She'd never felt the pull of motherhood, not even when she'd thought herself in love with Galvin.

Lily, reclining on a nearby cushioned rocker, removed her sandals and rested her bare feet on a footstool with a matching cushion. Closing her eyes and pressing her head to the back of the rocking chair, she smiled broadly. "It's as if we never parted, nothing has changed. You sit on the love seat while I take the rocking chair."

"Old habits are hard to break," Dana countered in a soft, calming voice. "You look wonderful, Lily. I must say that marriage and motherhood agree with you." The blending of Lily's African and Native American ancestry was evident in the rich darkness of her red-brown coloring, curly hair, and tall slender body.

Lily flashed a demure smile. "Thank you. I must admit that I've never been happier."

"When did you and Billy marry?"

"Three years ago."

"What took you so long? You've been in love with him since grade school."

Lily stared up at the whirling blades of a ceiling fan for a full minute, and then said, "I wasn't the first Mrs. William Clark." She ignored Dana's soft gasp of surprise. "Billy graduated high school, attended a college in Virginia, and was recruited by the FBI; after his graduation at Quantico, he met and married a forensic pathologist. He was assigned to a field office in Indiana, while his wife opted to remain in the D.C. area. It was only after Billy was transferred to Seattle that she followed him and they began living together as husband and wife. After fifteen years with the Bureau, he was promoted to a senior agent and transferred again. This time it was Los Angeles. Sandra, refusing to move again, returned to Virginia, filed for divorce, and remarried.

"Billy came back to Hillsboro to bury his dad, stayed a month, then returned to L.A. Less than a year later he was back—this time for good. The mayor appointed him sheriff after Mr. Newcomb fell and broke his hip while running after a young kid who'd jumped over the counter at the Piggly Wiggly to steal a pack of cigarettes for his trifling, deadbeat father."

"How's Sheriff Newcomb doing?" Dana had to ask, because Philip Newcomb had been the first person to come to Raven's Crest to view Alicia's body after Harry called to report her murder. The ex-sheriff would be at the top of her list once she began her round of interviews.

Lily shrugged a shoulder. "He walks with the aid of a cane. His wife attempted to sue the doctor who set his hip, saying he botched the operation. She lost the malpractice suit, and complains to any and everyone who will stand still long enough to listen to her."

Dana mentally catalogued this information on the ex-sheriff. "How did you and Billy finally get together?"

Grinning broadly, Lily told of Billy coming to pick up his nephew at the school where she taught second grade, promising he would stop by her house and catch up on old times.

"The catching up included Billy coming to see me whenever he wasn't working. He concocted the most outlandish excuses to stop by the school, claiming he was monitoring security."

Dana laughed, wrinkling her nose. "Security for an elementary school?"

Lily sobered quickly. "It's not that preposterous, Dana. We had an incident a few years back where a fifth-grader brought a gun to school with the intent of shooting another student because he'd spread a rumor about his older sister selling her body for drugs."

Shaking her head in disbelief, Dana said, "Whatever happened to kids settling their differences with their fists in the woods behind school property?" The most outrageous thing she and Lily had done was paint Hillsboro's meanest man's prize laying hen a bright blue on Halloween.

Lily shook her head. "That's a thing of the past. These kids will cuss you out, telling you quite explicitly where you can go, and then help you get there."

Dana smiled at her childhood friend. "You've done well, Lily. You always wanted to teach and you've accomplished that. And you always wanted to marry Billy, have his children, and you've also realized that."

Lily shared her smile. "I'm very blessed." She waved a hand. "Enough talk about me. What's been happening with you? Are you married? Seeing anyone? Do you have any kids?"

Dana's expression stilled, becoming somber. "No to all of the above. I was seeing someone for a couple of years, but it ended sometime ago."

"Did you ever go into nursing?"

"No." Her dream had been to become a nurse and assist her doctor in his practice. "I have an undergraduate degree in criminal justice and a master's in journalism. I'm currently an associate editor for a weekly newspaper."

Lily nodded, smiling. "I can see you as a reporter, because you used to write the most fascinating stories." They'd formed a club for which the girls developed a newsletter, and Dana had been selected as the editor in chief. "Where do you live?"

"Carrollton, New York. It's a small town not too far from Utica."

Lily told Dana that she'd asked her grandmother about her whenever she ran into her, but Georgia had never divulged any information about her granddaughter except to say she was doing well.

"After Miss Georgia took you away, she stopped coming to church, mostly keeping to herself. She'd drive into town to shop, or go to the post office, but didn't stop to talk to anyone. Everyone knew she went away for the summer, and we all suspected she went to see you, but no one could get up enough nerve to ask her where she'd been. Miss Georgia had a way of cutting her eyes at you that made you believe she would put a hex on you, your children, and your children's children."

"You're right," Dana confirmed. "All Grandma had to do was give me the *look* and I got it together. She said the hardest decision she ever had to make in her life was sending me away, claiming she wanted to spare me the hurt and shame of everyone talking and pointing their fingers at me because of what had happened to my parents."

Lily shifted uncomfortably on the rocking chair. She stared at her daughter, cradled against Dana's chest, rather than meet her gaze. "Do you really believe your father killed your mother?"

It was a while before Dana was able to form a reply. "There were times when I said I didn't know, but then there are the times when I can say with complete honesty that he couldn't have. My father was a doctor. He'd taken a pledge to save lives. And no matter how angry he was with my mother, I never saw him physically abuse her."

Lily nodded in agreement. "I just couldn't bring my-self to believe Dr. Nichols would ever hurt anyone. He was always so nice to all of us."

Dana met Lily's direct gaze. "I think I would've even-tually recovered from my mother's murder if my father hadn't committed suicide. After I was told that he'd hung himself in his cell, I cried for days. I cried myself to sleep for weeks on end. My aunt had to put cold compresses on my eyes every morning before I went to school to keep the other kids from staring at me.

"Then, one day, I realized Harry Nichols wasn't worth my tears. I'd convinced myself that he killed my mother, and then took the cowardly way out by taking his own life. My resentment and frustration escalated to loathing because I believed he'd become so self-cen-tered that he never considered how his suicide would affect me. I was in my twenties before I was finally able to talk about my fear of abandonment." What she hadn't resolved was the fact that she did not trust men.

"I did my share of crying, too," Lily admitted, her eyes filling up with moisture. "When I found out that Miss Georgia had taken you away to live with her sister, and that I'd never see you again, I cried so hard that I made myself sick. I begged Miss Georgia to give me your address, but she refused."

Dana wanted to tell Lily that her exile had been absolute, because her grandmother also refused to talk to her about her place of birth. Every summer when Georgia came north, Dana would ask her about Hillsboro, but would never get an answer to the ques-tions she sought. After a while she stopped asking.

Lily decided to change the subject. "How long do you plan to stay in Hillsboro?"

"I've taken a four-month leave. I'm expected back October first."

Lily's eyes narrowed. "Do you think it's going to take that long for you to close up this house?"

"I doubt it. I've extended my stay because I want to go over the proceedings of my father's trial."

Lily sat up straighter. "You plan to reopen your mother's murder case?"

A slight lifting of an eyebrow was the only movement from Dana as her gaze bore into Lily's shocked one. "Convincing the State of Mississippi to reopen the case will only become possible if I uncover enough evidence that will prove my father's innocence."

Changing the subject, they talked for another forty-five minutes, dissolving into paroxysms of laughter when they recalled some of the pranks they'd pulled on unsuspecting classmates and Dana's crush on Ross Wilson, Jr. A rush of heat singed her cheeks when she recalled how tongue-tied she'd become whenever she encountered the handsome young boy.

Lily said Ross, Jr., who'd lived in Miami since graduating college, had returned to Hillsboro four years ago to take over his father's real-estate business. Ross, Jr., had brokered the deal that brought the car-manufacturing plant to Hillsboro, thereby increasing the region's job base. Talk was circulating that residents wanted the wealthy, young bachelor to run for political office in the next mayoralty election.

Handing Danella back to her mother, Dana walked Lily to her car, waiting until the baby was strapped into a car seat in the rear of the late-model sedan, then hugged and kissed her friend.

"When am I going to see you again?" Lily asked.

"Do you plan to go to church Sunday?"

"Yes."

"I've decided it's time I give Hillsboro something to really talk about. I'll be at the eleven o'clock service. We can talk afterwards."

Lily chucked. "I'm going to get there early just to see everyone's reaction."

"You're bad, girlfriend," Dana crooned.

"No worse than you," Lily retorted, laughing.

Hugging Lily again, Dana waited for her to start up her car and back out of the driveway, waving until the car disappeared from view. Several cars were parked in driveways, but no one could be seen outside the eight houses lining the dead-end street. The heat had kept most people either indoors, or in air-conditioned offices or malls. Her grandmother's house did not have any air conditioners because Georgia complained the artificially cooled air was not conducive to her arthritic fingers. The crippling affliction had shortened her career as an accomplished seamstress and dressmaker. By her fiftieth birthday Georgia had stopped sewing altogether. She'd used the extra money to supplement the pension and widow's benefits she'd begun collecting following her husband's accidental death.

Dana turned to reenter the house, but stopped as she heard the sound of a car as it came closer. Looking around, she saw Tyler Cole maneuver into the driveway and turn off the engine to a black two-seater BMW roadster. Smiling broadly, he winked at her as he stepped out of the racy vehicle, shutting the door behind him with a solid slam.

He'd changed out of the shirt and slacks he'd worn earlier that morning into a pair of black linen walking shorts and matching short-sleeved shirt. Dana felt her mouth go suddenly dry when she glimpsed his strong legs and bare feet in a pair of imported woven black leather sandals. She was staring, but she couldn't help it. The black hair on his arms and legs, and the display of more crisp hair revealed by the open-necked shirt, shocked her with what had become a blatant exhibition of virility.

He took two long strides, stopping inches from her. The clean scent of his aftershave washed over her, weakening her knees. Closing her eyes briefly, she willed herself not to move. Her lids fluttered wildly before she was back in control.

"How did it go?" Dana did not recognize her own voice.

Tyler flashed a dimpled smile. "Wonderful. Mother and baby are doing well."

"What did she have?"

"A boy. A beautiful, healthy perfectly formed son."

Tilting her chin, she gave him a defiant look because she did not want him to know that she was lusting after him, that her whole being seemed to filled with a wanting she hadn't known—until now.

"Why are you here, Tyler?"

He lifted an eyebrow. "I told you I'd be back."

"You did *not* have to come back," she countered in a soft, no-nonsense tone.

"Yes, I did, because I want you to help me celebrate."

Her brow furrowed. "Celebrate what?"

"The delivery of the first healthy baby in my study. This baby's mother was the first woman whose pregnancy I confirmed once I took over as medical director at the clinic. I've followed her from the very beginning of her confinement to delivery. Her son proved a little stubborn when he refused to enter the world by the conventional vaginal method, but what's important is that he's here and he's healthy."

"You had to perform a C-section?"

Tyler nodded, smiling. "Well, Miss Nichols?"

"Yes, Dr. Cole?" Her voice was as soft and seductive as Tyler's.

"Are you going to help me celebrate?"

"What do you have planned?"

"I'd like to begin with a drive in the country. Then we can stop and take in a few sights."

"Are you sure about a drive in the country?" she asked. "What if you're paged?"

Holding his arms out from his sides, he turned around slowly. "See? No pager and no phone."

"What did you do with them?"

"I left them at home. I got another doctor to cover for me."

"But . . . but I thought—"

Tyler placed a forefinger over her parted lips, stopping her words. "Don't think, Dana. Please, just lock your door and come with me."

She went completely still. "You like giving orders, don't you?"

He looked at her, his gaze widening. "No. I don't like giving orders."

"But you do. At least with me."

His lids lowered as he bit back a smile. "I'm sorry if that's how you perceive me."

"I don't think you're the least bit sorry."

"Oh, but I am." His expression mirrored sincerity.

"I still don't believe you." Unconsciously, her brow furrowed. "I've tried to dissuade you from seeing me, but it is apparent you're quite willful once you want something. Don't say I didn't warn you if you compromise your reputation by being seen with me." Turning on her heels, she walked back into the house to retrieve her handbag and keys.

Tiny lines fanned out around Tyler's eyes as he smiled at her retreating figure. She looked delicate and extremely feminine in a dress. The soft cotton material clung to her curvy body, offering a hint of what lay under the fabric.

Did he want to see her naked?

Yes!

He wanted her naked and writhing under him in a passion he hadn't experienced in months; he wanted to caress the softness of her skin, inhale her delicate feminine scent, feel her heat, and taste her—everywhere, and he wanted to map her body with his hands and mouth until she was imprinted on his memory for an eternity.

Did he want Dana Nichols?

Yes! Despite her warning to stay away from her, his need to make love to her intensified with each second he spent with her. A muscle throbbed noticeably in his jaw as he clamped his teeth together. He whispered a silent vow. He'd always gotten everything he'd ever wanted—and in that instant he knew he wanted Dana Nichols, not just for sex. That he could get from any woman.

He wanted her just because of what he'd believed she'd become to him—his female counterpart.

Eight

Tyler held the passenger-side door open for Dana, waiting until she was seated and belted in before closing it. Rounding the convertible sports car, he slipped in behind the wheel, secured his own belt, and started it up with a minimum of motion. A rush of cool air swept over his face and body as he backed out of the driveway.

Within minutes he drove away from the cul-de-sac, heading for the local road. Several feet ahead of him, flashing red lights and ringing bells signaled the approach of a train coming from a westerly direction. He slowed, knowing he would not be able to make it across the grading before the freight train.

Shifting into neutral, he removed his left foot from the clutch, draped his right arm over the back of Dana's seat, and stared at her delicate profile. She hadn't put up her hair, and the lighter-colored strands shimmered like spun gold among the other tawny-brown strands. He curled his fingers into a tight fist to keep from touching her hair, knowing if he did he would be lost in the spell she unknowingly had woven to pull him in.

He'd become a prisoner of longing—one of his own choosing. He wanted to lie in Dana Nichols's scented arms just once—long enough to assuage the war of erotic emotions attacking him when he least expected them.

"While we're waiting, perhaps you can tell me why I should stay away from you." His voice was soft and coaxing. It was the same tone he used whenever he wanted a patient to relax and feel at ease during an internal examination.

Dana stared out the windshield, her gaze fixed on the flashing red lights. "It's apparent you haven't listened to what has been said about me."

Covering the brake, he unbuckled his seat belt. "I told you before that I don't make it a habit of listening to gossip."

Turning her head, she went completely still. Tyler had moved closer, close enough for her to feel the moist whisper of his breath on her cheek. Staring mutely at him, Dana was confused by the mixed feelings surging through her. There was no doubt she was attracted to the tall, handsome doctor, more captivated than she wanted or needed to be. However, she was only going to be in Hillsboro for four months—just long enough to uncover enough evidence to prove her father's innocence—just long enough to attempt to clear her family's name, but not long enough to become involved with a man—especially one as enthralling as the one sitting inches from her.

"I am the daughter of an alleged adulteress mother and an alleged murdering, pyromaniac suicidal father. And there's no doubt the murder-suicide of Alicia and Harry Nichols has topped Hillsboro's most-infamous-scandal list for the last two decades.

"I plan to remain in Hillsboro for four months— long enough to interview anyone who was involved in my father's trial and go through newspaper copy and court transcripts in an attempt to uncover the truth of what really happened that eventful day twenty-two years ago."

Curling his long fingers around the slender column of her neck, Tyler lowered his head and pressed his mouth to her ear to be heard over the roaring click-clacking sound of the passing freight train.

"What if you don't find what you want?"

The liquid gold in her brown eyes shimmered with unbidden moisture. Blinking rapidly, she willed the tears not to fall. "Then I'll leave Hillsboro knowing I've done all I could do to clear my family's name."

Tyler registered Dana's breathless whisper when she'd said *family's name.* The two words hit him in the chest like stones hurled from a powerful slingshot. He'd grown up with family name and family honor branded on his brain and in his heart. As a Cole, he'd had the expected code of behavior drilled into him at an early age. His father constantly reminded him of the legacy he'd been given and stood to inherit as the only son of the family's reigning patriarch.

Tyler hadn't gone into the family business, deciding instead on a career in medicine. However, becoming a doctor had not exempted him from his eventual responsibility of becoming head of the family once Martin Diaz Cole passed away. That fact did not disturb Tyler because he knew eighty-year-old Martin could be counted on to live at least until the century mark. Tyler's grandfather had died at 103, and his grandmother would celebrate her 102nd year of life this upcoming Christmas. His parents had become health buffs, to the point where they exercised every day and monitored everything they ate or drank, and there was no doubt they would continue to enjoy a long and healthy existence for many years to come.

Then I'll leave Hillsboro knowing I've done all I could do to clear my family's name. Dana's statement returned with vivid clarity. He wanted her to clear her family's name, but he didn't want her to leave Hillsboro. Not when he'd found himself ensnared in a web of seduction from which he could not and did not want to escape.

"Let me help you," he crooned.

Closing her eyes, Dana felt the runaway pumping of her heart in her ears over the roaring sound of the passing train. She shut out the sound ringing bells, the countless number of freight cars moving slowly along the tracks, the sight of the flashing red lights, and the drugging fragrance of Tyler's cologne mingling with the distinctive masculine scent of his flesh.

She forgot why she had come back to Hillsboro, that she'd just buried her last surviving family member, and that she was the last Hillsboro Sutton Nichols, as she gloried in the cool touch of Tyler Cole's hand on the nape of her neck.

"Help me how?" Her sultry voice had lowered noticeably.

"I'll help you get the best private investigator in the state."

Pulling back, Dana stared at him, noting his stoic expression. "I can't permit that."

"Why not?"

"I need to do this myself."

"What if you can't do it?"

"I can do it," she insisted stubbornly, "because this is what I've been trained to do."

"But you said you're a journalist."

"I am an investigative reporter."

Tyler blinked once as a shiver of uneasiness snaked up his spine. Reopening a case, especially a celebrated murder case in a small town, was certain to rekindle resentment while setting up warring factions among townspeople. And if Dana did prove her father's innocence, then would she attempt to uncover the guilty person or persons, thereby putting herself at risk?

"Will you let me know if I can help you—in any way possible?"

"Why, Tyler?"

He flashed a half smile. "I'm surprised you have to ask me that."

"But I *am* asking."

"Because I like you, Dana Nichols."

"You don't know me," she retorted.

"I like what I see."

"Is that all you have to go by? My looks?"

"It's more than enough. At least for now."

Dana shook her head. "No, Tyler, it's not going to work. I'm not going to become involved with you, then walk away like nothing ever happened."

"Then, don't leave," he insisted.

"I have nothing here to make me stay."

"What if I try and convince you to stay?"

"What are you offering, Dr. Cole? Marriage and a happily-ever-after?" She was barely able to keep the laughter from her voice.

"Maybe." Tyler wasn't certain where the single word had come from, but it was out and he could not retract it.

Dana sobered quickly, staring wordlessly at him, her heart pounding an erratic rhythm, stunned by his vacant response and expression. Moments later, her eyes crinkled in a smile.

"Thanks, but no, thanks."

Tyler stiffened as though she had struck him. It was the first time, even in jest, that he'd proposed to a woman, and his masculine ego wouldn't permit him to accept an outright rejection without an explanation.

"Have you ever been married?" he asked.

"No."

"Have you ever been in love?"

Dana hesitated for several seconds. "I thought I was."

"What happened?"

"It ended after a couple of years without much fanfare."

Tyler lifted an eyebrow. "You left him?"

"No," she replied honestly. "He left me."

Taking in a quick sharp breath, he shook his head in disbelief. How could a man leave a woman who looked like Dana Nichols? He'd found her perfect. She had it all—looks and brains.

"He was a fool, Dana."

"I don't think so. The relationship was going nowhere."

"Why? Because he wouldn't commit?"

She shook her head. "It was just the opposite. *I* wouldn't commit."

"Why not?"

Her lingering bitterness surfaced. "Because I don't trust *men*. What about you, Tyler? How old are you, and were you ever married?" Dana's voice faded to a hushed stillness as the last freight car rumbled past.

A slight smile softened his mouth as he gave her a lingering stare. "I'm forty-one, and I've never been married."

"Why not?"

"Because I've haven't met that special woman."

"Does she exist?"

"My mother says she does."

"And you didn't answer my question. Does she exist?"

Tyler lowered his gaze. "There was a time when I believed she didn't. But now I'm not so certain."

"Why?" Her voice was barely a whisper.

"That was before I met you, Miss Dana Nichols. Before I was complete blindsided by your incredible beauty."

"Tyler, please don't say—"

"No, Dana," he cut in softly, stopping her words. "Don't tell me what not to say, because I always say what I feel, not what someone wants to hear."

She shook her head. "Then what you want is not going to work."

He tightened his hold on her neck. "If it doesn't work, then it wasn't meant to be. But if it does work, then I believe we're in for the most exciting ride of our lives." His gaze bore into hers, seemingly challenging her to refute his quiet assurance.

His fingertips caressed the silken flesh covering her throat before his hand came down slowly. Turning away, he secured his seat belt. A smothering hush swelled inside the car, neither occupant attempting to break the silence. The heat of the blistering sun rose in shimmering waves off the iron rails, making visibility nearly impossible. The scorching rays had parched the grass, turning the landscape into a carpet of brown withered vegetation.

Shifting into gear, Tyler drove over the grading, ignoring the mocking voice inside his head that told him not to pursue Dana Nichols, that she was a woman he should stay away from. But he could not stay away from her because he did not want to stay away from her although she'd openly admitted she didn't trust men. Her declaration made him wonder if her distrust had stemmed from her father's betrayal. After all, the man had murdered her mother, then taken his own life, making her an orphan. It was obvious Dana had been faced with issues of loss and abandonment for most of her life, unlike Tyler, who'd grown up with both parents who'd nurtured and protected him until adulthood.

Tyler picked up a pair of sunglasses off the console, placing them on the bridge of his nose, and then pressed a button on the dashboard, turning on a CD player. The soft haunting sounds of an acoustical guitar with an accompanying muted trumpet filled the BMW. Increasing his speed, he maneuvered around a slow-moving tractor lumbering along the narrow road. The car shot forward in a burst of speed as trees, houses, and grazing livestock whizzed past in a blinding blur.

Closing her eyes and settling back on the leather seat, Dana lost herself in the music, the heat and sensually haunting scent of the man sharing her space. She wanted to tell Tyler to stop the car and let her out. She needed a few moments to herself to think— think about what he wanted from her and what she was able to offer him. He sought a relationship and she could not afford one—at least not at this time in her life.

"Tyler?" She hadn't opened her eyes.

"Yes."

"Do you want to sleep with me?"

His head snapped around, the car veering sharply to the right. Returning his attention to the road in front of him, Tyler straightened the wheel, regaining control of the vehicle. "What!" The word literally exploded from his mouth.

"You heard me."

"Did you ask me if I wanted to sleep you?"

"Yes, I did."

"Is that why you think I've asked you to go out with me?"

Dana opened her eyes. Her mouth was smiling even though her eyes were cold. His expression was a mask of stone. "Let's be adult about this," she said. "You can stop at the nearest motel and I'll assuage your curiosity about Alicia Nichols's daughter. I'm even willing to pay for the room."

She prayed he wouldn't take her up on her challenge, because there was no way she would be able to take off her clothes for Tyler, lie with him, and then walk away without a backward look. But if she did agree to see him during her stay in Hillsboro, she knew she had to assume control, set the limits of her involvement with him.

Slowing the roadster, Tyler maneuvered off the road onto to a narrow, dusty shoulder, turning off the engine. He pushed open his door, stepping out into the intense heat. Less than thirty seconds later, Dana stood on the side of the road with him, his fingers curled around her upper arms.

Pulling her up close to his chest, he struggled valiantly not to lose his temper. His dark face was set in a vicious expression as he clenched his teeth so tightly intense pain radiated in his jaws.

"You better never say anything like that to me *ever* again."

Dana's temper flared. "And don't you dare tell me what I can say. I merely asked you a question, and you have the most annoying habit of being evasive by answering my question with another question. Let's get something straight before we embark on something we may regret for the rest of our lives."

"What?" he ground out between his teeth.

"No head games, Tyler," she warned, her eyes narrowing.

His expression did not change. "What else do you want?"

"Complete candor with each other."

A half smile softened his mouth. "Anything else?" he drawled.

"No pleas for a commitment. I have a plan, but that plan doesn't include staying in Hillsboro, so don't ask me to stay. And last, but certainly not least, don't ask me to sleep with you."

Tyler stared at her, his expression now mirroring surprise and shock. He'd never met a woman like Dana Nichols. Whereas most women wanted a commitment from a man, she didn't. And because he wanted to date her, he would agree to her demands. Moreover, she'd challenged him, and he'd never had a woman challenge him.

He only had four months to convince her to stay in Hillsboro, and he planned to use anything and everything at his disposal to get her to change her mind.

A slow smile deepened the slashes in his cheeks. "You've got yourself a deal."

Dana's delicate jaw went slack as her mouth dropped open. She'd issued demands most men would've laughed at or rejected outright, yet Tyler had readily accepted them.

"Really?"

A chuckle rumbled in his broad chest. "Yes, really." Curving an arm around her waist, he opened the passenger-side door for her. "Let's get back in the car before we come down with heatstroke."

She slipped onto the leather seat, pulling the seat belt over her chest. She felt an unexpected warmth flow through her and it had nothing to do with the weather. She did not know how she knew it, but not only was Tyler Cole visually perfect, he was also extraordinary.

She'd come back to Hillsboro for a particular purpose, and nowhere in her plan did it include succumbing to a handsome doctor's sensual presence.

Nine

Tyler drove, enjoying the soft sound of music coming from the powerful speakers and the presence of the woman sitting beside him. After their roadside altercation, they hadn't exchanged a word. It was as if everything that needed to be said had been.

Dana had agreed to go out with him, but not without requirements. He'd readily agree not to engage in head games because he'd always found the exercise detrimental to any relationship. And he'd always been open and frank with any woman with whom he'd been involved. All of them knew outright not expect a declaration of marriage because of his nomadic lifestyle.

But all of that had changed since he'd come to Hillsboro. He had built a home, put down roots, and since coming face-to-face with Dana Nichols, he had unconsciously reassessed whether he wanted to spend the rest of his life alone.

He'd convinced himself that he had it all when deep down inside he knew he didn't. He had material wealth, had met and exceeded his professional expectations, but when he went home it was to loneliness. He kept up with his favorite sports teams, had a gourmet kitchen to concoct exotic dishes, and had set up a library filled with books and an intensive music collection. Occasionally a long-distance telephone call to a family member sometimes rounded out his day.

He'd ordered a Steinway piano, and had contracted to have an Olympic-size pool and basketball court installed on his property—items he now thought of as toys—toys to keep him amused when he wasn't working.

He'd thought his world perfect until he met Dana Nichols. A single glance at her beautiful face, the slight touch of her mouth against his, and the sound of her sultry voice calling his name had proven him wrong.

How ironic, he thought. He had come to Hillsboro to put down roots, while Dana had returned to her place of birth for a short stay.

It was also ironic that he'd agreed to a non-sexual relationship with her when his initial response to her had been wholly physical.

Shrugging a shoulder, he dismissed his musings, humming under his breath to a song on the compact disc. He turned onto MS 1—the Great River Road. The sluggish brown Mississippi River wound its way southward as he headed north. A sign indicating the number of miles to Greenville came into view.

"'The Delta begins in the lobby of the Peabody Hotel in Memphis and ends on Catfish Row in Vicksburg.' That's a quote from Greenville journalist David Cohn," Dana said in a drawling Southern cadence.

"This region has some fascinating history," Tyler observed.

"That's because of the Mississippi River. It has created the rich soil that made cotton production so profitable and Greenville a vital port used by the massive Delta plantations to ship their bales to market. But all of that changed during the Civil War battle for Vicksburg.

"Union soldiers burned Greenville to the ground. The citizens rebuilt the town, only to suffer a yellow fever epidemic in 1877. It was nearly destroyed by a disastrous flood in 1890, and then again in 1927. Levees finally solved the flooding problem after that."

"I don't think anyone would complain if we had a week of rain right about now."

Dana smiled at Tyler when he gave her a quick glance. "You're probably right."

He returned his attention to the road. "What made you decide to become a journalist?"

"It wasn't my first career choice." Her voice was low, calm as she told Tyler how she'd always wanted to become a nurse, how she'd been fascinated by her father's ability to assist in the healing of a patient. "I loved the antiseptic smell of hospitals and the efficient chaos of an emergency room."

"It's not too late for you to make a career change."

She shook her head. "At thirty-three I'm a little old to think about going to nursing school."

"That way of thinking is passé. I know men and women who waited until their forties to apply to medical school. It's a long and tough grind for someone in their twenties, but I discovered older students were much more mature and focused than their younger counterparts."

"How many older students were in medical school with you?"

"Two."

"Two out of a class of what?"

"Three hundred forty-eight."

"That's less than one per cent, Tyler."

"That's true. But both were women, African-American, single mothers, and both graduated in the top ten percent of the class."

Dana covered her mouth with her hand to stop the bubble of laughter spilling from her lips. The sound was infectious, and seconds later Tyler's deep rumbling laughter joined hers.

"Power to my sisters," she said, still laughing.

"Amen," Tyler intoned softly. "How did you get into journalism?"

"Mass communications was my minor as an undergrad."

"What was your major?"

"Criminal Justice. I'd become fixated with law because of my father's trial. My grandmother, in her need to protect me from my parents' murder/suicide, overcompensated by not allowing me to visit my father in jail, or going to court for his trial. She even forbade me to read the *Hillsboro Herald*, which put out special daily editions for the duration of the trial. I'd immersed myself in the study of criminology like a first-year law student, staying up nights going over cases, researching interrogation techniques and evidence gathering. My college social life was practically nonexistent. If I wasn't in my room studying, then I could be found in the library.

"One day I fainted while walking to class, and spent two days in a local hospital, undergoing a battery of tests. The reason for my collapse was sleep deprivation and malnutrition. My advisor came to see me, suggesting I seek out a therapist after I'd begun crying and couldn't stop. I took her advice, stayed in counseling for two years, and learned how to cope with losing my parents."

Signaling, Tyler turned off onto a county road, following signs advertising a restaurant that served the best seafood in the state. He'd listened to Dana as she disclosed her anguish and frustration, wanting to stop and pull her into his arms. He wanted to tell her that she had nothing to fear, that he would protect her. But he hadn't because he knew instinctively she would reject his overt display of empathy.

A slow smile softened his features, because now he

knew why he'd been drawn to Dana Nichols. Not only
was she beautiful and intelligent, but also decisive, independent, and feisty. Qualities he admired in a
woman—qualities found in the women in his family.

His fingers tightened around the leather-wrapped
steering wheel. The word *family* jumped at him again.
What was it about Dana that evoked a longing to make
her a part of his life, his family? She'd already laid
down the ground rules: She would remain in Hillsboro
for only four months—hardly enough time for him to
get to know her or she him, and there was to be no
physical involvement. That wouldn't have proved a
hardship if he hadn't been celibate. He was able to
keep his erotic thoughts at bay during his waking
hours, but it was at night when he went to bed alone
that his traitorous thoughts played havoc with his body.
Tossing and turning restlessly, he'd lay awake for
hours, trying to mentally will his rigid flesh to a flaccid
state. He tried concentrating on anything but Dana,
but the sound of her voice and the vision of her golden
eyes returned with vivid clarity, until he finally left his
bed to sit in the breakfast room and drink black coffee.

He stole a glance at Dana's delicate profile, silently
cursing her. She'd become hazardous to his health because he couldn't sleep, had resumed his marathon
coffee-drinking sessions, and for the first time in a very
long time, he considered taking care of his own sexual
needs rather than release his passions in a woman's
scented body.

"You say therapy helped you cope with your fixation
with your parents' tragic demise, yet you're going to
spend four months researching their murder/suicide."

Biting down on her lower lip, Dana felt a throbbing
pulse against the ridge of her teeth. She knew researching Harry's murder trial would reopen all wounds. But
she was no longer a child, vulnerable and emotionally

defenseless. Her grandmother had done what she thought was best to protect her, not knowing the exile would prove more damaging than supportive.

"I need closure, Tyler. My parents are dead. The great-aunt who'd become my guardian died during my junior year in college, and I just buried my grandmother earlier this week. I'm the last of the Hillsboro Suttons and the Nicholses, and once I leave Mississippi I don't want to look back."

Tyler wanted to tell Dana that she did not have to constantly remind him that her stay in Hillsboro would be a short one—that she would probably leave at the end of October or the beginning of November. *Four months.* He had only four months to execute his own plan in which he would convince her to stay in Hillsboro—forever.

Downshifting, he maneuvered off the paved road onto a rutted one leading up a steep hill. Looking around her, Dana noticed the towering pine trees growing closely together nearly blotted out what was left of the fading sun. Twilight had fallen.

"Where are we going?"

"I'm going to stop so we can get something to eat."

She shrugged a bare scented shoulder, settling back to peer at the changing landscape through the windshield. Everything was still green in this part of Mississippi. It was as if the area hadn't been affected by the lingering drought. But she knew that even if the trees were still green, the ground was bone-dry. One carelessly discarded lighted match or one strike of lightning was certain to turn the woods into a raging inferno.

Dana heard the sounds of music, blaring car horns, and raucous laughter before she saw the enormous structure constructed of thick, massive logs. Standing in a cleared area was the largest log cabin she'd ever

seen. It more closely resembled a longhouse than a
cabin. Blinking colorful neon lights glaringly identified
the establishment as Three J's.

A lot set aside for parking was filled with pickups,
sport utility vehicles, and several farm vehicles. Men
and women were getting out of trucks and tractors,
dressed in suits, jeans, T-shirts, skimpy tank tops,
shorts, and dusty footwear.

Tyler pulled into a space next to a tractor and
parked. He came around the low-slung car, holding
the passenger-side door open for Dana. Extending his
left hand, he waited for her to place her hand in his.
He noticed the indecision in her gaze, which vanished
as she placed her hand on his outstretched palm.
Tightening his grip, he pulled her to her feet, curved
an arm around her narrow waist, and led her to the
door to Three J's. It took several seconds for his eyes
to adjust from coming out of the encroaching darkness
into the muted lights inside the eating establishment.
He felt Dana stiffen, and he pulled her closer to his
side.

Dana went completely still, her gaze widening as she
took in the sights and sounds inside the restaurant. An
enormous colorful jukebox was the space's focal point.
Specially made, it covered about thirty feet of one wall,
and was filled with hundreds of compact discs. The
interior was dimly it, as if everyone who'd ventured
through its doors came to hide from the outside world.
Strategically hung light fixtures with three globes were
reminiscent of those identifying pawnshops.

Tyler saw the direction of Dana's stunned gaze. Lowering his head, he said softly, "It holds three thousand
CDs." He'd answered her unspoken question. "Three
J's stands for Jesse's Juke Joint, and as a family-owned
business, they're known for serving the best seafood

in the state. They even have their own catfish farm out back," he whispered close to her ear.

Tilting her chin put her mouth dangerously close to his. "I thought you said we were going for a drive in the country, then stop to take in a few sights."

He smiled, and the lines around his eyes deepened attractively. "You'll get to see sights here that you probably won't see anywhere else in the state," he said cryptically.

Dana had to admit Tyler was right about unusual things to see. They sat a table for two in a dimly lit corner as the humongous jukebox blared out blues, rock and roll, hip-hop, and R&B tunes covering nearly seventy years of music. The blues was the sound of the Mississippi Delta, the South Side of Chicago, and a million juke joints all over the country.

The music was as eclectic as Three J's patrons. Well-dressed businessmen, farmers, truckers, and office workers crowded tables, drinking pitchers of beer and devouring mounds of steaming crawfish, steamed crabs, and crispy strips of fried catfish with an accompanying Dijon mustard sauce with a hint of horseradish hot enough to wake up one's untried taste buds. The restaurant's specialties included a shrimp cocktail made with sweet Gulf jumbo shrimp, soft-shell crab sandwiches on sourdough bread with a spicy mayonnaise, sweet-and-sour cole slaw, spicy collard greens, hot buttered biscuits and corn bread, fried chicken, and baked country ham and sweet-potato fries.

A quartet of pool tables was set up in one corner, several dart boards in another, and half-a-dozen video games in a third. Eight flat-screen televisions crowded every available wall space, all of them tuned to different channels with the sound muted. And whenever the

mood hit, couples would get up and dance to whatever
was playing on the jukebox.

A middle-aged couple danced to Marvin Gaye's
"Sexual Healing," moving sensuously to the classic
R&B tune. The woman wound her arms around her
partner's neck, her hips grinding heavily against his
without moving her feet.

"Ya'll know ya'll too old for that foolishness," a
woman with a raspy voice called out. "Take that ole
nasty stuff home, Vilma. Don't ya'll know there's decent people up in here?"

Vilma raised her head from her partner's shoulder,
rolled her eyes, while sucking her teeth loudly. "You
just mad 'cause you don't git none, that's all. If you'd
took care of your man like I do mine, then you
wouldn't be running off at the mouth about somethin'
being nasty."

Everyone laughed at Vilma's comeback, Dana laugh-
ing with the others. She found herself humming along
with John Lee Hooker's "Boom Boom," Bobby Blue
Bland's "Turn On Your Love Light," Muddy Waters's
"I'm Your Hoochie Coochie Man," and B.B. King's
"The Thrill Is Gone."

Tyler nodded his head in time to the music, singing
softly under his breath, "I got twenty-nine ways to make
it to my baby's door. If she need me bad, I can find
about two or three more."

"How do you know all these songs?" she asked Tyler
after Willie Dixon's "Twenty-nine Ways" ended.

Lowering his gaze, he smiled the sensual smile she'd
come to look for. "I try to come here every Friday
night. It's funky and unconventional, and the best way
I know to unwind at the end of a work week."

He came to Three J's because he could be Tyler and
not Dr. Cole. He was just another customer who came
to eat and listen to music. There were occasions when

he got up to dance with a woman, but most times he preferred sitting alone, watching everyone enjoy themselves. He liked their policy of leaving menus along with what was known as a Three J's purchase order on the table. All a customer had to do was check off his selections, leave it on the table, and a server would come by and pick it up. Pitchers of wine, beer, or soda were compliments of the house.

The distinctive voice of Etta James crooning "At Last" flowed from the speakers, and Tyler stood up, extending his hand to Dana. "Dance with me, please."

Rising to her feet, she permitted him to lead her out to an area set aside for dancing, moving into his strong embrace. Closing her eyes, she rested her forehead on his shoulder, melting into his unyielding strength.

Tyler was a good dancer, and she followed his lead easily. Her arms curved around his waist as she moved closer, reveling in the sense of protectiveness she found in her dance partner's embrace. She'd permitted Galvin to make love to her, hold her close throughout the night, yet he never was able to make her feel totally protected. It was as if he withheld a part of himself to conceal his own vulnerability.

But it was different with Tyler. Wrapped in his embrace, cradled gently to his heart, made her feel safe, as if she had nothing to fear—seen or unseen. It was as if he was in total control of himself and his world around him, and she would have nothing to fear if she opened up and allowed him to become a part of her existence.

Hadn't she told herself that she was prepared to smile, flirt, and do everything short of using her body or bribing someone to get what she wanted to unravel the events beginning with her mother's murder? And hadn't Tyler offered to help her secure the best private investigator in the state? But distrust, suspicion, and false pride had kept her from accepting his assistance.

Without warning, a sense of strength came to her as any misgivings she harbored dissipated. She'd lived with pain and loss for two thirds of her life, which kept her from living and loving freely.

Galvin's deception had wounded her even though she knew he'd attributed his decision to a desire to go back to a former girlfriend. He'd asked the one thing from her she hadn't been able to give: a declaration of love. She'd felt in her heart that she'd loved Galvin, yet had been unable to verbally express her love.

"Tyler?"

Resting his chin on the top of Dana's head, he exhaled a long sigh of contentment. He'd felt a bottomless peace holding her in his embrace, their hearts beating in perfect rhythm.

"Yes, darling?" He went completely still, missing a step. Recovering quickly, he spun Dana around and round. The passionate endearment had just slipped out of its own volition.

"What is it, Dana?" His tone was neutral, lacking emotion.

She stared up at him, trying to make out his expression. "I've changed my mind."

There was a pulse beat of silence before he spoke again. "What about?"

She forced a smile. "I'm going to accept your offer to help me find a private investigator."

He lifted an eyebrow, nodding. "Have you changed your mind about anything else?"

Dana knew he wanted her to stay longer than four months, but she couldn't. She was fortunate the *Chronicle*'s publisher had approved her leave, knowing he had only agreed because she usually worked a four-day workweek during the summer months.

"Not yet."

There was a gentle softness in her voice that swept over Tyler like a rush of cool air over his face on a hot, sultry day. Swinging her around again in an intricate dance step, he pulled her closer and breathed into her ear.

"I should warn you that I'm a patient man, Dana. A *very* patient man, who's willing to do whatever it takes, within reason of course, to make you change your mind."

There was something about Tyler that drew Dana to him, but on the other hand he had a maddening hint of arrogance that made her wary. And there was no doubt he was spoiled, used to getting his way.

"Are you an only child?" she asked.

The song ended and he led her back to their table. "No. Why would you ask that?"

"If you're not an only child, then you must be the only son."

He seated her, lingering over her head. Their server had picked up their order. "Now, who's the one answering a question with a question?"

Waiting until he was seated across from her, Dana gave him a direct stare. "You're spoiled, Tyler Cole. You're used to getting your way, aren't you?"

"No." His expression was stoic.

She wrinkled her nose, charming him with the gesture. "Yes, you are," she crooned.

Reaching across the small table, he ran a forefinger down the length of her short nose. "You're wrong about that, Dana, because I can't get my way with you."

"I'm probably the first woman who has ever turned you down."

He sobered, his gaze caressing her face before it shifted lower to her chest. Slowly, boldly, and seductively he looked her over, stoking and bringing to life a banked fire that Dana had long forgotten existed. And as she studied the lean dark-skinned face of the man who made her feel desire with only a glance, she chided herself for challenging him. Had she gone too far?

"No, Dana." Tyler's quiet voice floated across the space separating them. "You're not the first woman to reject me. But you are the first woman I've met that I want to get to know—really know."

"That's impossible." Her voice was a hushed whisper.

"Why?"

"I'm only going to be here four months."

He leaned closer. "That's enough time. "

"Are you sure?"

"Very sure."

She blinked once. "Okay, Tyler, you're on," she said, accepting his challenge.

Lowering his lids, he smiled, a sweep of thick black lashes touching a pair of high cheekbones. "We go all the way, Dana."

"All the way," she repeated seconds before he rose from his chair, hunkered down, and covered her mouth covered with his, sealing their pledge, while leaving her mouth burning with a fire that refused to go out.

Dana returned Tyler's kiss with a hunger that belied her outward calm. His kiss was gentle, as gentle and soothing as his comforting hands and voice. She longed to part her lips and trace his mouth with her tongue, but as soon as the notion entered her head, she jerked back as if burned.

She was on fire—her face, mouth, chest, and every place below her waist. The pulse in her throat fluttered uncontrollably, and she was certain Tyler would be able to count the beats without touching her.

"Please pour me a glass of beer." She needed something cold, anything to cool down the inferno sweeping throughout her fevered body. Tyler picked up the pitcher of beer, filled a mug, and handed it to her.

She took a swallow of the cold brew, grimacing slightly as she placed the glass on the scarred table. She'd acquired a taste for beer, but found Three J's beer too bitter for her palate.

Tyler noted her expression, smiling. He was pleased Dana had lowered the barriers so he could convince her that his intentions were honorable. He would be a liar if he denied he didn't want to sleep with her; however, that was no longer important or a priority now that she'd agreed to see him whenever their schedules permitted.

He knew he was drawn to Dana because she had an air of self-confidence and a sense of who she was, which meant she was a woman who was certain to meet him as an equal.

He sat down again, pulling his chair closer to hers. Picking up her mug, he took a long swallow of the beer, which went down cold and smooth. He put down the mug and filled a glass with soda, handing it to Dana.

Smiling broadly, he touched his mug to her glass. "Here's to your homecoming."

Dana glanced up as a waiter approached their table, balancing a tray on one shoulder. She refused to register the significance of Tyler's toast. If she'd glanced at his face at that moment, she would've noticed the look of implacable determination in his expression.

It was a look those who knew Tyler Simmons Cole well would recognize. A look Dana Nichols would come to know well in the days, weeks, and months to come.

Ten

Dana returned home exhausted and exhilarated. She'd eaten until she couldn't move, and then danced with Tyler for the next two hours. She'd asked to drive his car on the return trip, and he'd willingly complied. He'd sat beside her, eyes closed as she expertly shifted the gears in the racy BMW. The easily handling and the agility of the roadster made it a joy to drive.

Standing in the entryway, she smiled at Tyler. He stood motionless, staring down at her. "Thank you for a wonderful evening," she said.

Pushing his hands into the pockets of his shorts, he angled his head. "I should be the one thanking you for celebrating with me."

"Do you mind if I asked for a rain check for tomorrow night? I don't think I can take two consecutive nights of dinner and dancing."

"We don't have to go out."

"What's the alternative?" she asked.

"I can pick you up after I close the clinic, and we can hang out together at my place. I'll cook something simple and then we can relax."

Dana drank in the sensuality that made Tyler Cole who he was: tall, dark, handsome, and confident. He was so at ease with his rightful place in the world that it frightened her a bit. She knew she was Dana Nichols, but was uncertain about her future. She was a journalist, and a very good one, but did not know whether five years from now she would be content to remain with a small weekly. Her experience had helped her periodical win a Pulitzer, but that was the *Chronicle*'s achievement. What about hers? What did she want for herself? Her future?

She had never questioned herself before meeting Tyler. What was it about him that evoked an air of uncertainty? Was it Tyler or was it Hillsboro?

"I'd prefer that, thank you," she said.

Bending over, he pressed a kiss to her cheek. "I'll pick you up around four."

He wanted to give himself enough time to see his last patient, then preview the charts for the patients with scheduled appointments for the coming week. And with the birth of the first baby in the study, he would begin entering the child's data into a database set up by the U.S. Department of Health and Human Services. He was certain there would be knowing smiles once he listed the baby's name because the mother had elected to give her son the middle name of Tyler. He wondered how many more Tylers there would be before the five-year study ended.

Dana nodded. "I'll see you tomorrow."

Dana's sultry voice had dropped an octave, making Tyler realize he didn't want to go home. He wanted to stay with her, spend the night in her perfumed embrace. Dancing with her, holding her close to his body had offered a temporary respite for his sexual frustrations. He'd gloried in the soft curves of her lush body, committing the feel and smell of her skin to memory. She was slender, but not skinny. The fullness of her breasts, the distinct indentation of her waist, and the curve of her rounded hips were blatantly female.

He backed out of the entryway, smiling. "Good night, Dana."

She wiggled the fingers of her left hand. "Good night, Tyler."

He was there and then he was gone, the sound of his car's engine fading into the quiet night.

Dana closed and locked the door. Biting down on her lower lip, she closed her eyes and inhaled deeply. She felt like Cinderella meeting her prince for the first time. Spending time with Tyler, dancing and talking about inconsequential events, was something she'd missed in her dealings with the opposite sex. She had dated a few men other than Galvin, but most times she couldn't wait for the night to end so she could go home alone and crawl into bed with a book.

She hadn't realized how much she liked to dance until she found herself in Tyler's arms. He'd confessed that he didn't get out much, but she doubted that because he was familiar with most of the latest dance steps. She'd sat out while he gyrated with the other patrons, executing the steps to the cha-cha version of the electric slide. Her face was burning when he returned to their table because she'd tried imagining him completely naked, dancing for her, while regretting her demand that he not ask her to sleep with him.

She opened her eyes, staring at the door. Did she want to share Tyler Cole's bed?

"Yes," she whispered, her eyelids fluttering wildly.

She wanted him—more than she had ever wanted any man. He was a stranger, yet she still wanted him.

Turning, she left her tiny purse and keys on the table, then made her way to the staircase and her bedroom. The heat in the house was stifling but not unbearable. It had taken Dana less than a week to become acclimated to the Southern heat.

Walking into her bedroom, she stripped off her clothes, leaving them on the wooden bench at the foot of her bed. She went into the bathroom, brushed her

teeth, washed her face, and then returned to the bedroom and fell across the bed. The rotating blades of
the ceiling fan cooled her body. However, it failed to
cool her thoughts as she dreamed of Tyler Cole
throughout the night.

Dana awoke at dawn, her body moist, breathing labored, chest rising and falling heavily, and moaning
softly from the aftermath of an erotic dream that had
left the area between her thighs wet and pulsing.

Rolling over on her chest, she lay, waiting for her
traitorous body to return to a normal state. It was another ten minutes before she left her bed, temporarily
dismissing the pleasurable feelings brought on by the
dream.

It's because I haven't had sex in a long time, she mused
as she stood under the cool spray of a shower. "Who
are you kidding, Dana?" she said aloud, reaching for
a tube of shampoo from the shower caddy.

She did not want to lie, especially to herself. The
return of sexual desire was attributed to one man—
Tyler Cole.

Not wanting to sleep with Tyler had nothing to do
with not being attracted to him. It was simply that
when she left Hillsboro, she did not want any regrets.
She wanted to walk away without looking back. It was
safer that way.

She shampooed her hair, adding an instant condi-
tioner, then lathered her body with a scented body
wash. Lingering under the cooling water, she rinsed
her hair and body before stepping out of the tub.
Wrapping a towel around her head, she let the moisture on her body nearly evaporate before spraying on
Chanel No. 5 sheer-moisture mist. The distinctive fragrance had been her mother's favorite, and every

Christmas Georgia had sent her an ample supply of soap, crème cologne, perfume, body powder, and the moisture mist to last her for a year.

Deciding it was too hot to sit under a dryer or blow-dry her hair, Dana decided to let it air-dry. Then she would put it up in a ponytail or a twist. She'd noticed a full-service beauty salon when she'd gone downtown, and planned to call Hot Chocolate for an appointment for a manicure, pedicure, facial, and trim.

She pulled on a pair of bikini panties, an oversized T-shirt, and a pair of old shorts, deciding to tackle another closet before it got too hot to do anything more than sit on the back porch.

The telephone rang and Tyler reached for the receiver as he read the last entry in the first chart stacked on his desk. "Health Clinic, Dr. Cole speaking."

"Lighten up, brother. You don't have to sound so formal. Save that Dr. Cole business for your patients."

A warm smiled tilted the corners of Tyler's mouth upward, and he closed the chart. "Someone of us have to work for a living, slacker."

"Stuff it, Ty. Some of us have to work because we weren't born with diamond-encrusted platinum spoons in our mouths."

"Did you call me to harass me, Wade?"

"I called you to remind you that we're all getting together at my place on Sag Harbor over the Labor Day weekend."

Opening a desk drawer, Tyler pulled out a planner, turning to the month of September. He'd blocked out the first weekend with a question mark. He and three of his best friends from medical school usually got together once a year for a brief reunion.

"I thought we were going to meet at Keith's cabin."

"That was before Denise decided she wanted to re-decorate. Tell me something, Ty. How do you redecorate a cabin so far back in the Massachusetts woods that she and Keith get lost every time they go there?"

"Now, I know you're not asking me to explain Keith's wife."

"Speaking of wives—"

"No, Wade," Tyler said, interrupting him, "I'm not married."

"Damn, Ty," Wade groaned, "I heard Southern women are hot."

Ignoring his friend's comment about Southern women, Tyler thought about Dana. She may have been Southern-born, but she hadn't lived in Mississippi for more than two decades. He thought of her as sexy and sensual rather than *hot*.

"The only thing that's hot down here is the weather. We haven't had a drop of rain in eight weeks."

"That's serious, but you're making me look bad, brother."

Tyler's expression changed, becoming somber. "Why?"

"I have a bet with Keith and Al that you'd be either engaged or married before the end of the year."

"How much did you wager?"

"A thousand."

"If you have a thousand dollars to throw away, then you should give it to a worthwhile charity."

"Does this mean you're not going to tie the knot?"

"It means you should stop gambling and mind your business, Dr. Wade Robinson."

A hearty laugh came through the wire. "Are you holding out on me, Dr. Cole?"

"Good-bye, Wade."

"Don't hang up, Tyler. Are you coming?"

The furrows in Tyler's forehead disappeared. "Of course I'm coming."

"Tammy wants to know if you're coming alone, because if you are, then she'd like to hook you up with her cousin."

"Tell Tammy thank you for thinking of me, but I can find my own company for the weekend."

"I promised her I'd ask."

"And you did."

"Everyone's either coming in late Thursday or early Friday."

Tyler stared at the blocked-out dates on the planner. "I'll probably get there Friday."

"I'll look for you then."

"Thanks for the invite. You guys are welcomed to come to Mississippi next year."

"Bring pictures of your place when you come."

Tyler exchanged pleasantries with his friend for another three minutes before ringing off. It had become an annual event for the four of them to get together for either the Fourth of July or Labor Day holiday weekends.

It had begun with four medical school students, then four doctors. After a few years the group increased to include fiancées, and finally wives and children. Tyler had been the last holdout. He did not have a wife or children, but he never thought of his single status as a liability. He merely ignored his friends' wives' references to *"hooking"* him up with their single female friends or relatives.

And he wasn't amenable to blind dates, because he preferred making his own choice when dating. Reopening the chart, he stared at his notations with unseeing eyes, wondering how Dana would react if he invited her to go to New York with him for the holiday weekend.

He sighed audibly, and his expression softened. There was one way to find out, and that was to ask her, but he decided to wait until they were better acquainted.

Remembering his promise to help her, he picked up the telephone receiver, dialing the area code for Washington, D.C. His call was answered on the second ring, a familiar deep male voice offering a warm greeting.

Tyler's smile widened. *"Hola, primo."*

"What's up, Tyler?" Michael Kirkland returned in the same language.

"Not much, cousin. How's the family?" Tyler asked, continuing in Spanish. He hadn't had the opportunity to speak the language very often, and feared he'd lose his facility if he didn't practice it.

His Cuban-born grandmother had taught him and his sisters the language, which had proved invaluable whenever he treated Spanish-speaking patients as an intern and resident.

"Everyone's great. Teresa began walking on her own yesterday, so Jolene and I spent most of the morning moving things out of her reach. She's also trying to talk. I must admit fatherhood is better than I'd ever imagined it would be."

Tyler smiled. "So, you like being a daddy?"

"I love it. I can't wait for the next one."

"How's Jolene?"

"Other than a little fatigue, she'd feels and looks wonderful. Right now she and Teresa are taking a nap."

"She told me you guys decided to expand your house."

"We're adding three more bedrooms and a guest cottage that can sleep at least four. The last time Emily and Sara came to visit, their children were sharing beds, so I thought a little expansion was in order."

Michael's sister Emily Delgado was now the mother of three. She had two sons, Alejandro and Mateo, and a daughter, Esperanza. Sara Lassiter, Emily's sister-in-law also, had three children—a son, Isaiah, and twin daughters Nona and Eve.

"Did you and Jolene plan this pregnancy so you could have a Christmas delivery?" Tyler teased.

"That's what *abuela* said when we told her. She said if the baby's born on her birthday, then we should name it after her."

Marguerite Josefina Diaz-Cole would celebrate her birthday December 27, and in six months the entire Cole clan would gather in West Palm Beach, Florida, to honor their matriarch and commemorate her 102nd year of life.

"What if you have a son? I don't think he would appreciate being called Marguerite," Tyler teased.

"I don't think that would be a wise decision if Jolene and I hope to raise an emotionally stable boy."

"Do you want to know the sex this time?" Michael and Jolene had elected not to know the sex of their first child until Tyler delivered a beautiful little girl who looked enough like Michael's sister Emily to be her daughter.

"I know I do. I'd asked Jolene, but she hasn't told me what she wants one way or the other. You know we'd like you to deliver this one, too."

"I'd be honored, but you're going to have to make arrangements with a hospital in West Palm."

"No problem."

Picking up a pen, Tyler made circular notations on a pad. "I need your help, Michael."

His cousin had given up a military career to teach at a Virginia military institution. Michael, like his father before him, had attended West Point, and subsequently joined the Pentagon's Defense Intelligence Agency. Joshua Kirkland had retired as a colonel and Michael a captain. However, Michael had added a law degree to his impeccable military credentials, which qualified him to teach military law.

"Sure. What do you need?"

"The name and telephone number of a private investigator. I want someone to look into a twenty-two-year-old murder case."

There was a noticeable pause before Michael's baritone voice came through the wire again. "I don't know a PI, but I do know someone who might be able to help you out. His name is Merrick Grayslake. He used to work for the Company."

"The Company?"

"CIA," Michael explained.

Tyler forced a laugh. "I don't think I'm going to need someone trained in covert activities."

"What you need is the best when it comes to scrutinizing facts and data, and Gray was and is still one of the best I know."

"I'll take your word for it, *primo*. Give him my home number and tell him to call me. Let him know money is no object."

It was Michael's turn to laugh. "If I tell him you're my first cousin, then he'll inflate the fee so much that you'll be forced to file for bankruptcy."

"I repeat, money is no object."

"Back it up, *primo*. Does this have anything to do with a woman?"

"Why would you say that, Michael?"

"Because I've never known you to be such a spendthrift. I don't know whether you're aware of it, but there's a family joke about the rituals you go through before you settle on your annual charitable donations."

"That's because when I decide to share my wealth, it should be for a worthy cause. What I don't want to do is throw it away."

"I hear you," Michael intoned. He'd donated a generous portion of his own personal assets to his wife's crusade to help women reclaim their lives from the vicious cycle of substance abuse and domestic violence.

"Thanks, cousin, for helping me out. I'll see you for Thanksgiving."

"I'll be looking for you. You're always welcome to bring a guest if you want."

It was always the same. Every time someone invited him for a gathering, he was told to bring a guest, and because he'd always come alone, he always thought they would tire of extending the offer. But they didn't.

"Gracias y adiós."

"Adiós, Tyler."

Tyler hung up, reaching for a chart at the top of the pile. He had to complete his review of the charts before he left to pick up Dana. Twin dimples winked attractively as he recalled the feminine lushness of her body pressed to his when they'd danced at Three J's. Holding her close, inhaling her fragrance, feeling her heat had become a sensual feast for his senses. A feast he wanted to partake of over and over again until satiated.

Eleven

Dana shivered, despite the intense heat, staring at Tyler as he stared back at her through the finely woven mesh strung tightly over the door. Something in his stance, his expression, silently communicated she was seeing Tyler Cole for the first time—the real Tyler Cole.

His obsidian gaze was unwavering, intense, adding more heat to her already warm cheeks, and she found his nearness both disturbing and exciting. She'd known him less than a week, although it seemed much longer. He'd come into her home, and she'd gone to his. They'd shared several meals and danced together. He'd also kissed her, and she'd returned his kisses.

She'd found him soft-spoken, even-tempered, generous, and compassionate, and she responded to him despite her resolve not to become involved with a man. She'd agreed to date Tyler, while permitting him to become a part of her existence, but she had to ask herself, was she involved with him? That question had haunted her as she went through a hatbox of letters her grandfather had written to her grandmother during their courtship phase.

Daniel Sutton had poured out his heart in those long-ago written missives, declaring an undying love to the young woman who'd captured his heart. He'd waited for Georgia to celebrate her eighteenth birthday before claiming her as his wife. There were more than four-dozen letters from Daniel to Georgia, and while Dana had searched several other hatboxes for correspondence from her grandmother to Daniel, she could not find any. She found it strange because rarely had a month gone by when she did not get a letter from Georgia.

Without warning, Tyler smiled, the even whiteness of his teeth dazzling in his dark face. There was enough eroticism in his expression to melt away her defenses. Her emotions seemed out of control, her head swirling with doubts. She wanted Tyler Cole.

She wasn't certain whether she wanted or needed him to assuage the sensations attacking her celibate body simply because of his statement: *We go all the way.* Did going all the way translate into a sexual liaison or an eventual commitment? Dana knew she could sleep with Tyler without committing to a future with him. However, she wondered, would he accept one without the other?

"Are you coming out, or do you want me to come in?"

The soft drawling sound of Tyler's voice broke the spell as Dana offered him a sensual smile, unknowingly quickening his pulse. "I'm coming out." Reaching for her tiny purse on the drop-leaf table, she unlatched the screen door, opened it, and then closed the solid oak door behind her.

Cradling her elbow, he led her to his truck, helped her in, and then slipped in behind the wheel. He hadn't turned off the ignition, and cool air flowed from the vents.

Tyler backed out of the driveway, mindful of the young children playing in the street. He accelerated, heading west, his gaze fixed on the sky. Dark clouds were forming in the blistering white sky.

"It looks as if it's going to rain," he remarked casually.

Dana's gaze narrowed as she studied the heavens. There was a greenish glow that made everything appear iridescent. "I don't like the look of the sky."

Tyler glanced at her profile. "What's wrong with it?"

"We're in for some bad weather. Probably a thunderstorm with hail."

That's if we're lucky, she mused. She remembered the same type of sky as a child before a tornado touched down on a town to the east of Hillsboro. A month after the twister had hit, the inhabitants were still reeling from its devastating effects. Homes were leveled, the roof of the church had been blown away, all of the windows in the schoolhouse were shattered, and the countryside was littered with debris. The most appalling sight had been the number of dead livestock. Cows, horses, hogs, and chickens lay bloated and decomposing miles from where they'd grazed.

Tyler crossed the railroad grading, heading in the direction of the river. He returned a wave from a man on a slow-moving tractor, going in the opposite direction. Then he gave Dana a quick glance. She sat, her hands cradled in her lap, staring out the side window. She reminded him of a young college student with her bare face and hair brushed off her face and secured in a ponytail. She'd elected to wear a sleeveless orange linen dress that skimmed the lush curves of her body, and a pair of matching espadrilles.

He forced himself to concentrate on his driving rather than stare at his passenger. Today Dana looked more delicate than he had ever seen her—delicate and vulnerable. Without warning, an urgent need to protect her at any cost surfaced, a need stunning him with its intensity.

He'd never had to look after or protect anyone—not

even his sisters. That task was left to their father. Why, he wondered, at forty-one, did he suddenly feel the need to take care of someone other than himself; and why Dana?

You're falling for her, an inner voice taunted. He was falling and falling hard, and again he had to ask himself—why Dana?

Moreover, Tyler knew without a doubt that Dana was the one—that special woman who could get him to reevaluate who he was and whether he wanted to spend the rest of his life alone.

His gaze narrowing, he turned off onto the private road leading to his property. Rows of newly plants trees stood like sentinels on guard duty. They would've wilted in the extreme heat and lingering drought if he hadn't installed an automatic underground sprinkler system. It was programmed to activate twice daily, so trees, the endless expanse of lawn, flower, and vegetable gardens, and the orchard were provided with the moisture needed to remain lush and verdant.

His lifestyle appeared orderly, nearly perfect. Or was it? he had to ask himself. Appearances were deceiving, because in reality his life was far from perfect. He'd acquired the characteristics that signaled success, but real success had only come from his profession. Nowhere in his personal life had there been an iota of success.

He didn't know why, but he'd shied away from commitments because he'd told himself it would interfere with his work. Dr. Tyler Cole had convinced himself that he didn't want a woman, didn't need one except for physical release; but since interacting with Dana, he knew he'd lied to the universe and to himself.

Did he want a wife?

Did he want children?

The two questions bombarded him like the rhythmic

pounding of a bass drum in a holiday parade, until he felt like shouting, *Yes, I do!*

He did, and what he had to uncover was why now.

Reaching up, he pressed a button on the visor, and the door to the three-car garage opened silently. He pulled in, parked, leaving an empty space between the truck and the BMW roadster.

Dana waited for Tyler to come around and assist her getting out of the vehicle. She much preferred his low-slung convertible. It was built low to the ground, and she did not have to wait for him to lift her until she gained her footing, or endure the pleasurable sensations whenever their bodies touched.

Being that close to Tyler, inhaling his intoxicating masculine scent, reveling in the strength of his muscular arm around her waist whenever she was cradled in his embrace, made her ovaries ache. At the same time she was astounded by the sense of protection he offered her. He closed the truck's door with one hand, the other resting against the small of her back.

Tilting her chin, Dana stared up at him, smiling. "I hope you don't mind, but I'd like a tour of your property before we go in."

Lowering his head, Tyler brushed a light kiss over her parted lips. "Okay."

Hand-in-hand, they walked out of the garage, the doors closing automatically after they'd moved beyond the beam of a motion detector. Overhead, the sky darkened as angry clouds gathered in the distance. Intermittent flashes of lightning sliced the heavens.

Dana continued to watch the sky at the same time an uneasy feeling swept over her. The familiar scent of the Mississippi River wafted in her sensitive nostrils.

"I smell the river. It's definitely going to rain," she predicted.

"I'll show you the garden, then we'll go in," Tyler said, leading her around to the back of the property. The winding path of rose-pink brick was a soft contrast to the dark green grass.

"What's that?" she asked, pointing to a separate building several hundred feet away from the garage. The design was the same as the main house, but on a much smaller scale.

"That's the guest house. It has several suites, each with a bedroom, adjoining bath, efficiency kitchen, and a living/dining area."

"You must expect to do a lot of entertaining."

Tyler gave her fingers a gentle squeeze. "I come from a very large family."

"How many children did your parents have?"

He directed her around the barricades where workmen had dug a deep hole for what would become an in-the-ground pool. Set back from the hole was a pool house. Made of pure white marble, it looked like a Grecian temple, shimmering eerily in the ominous afternoon light.

"Three: two daughters and a son. When I say family, I mean all of the Coles, which includes in-laws, aunts, uncles, and cousins. My grandparents had five children between them, eighteen grandchildren, thirty-six great-grandchildren, three great-great grandchildren, and my younger sister is expecting the fourth."

Dana averted her head, blinking back the moisture welling up in her eyes. Tyler was only one of a number of Coles, a family with a legacy, while she was the last in the bloodline of Mississippi Suttons and Nicholses. After she passed away her DNA would end with her.

Biting down on her lower lip, she drew in a deep

breath and within seconds was back in control. "What color have you planned for the pool tiles?"

"Lapis blue."

They continued along a winding slate path, which led to a verdant forested area with an overgrowth of trees, flowering bushes, ferns, and clinging vines. Ancient oak trees festooned in shrouds of Spanish moss competed with fruit trees, which showed evidence of putting forth their early summer blooms. Large clay pots overflowed with a lavender and green display of hyacinths, anemones, lilacs, and pansies. Pale white roses, peonies, muscari, lisianthus, and viburnum spilled from a quartet of massive pots at the entrance to a section where several Japanese magnolias shaded a narrow path leading into a large field of wildflowers blooming abundantly in their natural state.

The temperature in the garden seemed at least ten degrees cooler, and Dana knew it was the perfect place to begin or end a day. Pulling her hand from Tyler's protective grasp, she bent down to inhale a profusion of blue hydrangeas growing amid a carpet of daffodils.

Placing her hand on the ground, she trailed her fingertips over the cool, dark earth. Here, everything was moist, alive, while the rest of Hillsboro withered. Another section, surrounded by circles of stones, revealed an herb garden. The distinctive scent of mint, basil, thyme, and rosemary perfumed the warm humid air.

"It's so pastoral." Her voice was low, filled with awe. "This is probably what the Garden of Eden was like."

Tyler hunkered down next to her, pointing to his left. "There's an underground stream about fifty yards from here which keeps the ground moist. I'm surprised it hasn't dried up like all of the others around here."

She glanced at his distinctive profile, admiring the

finely defined bones making up his handsome face. "What if it did dry up?"

"I had several wells installed on the property to off-set that problem." He stood, easing Dana up with him. "This is one of my favorite places. Come with me," he urged softly, cupping her elbow. He led her through the field of flowers.

Dana followed him through what she'd come to think of a jungle, stepping out into a cleared area where a gazebo sat on a grassy lawn, the structure resembling the top layer of a wedding cake; the sight elicited a soft gasp from her.

The gazebo overlooked a picnic area. She surveyed a large barbeque pit with a chimney rising at least six feet in the air, stone benches, and four outdoor patio tables, each with seating for six, shaded by massive umbrellas in the same sailcloth fabric covering the backs and seat cushions of the teakwood-trimmed chairs. The patio was made up of massive blocks of black marble.

She pointed to a large slab of concrete. "Is that going to be a tennis court?"

Smiling, Tyler shook his head. "No. A basketball court."

She grinned at him. "You weren't kidding when you said you play, as you call it, B-ball."

He wiggled his eyebrows. "You'll find out just how serious I am once the court is completed. I plan to practice throwing three-pointers until I can do it with my eyes closed."

"What are you training for?

"I've challenged a cousin to a three-throw contest. Right now Gabe holds the family record for the highest number of three-pointers in a game. He calls himself the Reggie Miller of three-pointers, but I'm out to prove him wrong."

"Is he that good?"

Tyler shrugged a broad shoulder under the finely woven fabric of a creamy lawn cotton shirt that was an exact match for a pair of tailored linen slacks. "He's good, but he's no Reggie Miller."

"Did he ever try out for the NBA?"

"No. He's happens to be a gifted musician."

"Did you ever think of playing ball professionally?"

Shaking his head, Tyler said softly, "The only thing I ever wanted to be was a doctor."

Dana lifted an eyebrow. "Did you ever think you might not score high enough on the MCATs to get into a medical school?"

He gave her a long, penetrating stare, then said, "I never thought I would not become a doctor."

It was Dana's turn to stare as she leisurely studied Tyler's face, feature by feature, looking for arrogance in his expression; what she did recognize was self-confidence and privilege. Even if Tyler Cole hadn't become a doctor, she knew he was privileged.

This was evident by the design of his home, its furnishings, guest house, vehicles, and the added amenities of an Olympic-sized swimming pool and professionally designed gardens. Even his manner of dress was classic and elegant.

I never thought I would not become a doctor. His statement told her all she needed to know about the man who'd pulled her into a vortex of desire from which she did not want to escape. It was obvious that if he wanted something, he would let nothing stop him from attaining his goal.

And it was apparent he wanted her—for what purpose, she wasn't certain. She'd tried to discourage him from seeing her, but to no avail, and she had concluded she would go along for the ride until it ended. The only thing she would not consider at this time was staying in Hillsboro after she'd cleared her father's name.

A sensual smile curved her mouth as she drank in the devastating virility Tyler projected. Taking a step, she moved closer, placing a hand on his forearm. "Your property's incredible. I know you will spend many wonderful years here."

The instant Dana touched him, Tyler longed to carry her back into the lushness of the garden, lower her to the earth, and make love to her until time ceased to exist for them; he wanted to join their bodies, making them one for all time, while pouring out his passions in her fragrant body until he forgot where he began and she ended.

Was he actually falling in love with her?

Yes!

Had she forced him to question his attitude toward marriage?

Yes!

And did interacting with her elicit the yearning to father a child?

Yes!

A delicate golden-eyed woman he hadn't known a week had unknowingly slipped under the barrier he'd set up to keep all women at a distance—women he would sleep with but not commit to, women who had become recipients of his lust, but never his love.

He knew what he felt for Dana was not lust, because that emotion was more than familiar to him. However, it was the surprisingly extraordinary feelings of elation and anticipation whenever he was in her company that had him coming back to her again and again.

He took a step, curving an arm around her waist. His free hand cupped her chin, raising her face to his, while his eyes made passionate love to her face. "You are so incredibly beautiful, Dana." There was no mistaking the awe in his voice. The seconds ticked off as he stared into her golden gaze, his head coming down slowly, his moist breath mingling with hers.

Dana closed her eyes briefly, then opened them, her gaze widening, a shudder of shock and fear sweeping over her. "Tyler." Her voice was barely a whisper. "Look."

Turning slightly, he glanced over his shoulder, his gaze fixed on the dark, distinctive shape of a funnel cloud racing swiftly across the horizon. It was heading in a southerly direction. Reacting quickly, he captured Dana's hand, pulling her roughly to his side.

"Let's get out of here."

There was no way she could estimate how close the twister was to them, but one glance revealed it was moving quickly, growing larger and gathering strength as the sound of the wind matched that of a runaway freight train.

She stumbled, nearly pitching forward, and would've fallen if Tyler hadn't tightened his grip on her hand. He pulled her along, shouting at her, but the words were snatched from his lips as the tornado moved in their direction.

The wind ripped the elastic band from her hair, whipping the strands around her face and into her eyes. Why hadn't she noticed the lightning had stopped after ten minutes? Why hadn't she been more vigilant? She had spent the past two thirds of her life in upstate New York where twisters were rare occurrences. But in throughout the Midwest and South, tornadoes were not only common but also very probable.

We're not going to make it! We're going to die! The ominous prediction echoed in her head over and over as the buffeting wind ripped at her clothes and assaulted her body. Massive branches of ageless trees dipped and swayed like tender saplings, leaves were stripped from

trees and brushes, and petals from flowers danced
wildly in the air like pieces of colorful confetti. Dana
felt her lungs burning as she forced her legs to move
faster, refusing to believe she'd returned to Hillsboro
to die. The faster she ran, the more her confidence
spiraled. As long as her legs were moving she knew
she was still alive. They had to make it back to the
house and shelter.

Tyler picked Dana up with one arm as if she were
a child, not breaking his stride. He was breathing heavily when he came to a stop, halfway between the house
and garden, bent over, and pulled on a large iron ring
attached to a slab of concrete. It took two attempts
before he was finally able to lift the door to what he'd
discovered before was a tunnel.

The sky was nearly black, but not black enough to
obscure the frightening sight of the tremendous funnel coming dangerously close to the ground. They had
to get underground before the tornado touched down,
sweeping up everything in its deadly path.

"Get in!" he shouted close to Dana's ear, doubting
whether she could hear him over the roar of the wind.

Dana saw Tyler's mouth move, but no words came
out. The wind had snatched them from his tongue.
Gritting his teeth tightly, he threw her over one shoulder, holding her legs tightly as he stepped back into
the hole. His foot slipped, and he quickly regained his
balance as he moved down a crude wooden ladder.
The last rung broke under his and Dana's weight. Setting her on her feet, he climbed up the ladder, reached
up using both hands, and pulled down on an inner
iron ring, closing the slab of concrete. Within seconds
he'd shut out the fury of nature raging out of control.

Complete darkness descended on Dana, and she began shaking uncontrollably, reaching out for Tyler.

Even though she was out of danger from the storm, she couldn't stop trembling.

"Tyler." His name was a muted whisper. "Tyler!" she screamed over and over, her voice bouncing off the earthen walls held back by wide planks of wood.

Tyler moved toward the sound of her voice, touching her shoulder and pulling her against his chest. "It's all right, darling. You're safe, sweetheart," he crooned in her ear.

Dana buried her face against his shoulder, biting down hard enough on her lower lip to draw blood. She felt the blackness closing in, suffocating her. She was dying, buried alive.

Tyler grimaced against the stabbing pain in his chest. Dana's fingernails dug into his flesh as she tightened rather than loosened her grip on his shirt. Gripping her hand, he forcibly wrested it from his shirt. He needed to get to a lantern he'd left in the shaft after he'd discovered its existence.

"No, Dana," he whispered harshly. "Please let me go, baby. I have to get a light."

"Tyler," she sobbed, "please don't leave me. I don't want to be alone."

Her shaking increased as tears stained her cheeks. As long as he held her she knew she would be safe. Rising on her toes, she pressed her open mouth to his, devouring it. She felt his heat, tasted the texture of his tongue.

Tyler reacted violently to Dana's assault on his body and his senses, knowing she was close to becoming hysterical. "No, Dana," he mumbled against her marauding mouth. She was kissing him, and the flesh between his legs hardened quickly, refusing to follow the dictates of his brain.

And what did she mean about not wanting to be

alone? He wasn't going anywhere. All he wanted to do was search the underground tunnel for the lantern.

Tightening his grip on her shoulders, he shook her. "Stop it, Dana. I'm not going to leave you. But I have to let go of you to find a light."

"No-ooo." The single word came out in a lingering sigh.

"Ouch!" he gasped audibly. Her fingernails bit into his back through the delicate fabric of his shirt.

Tyler knew he had to free himself from Dana's punishing grip before her sharp nails gouged his flesh. Tempering his superior strength, he forcibly pulled her arms down, holding her against his side in a punishing grip. He pulled her along with him as he took tentative steps near what he thought was the entrance to the tunnel, while Dana fought him like an enraged cat.

He found what he'd been searching along a wall, picked it up, and pressed a switch with one hand. A beam of light lit up their darkened sanctuary. His heart nearly stopped when he looked at Dana's grief-stricken expression.

Her eyes closed, her bloodied lower lip trembling, tears coursed down her cheeks. Bending slightly, he placed the lantern on the dirt-packed ground, and then swept Dana up in his arms. Holding her to his chest as if she were a child, he rocked her gently.

"Cry, baby," he crooned softly. "Let it all out."

Dana heard the soothing male voice, a voice that sounded like her father's, and she did cry. She cried for the years she'd spent exiled from her home; cried for the loss of her mother and all she should've shared with her: the onset of her menses, the strange emotions she felt whenever she saw a boy she liked, the loss of her virginity, and the mother-daughter talks that would never be. She shed tears because the first man she'd loved had betrayed her with a single act of cowardice when he'd elected to take his own life rather than fight for it. She sobbed because her dream of becoming a nurse to assist Dr. Harry Nichols in his practice had vanished once a Greenville jury rendered a guilty verdict in *Mississippi v. Nichols* for murder and arson.

Sitting down on the floor next to the lantern, Tyler held and rocked Dana until her sobs subsided and were replaced by dry heaves. He pressed a kiss to her mussed hair, inhaling the flower-scented fragrance clinging to the heavy strands. His lips continued to explore her hair, moving down to her ear, and still lower to the column of her velvety neck.

He was totally unaware that his attempt to comfort her had become an overture to seduction. Dana's arms tightened around his neck and she turned her face, tentatively pressing her mouth to his. The caress of her lips on his mouth enflamed his body as he returned the kiss, his tongue probing gently until she parted her lips and permitted him complete access to the honeyed sweetness she'd guarded jealousy for many years.

The storm, which raged outside, slipped between the slight opening around the concrete, igniting a hunger neither Dana or Tyler knew they were experiencing.

Easing her backward and cradling her head on his arm, Tyler moved over her body. The fingers of one hand feathered over her cheek as he drank deeply from her moist mouth.

His kiss was healing, comforting, bringing heat where there was cold. It signaled a beginning for Dana, a beginning where she had to confront her past in order for her to face her future—regardless of her investigation's outcome. She had to learn to trust—to trust and to love all over again—for the second time in her life. The first time had been as a child when she'd loved and trusted her parents unconditionally; however, all that had changed with three bullets. Three gunshots fired at point-blank range and twenty-two years of exile.

Now, she wanted to live and breathe freely, without the unbidden memories that continued to haunt her; wanted to love and trust, and plan for a future that included a husband and children; and she wanted to give into the gentle yearning and fall in love with Tyler Cole. Why him, she didn't know. Why him, she no longer cared.

"Love me," she whispered against his warm throat.

Tyler went completely still, cradling her face between his hands. "Do you know what you're saying?"

"Yes. I know exactly what I'm saying. I want you to make love to me."

"Here? Now?"

"Yes." The single word was firm, resolute.

"I want to make love to you, Dana" he confessed softly. "I wanted to make love to you the first time I saw you, but . . ." His words trailed off.

Dana felt her face burn with shame. She'd begged him to make love to her—assumed he wanted to make love to her. Pushing against his chest, she attempted to free herself.

"Please, let me up."

"No, Dana. Hear me out. I want you. I want you more than I've *ever* wanted any other woman I've met or known. However, I will *not* become someone to warm your bed because your hormones are running amuck. I won't sleep with you, and then stand by and watch you walk away from me in four months. That's not who I am. I need you to tell me now if I'm going to become a part of your life."

Dana's mind floundered. She'd stripped herself

bare, begging a man to make love to her, and he'd refused her offer. Vertical lines appeared between her eyes. "What are you asking, Tyler?"

"Total commitment." He'd uttered the words he'd never said to any woman—words he'd never said aloud. They were out, he couldn't retract them, and he felt free, freer than he'd ever been in his life.

Dana's breath caught in her throat, not permitting her to speak as she forced her confused emotions into a semblance of prudence. She managed a nervous laugh. "Are you talking about marriage?" He nodded. "Why? I don't know you, and you don't know me," she continued, her words falling over themselves as they spilled from her lips.

Lowering his head, Tyler pressed a tender kiss at the corner of her mouth. "Don't you believe in love at first sight?"

She shook her head. "No. I . . . I don't know. I've never actually been in love." And she hadn't—not with Galvin or with any other man.

He chuckled softly. "Neither have I."

"Why me, Tyler?"

There was a noticeable pause as the sound of their breathing was heard over the staccato tapping of rain and hail on the concrete slab above their heads. Water seeped around the edges of the stone, forming pools on the dirt floor.

"I don't know, Dana." Tyler's voice resonated a somber timbre. "One thing I know is it's not because of your looks. It's true what you said about us not knowing each other. But I do know what I feel. What I feel for you is real, as real as the storm that forced us to seek shelter in this tunnel." He kissed her again. "Give me time to prove to you that my intentions are honorable."

Her eyes swam with unshed tears. "I didn't come back to Hillsboro to fall in love."

He smiled at her in the dim light. "Are you falling in love with someone?"

"Maybe," she said teasingly. One thing she was certain of was her desire for him. She wanted him more than she'd ever wanted any man."

"We *will* make love, Dana, but only when the time is right and when I can protect you. I don't plan to become a baby's daddy. I want to be a husband and a father. Preferably in that order."

She managed a sad smile, her gaze awash with golden lights. "You have everything figured out, don't you?"

"I'd be a sorry something if at forty-one I didn't know what I wanted."

Dana closed her eyes. "I also have a plan, Tyler."

"Include me in your plan," he whispered passionately.

"I . . ."

His kiss stopped her mild protest. "Will you include me, darling?" He placed small nibbling kisses around her mouth, frustrating her.

She wanted him to stop teasing her and kiss her with passion—a passion she knew would be all-encompassing. "Yes," she breathed out into his mouth as it moved over hers.

There was promise and resignation in the single word. Wrapping her arms around Tyler's neck, she went pliant, giving into the desire that simmered just below the surface.

The man cradling her to his heart was offering her a second chance to love and to trust, and she was going to accept it as willingly as she accepted his healing kisses.

He reversed their positions, her legs sandwiched in

between his. They lay together on the dirt floor, unaware that their ancestors had done the same centuries before while they awaited freedom.

Closing her eyes, Dana rested her head on Tyler's broad shoulder. *You're home,* a voice whispered to her. Home wasn't Hillsboro, Mississippi.

It was Tyler Cole.

Twelve

Dana and Tyler became aware of the silence and stillness simultaneously. She scrambled off his body, coming to her feet.

"It's gone." Her dulcet voice was calm, thankful.

Tyler stood up and walked over to the wooden ladder. "I'm going up to take a look."

Inhaling deeply, he mentally prepared himself for the worst, expecting property damage; what he was not prepared for was the loss of human life. As soon as he lifted the concrete slab he heard the sirens. They were a long way off, but they still could be heard in Hillsboro. It was apparent the tornado had touched down—where was the question.

Hands splayed on his hips, he surveyed his property, whispering a silent prayer of thanks. Except for a few downed tree limbs, everything was still intact. He'd been spared.

He returned to the tunnel, holding the lantern aloft while Dana climbed the ladder. Waiting until she reached the top, he turned off the lantern, left it near the entrance, and then retraced his steps, placing the covering over the opening.

Dana stared up at the heavens. The rain had stopped, the sky had brightened, and watery rays of sunlight peeked through fluffy white clouds. Large hailstones were melting quickly in the suffocating heat.

The sound of the wailing sirens chilled her, and she curbed the urge to place her hands over her ears as she'd done as a child.

The compact cellular phone clipped to Tyler's waist rang. Vertical lines furrowed his forehead when he stared at the display. It was the county hospital. Depressing the TALK button, he said, "Dr. Cole."

He listened to the authoritative voice coming through the tiny earpiece telling him the twister had hit Calico, and the governor had declared a countywide emergency. Civilians were not permitted on any county roads, a six P.M. curfew was in effect, and all medical personnel were ordered to report to Calico to assist the injured. It was nearly five-thirty, and the curfew was scheduled to go into effect within half an hour.

"I'll be there as soon as I can." He ended the call, and then turned to Dana, taking her hand. "I have to go to Calico. But first I'm going to shower and change my clothes." Taking long, determined strides, he headed toward the house, pulling her along with him. "I want you to stay here until I get back."

Dana quickened her pace to keep up with him. She was practically running. "Can't you drop me off home? I need to wash and change my clothes."

"No. There's a county emergency, which means civilians aren't allowed on the roads. Besides, there's also a six o'clock curfew."

"But I'm going to stay indoors."

"I'm not willing to risk you getting arrested, Dana. Give me the keys to your place, and if I can I'll pick up something for you." There was a thread of steel in his voice she'd never heard before.

Waiting for him to unlock the front door to his house, she stared at his profile. His mouth was set in a tight grim line, while a muscle quivered in his lean jaw. She'd challenged Tyler before, speaking her mind, but something told her this was not the time to engage in a verbal confrontation. The telephone call had transformed him so that he'd become a complete stranger. Within seconds Tyler had disappeared, Dr. Cole taking his place.

Tyler unlocked the door, resetting the code on the alarm system on a panel in the entryway, handing Dana his keys. "I'm going to leave these with you in case you get cabin fever. However, I'll need your keys."

She stared up at his grim expression. "They're in my purse. I left it in your truck."

"I'll get it before I leave."

"What time do you expect to come back?"

"I don't know," he replied, pulling the hem of his shirt from the waistband to his slacks. Leaning over, he kissed her cheek. "I have to change."

Dana nodded numbly, watching him mount the curving staircase. Her shoulders slumped as she stared down at the smudges and stains on her shoes and dress. She'd wait for Tyler to leave, then shower and wash her clothes.

Tyler forced himself to remain upright. It was past midnight, and he'd been on his feet for more than six hours, refusing to acknowledge fatigue. The F3-category tornado had touched down on Calico, leveling most of the town. The only building left intact had been the bottling factory.

The county hospital's emergency room resembled a MASH unit. The injured lay on beds, stretchers, and gurneys; the numbers swelled until they filled every room and corridor in the three-story medical facility. After running of out space inside the hospital, they laid patients on makeshift cots on the lawn, where powerful flood lamps and a generator had been rigged up to provide light for the hospital staff to treat the injured. Tyler had been assigned to triage, along with a cardiologist and an internist. He'd diagnosed broken arms, legs, concussions, fractured skulls, jaws, and ruptured spleens and kidneys.

An area behind the parking lot had been set aside as a morgue for those who hadn't survived the deadly storm. Many had been found trapped under fallen debris, others in vehicles that had been hurled hundreds of feet from their original location.

Tyler had forced himself not to glance at the sheet-covered corpses. Despite the antiseptic smell wafting in the warm night air, the odor of death prevailed.

"Dr. Cole, you're needed over here!" A nurse with a blood-covered uniform gestured wildly to him.

Skirting a dazed man sitting on the grass cradling an injured arm to his chest, Tyler rushed over to the nurse. Leaning over, he peered at a young woman holding her distended stomach as she moaned softly. Her light-colored slacks were soaked with her own blood. He recognized her immediately. She was Miranda Connelly.

He ripped off his latex gloves. "Nurse, get me a clean pair of gloves, undress this patient from the waist down, and cover her with a sheet." He had to discover how far along she was in her labor.

The nurse moved to a nearby cart, grabbing the items he'd requested; she covered the lower portion of Miranda's body with the sheet and removed her slacks and blood-soaked underpants.

Reaching under the sheet, Tyler parted his patient's knees, inserting a finger into her vagina. His heart sank. She'd dilated four centimeters. He had to deliver her baby despite the risks. Miranda was only twenty-six weeks into her confinement, her unborn son weighing about two pounds.

"Mrs. Connelly?"

Miranda opened her pain-filled eyes, staring up at the familiar face looming above her. "Dr. Cole." His name had come out in a breathless sigh.

"I'm going to have to take your baby."

Tears stained her pale cheeks as she shook her head. "It's too soon."

"He's not full-term, but we have to give him a chance to survive." She tried to sit up, but Tyler placed a hand on her shoulder, easing her back to the cot. "You can't get up."

"I need to see Chuck. I want him with me."

"Where is he?"

"Someone took him to get stitched up. He took a large piece of glass to the side of his neck. He's lucky it didn't cut an artery."

"We'll try to find your husband," Tyler said, hoping to put her at ease. Removing his gloves, he motioned to the nurse. "Tell Dr. McCann I need an operating room for a C-section. I'll also need a neonatal team standing by. And please have someone page a Charles Connelly."

The nurse nodded. "Yes, Doctor."

Dana lay in bed, struggling to stay awake. A clock on the bedside read twelve-ten. Clad in a white T-shirt belonging to Tyler, she inhaled the fragrance of his cologne clinging to the pillow under her head, closed her eyes, and fell asleep, her right arm resting on the open pages of the book she'd been reading.

She'd tried amusing herself during his absence, hoping to remain awake long enough to ask him about the damage from the tornado. She took a leisurely tour of his home while awaiting his return, totally awed by its magnificence.

She searched through the drawers in a massive walk-in closet for something to cover her nakedness, took a shower, put her clothes in the washing machine in the laundry room off the kitchen, and then prepared a light snack for herself. She cleaned up the kitchen, and then wandered throughout the large structure, beginning with the first floor.

At the rear of the house, an unfurnished space with glass walls would eventually become a conservatory. Another room facing east had been set up as a library/music room. Built-in floor-to-ceiling cherrywood bookcases with sliding ladders were crowded with volumes ranging from anthropology to zoology. One wall held hundreds of DVDs, CDs, videotapes and audiocassettes, the latest state-of-the art stereo component system, and a large flat-screen television.

Dana found herself transfixed by a large, handcrafted, gemstone globe inlaid all around with semiprecious gems. She spent three quarters of an hour tracing each country, which was represented by a gem. Canada was mother of pearl, India green aventurine, and Paraguay red jasper. The oceans and seas were depicted in black onyx, and the meridians by silvery wires. A leather-bound unabridged dictionary from the nineteenth century lay atop a mahogany library stand. There was no doubt the antique library stand was as old as the book it cradled.

A quartet of hand-cast bronze-layered plaques was positioned on a wall, two inscribed in English, the other two in Latin. Reading the plaques revealed a lot about Tyler Cole.

Be still then, and know that I am God. The inscription inspired by Psalm 46:10, this simple phrase invoked silence, mindfulness, contemplation, and prayer.

Another, with a quote from Michelangelo, read: *I am still learning.*

She read the Latin, making a mental note to ask Tyler to translate *Vocatus atquenon, Vocatus Deusaderit,* and the palindrome: *Sator arepo tenet opera rotas.*

After perusing the room, she had selected a movie, settled down on a comfortable club chair, and watched it in its entirety.

A clock on the fireplace mantel had chimed eleven-thirty when she finally retreated to the upstairs bedroom with a hardcover mystery novel tucked under her arm.

The master bedroom suite on the second floor was the only one of the four completely furnished. The king-sized mahogany sleigh bed and exquisite bed dressing were the room's focal point. A blue-gray knotted silk quilt, hand stitched with intricate diamond shapes, each surrounding a circle that mimicked a small knot, and matching pillow shams created a pearly luster and an antique appearance. Pale gray silk panels covered floor-to-ceiling mullioned windows. A mahogany desk and matching chair were nestled in a sitting area along with twin club chairs and ottomans in a black, white, and gray velvet and silk striping. The effect was sophisticated masculinity.

She had been intrigued by a spiral staircase, which led from the bedroom to the seating area. Climbing the staircase, she discovered a private little dormered loft with a scenic view of the Mississippi River in the distance. The reproduction of a sixteenth-century Dutch colonial bench was only object in the space. She sat for a few minutes, staring at the darkened landscape, her mind drifting back to another era.

Each of the four bedrooms had adjoining baths, utilizing varying shades of the color scheme selected for the bedrooms. The walls of the smaller bedrooms were covered with Smithsonian patterned wallpaper, reminiscent of a bygone era. Two of the smaller bedrooms were partially furnished with tables, chairs, and lamps, while the last one stood completely empty. She remembered Tyler saying the house was only partially furnished and that he awaited the arrival of furniture for more than half the rooms.

Sunrise was still an hour away by the time Tyler maneuvered his SUV into its bay in the garage. He was beyond being tired—he was exhausted. He'd left the hospital when a team of doctors arrived from several hospitals in the state's capital. All of them had had to be airlifted in because only one road leading into Calico had been cleared, and only for official emergency vehicular traffic.

He'd delivered the Connelly baby, but had remained in the hospital's tiny neonatal unit watching the machines monitoring the two-pound, six-ounce infant's fight for survival. Someone had located Charles Connelly in time for him to witness his son's birth. Tyler reassured the new father that each day his son remained alive was looked upon as a miracle, quoting a favorite line from Willa Cather's *Death Comes for the Archbishop. Where there is great love there are always miracles.*

He craved a hot shower, at least four hours of uninterrupted sleep, and Dana Nichols. He hadn't remembered he had to stop at her house to pick up clothes for her until he was halfway home. Reversing his direction, he made it to her house, and after searching two bedrooms, found hers. He shoved a pair of sandals and running shoes into a canvas bag he'd found in a closet. He opened dresser drawers, pulling out panties, bras, T-shirts, jeans, and shorts, adding them to the bag. Lastly, he picked up several bottles of perfume, creams, and personal hygiene products, put them in the bag, zipping it.

Hillsboro was ominously quiet. Tyler hadn't encountered anyone on the road, except for several police cars parked along the shoulder, their lights flashing in the dark. Every house he passed was unlit. It was as if everyone quietly mourned the loss of life and property in the town several miles away. If the twister had turned north rather than south, then it would've been Hillsboro residents who would be found picking through the remains of what would've been their life possessions for something to salvage, or making arrangements to bury their loved ones.

Tyler's step was slow and heavy as he walked the short distance from the garage to the house. It wasn't until he unlocked the door and pushed it open, flicked a switch turning on the overhead chandelier, that he felt a rush of gratitude sweep over him. It was times such as this when he was grateful for his profession. He'd always thought of his ability to aid in healing as a special gift from God. And tonight his gift had been manifested over and over as he tended the injured, while helping to bring another life, albeit fragile, into the world.

Leaving the bag with Dana's clothes on a table in the entryway, he slowly made his way up the staircase. The soft golden glow from a table lamp at the far end of the second-story hallway illuminated the space. He smiled, weariness etched into the lines ringing his nose and mouth as he made his way down the hallway to his bedroom. Dana had left a light on for him. Peering into the bedroom, he made out the outline of her body under a sheet.

He decided to use the bathroom in one of the other bedrooms to shower and brush his teeth, not wishing to wake or startle her. Fifteen minutes later his eyelids were drooping when he walked into the master bedroom, lifted the sheet, and slid into bed next to the woman who'd captured his heart with only a glance.

Dana felt the heat and the arm thrown over her hip. She stirred restlessly, turning toward the source of heat. Her eyelids fluttered wildly as a whisper of warm breath caressed her forehead.

"Tyler?" Her voice was heavy with sleep.

"Go back to sleep, baby. We'll talk later."

Snuggling against his heat and strength, she complied, returning to the comforting arms of Morpheus.

Thirteen

Dana rubbed the tip of her nose, hoping to swat away whatever it was tickling her. She loathed opening her eyes to get up. Something brushed against her nose again, and this time she opened her eyes, encountering the dark amused gaze belonging to Tyler Cole.

Gasping, she inched away from him, but was thwarted from putting space between their bodies as he tightened his grip on her waist. Her face had been pressed against his hair-covered chest.

Streams of bright sunlight filtering through the pale gray panels lining the windows provided enough light for her to see the stubble of black hair on Tyler's lean jaw. Smiling, he shifted, bringing her belly into direct contact with his groin. He had come to bed naked!

Pulling back her hips as naturally as she could, she smiled up at him. "Good morning."

Tyler returned her smile with a dimpled one. "That it is, beautiful, especially if I can wake up with you in my bed every morning." Lowering his chin, he dropped a light kiss on the top of her mussed hair.

Dana glanced up at him through her lashes. The dark smudges under his eyes indicated fatigue, but rather than detracting, they enhanced the large, intense, deep-set eyes framed by long black lashes. She found his gaze hypnotic.

"At what time did you get in?"

"A little before four." It was now after eight.

"How bad is it?"

Sighing, Tyler released her, shifted, and folded a muscular arm under his head. He stared up at the ceiling. "There's a lot of property damage."

Rising on an elbow, Dana studied his grim expression. "Any fatalities?"

"Unfortunately, yes."

Closing her eyes, she rested her cheek on his solid shoulder and said a silent prayer. Both of them were silent, each lost in their private thoughts.

"There were a lot of broken bones and lacerations from flying glass," Tyler continued slowly, choosing his words carefully. "There was also a birth. A tiny little boy who weighed in at a little over two pounds."

Dana sat up, smiling. "A preemie?"

Turning his head, he looked at her. "Three months premature."

"Do you think he'll make it?"

"The next few weeks are very critical. If he gains weight, then we are hopeful he can make it. Of course there's still the problem of his underdeveloped lungs. The doctors in the neonatal unit will monitor his progress very closely. I'm certain they're going to recommend transferring him to a hospital in Jackson."

"Why move him at all?"

"There's a hospital there that specializes in treating low birth weight babies." He knew he would be the one to break the news to Connellys, hoping they wouldn't balk in giving their approval to move their newborn to a more qualified facility.

"Why don't we have a similar unit at our county hospital?"

Lowering his arm, Tyler gently pulled Dana against his body, her hips pressed to his groin. He smiled.

She'd said *our* instead of *the* county hospital. Could he hope she was beginning to regard Hillsboro as her home?

"Maybe that will change in the future."

Dana held her breath when she felt the flesh between Tyler's legs stir against her buttocks. She didn't know if she was ready for him, unlike the day before in the tunnel. Fear and desperation had replaced common sense when she'd begged Tyler to make love to her. But now in the bright sunlight, in the warm, protective grasp of his arms, she felt shy.

"Do you have to go back to the hospital today?"

"No. However, I'm still on call for the next thirty-six hours." He covered her smooth legs with one of his. "Would you mind if we stay in bed a little longer?"

She gave him a long, penetrating look over her shoulder, her heart turning over when she saw the longing in his gaze. "No, Tyler, I don't mind." At that moment she did want to stay with him, in his arms, in his bed for a long, long time.

His left hand feathered up her thigh and under the T-shirt, fingers splaying over her hip. His hand burned her sensitive flesh through the delicate fabric of her silken panties.

Tyler buried his nose in the gold-streaked strands flowing over the pillow next to his, inhaling the very essence that was Dana Nichols. They lay together, wrapped in a cocoon of gentle intimacy almost as satisfying as the aftermath of a passionate coupling. He hadn't made love to her, yet felt satiated. What he was experiencing with Dana he'd never shared with any other woman.

Women who'd shared his bed in the past were usually interested in one thing: sex. One or two had wanted more, but he had never been able to commit— not when his research projects had garnered so much

of his time. Most of his time had been spent at the
laboratory entering and analyzing the data he'd spent
thousands of hours gathering. He and the members
of the research teams had studied the effects of differing drugs, enzymes, and chemical changes in pregnant
women. He was one of the lead doctors on a study of
endometriosis, GTN—abnormal pregnancies with a
cystic growth of the placenta, and IUGR—the inade-
quate growth of a fetus during the last stage of pregnancy.

He woke up each morning thinking of the work
he'd done the night before. It was only when the labs
closed for holiday vacations that he permitted himself
to step away from his world of research. He always returned to Florida the last two weeks of the year to
reconnect with his family. In West Palm Beach he was
Tyler Simmons Cole, son of Martin and Parris, brother
to Regina Cole Spencer and Arianna Cole Kadir, and
uncle to Clayborne and Eden Spencer. As Tyler, he
interacted with his grandmother, brother-in-law, aunts,
uncles, and numerous cousins.

He and his unmarried cousins, who usually visited
trendy nightclubs, returned home with the sunrise,
slept late, frolicked in heated pools, played tennis, and
often engaged in spirited competitive basketball
games. It was also the time to bet good-naturedly on
professional and college football teams. The wagers
were always done in secret, because the family matriarch forbade gambling in any form.

Dana felt some of her uneasiness dissipating as she
lay in Tyler's protective embrace, marveling that he
hadn't attempted to make love to her even though his
hardness throbbing against her hips indicated he was
fully aroused. She had to admit that the surging heat

and size of his prodigious sex was definitely a turn-on, and there was no doubt Tyler Cole was a virile man in the prime of his life.

As a young girl she remembered knocking on the door to her parents' room, waiting for them to acknowledge her presence. She'd race into their bedroom, jump on the bed, and lay atop the sheets between them. There were occasions when her mother's face was flushed with excitement, and it wasn't until years later that she realized her mother's expression reflected a satiated woman who'd experienced what it meant to be born female. It was a time when one could conclude with a single glance that Harry and Alicia had been very much in love with each other.

Was that how it had been between them before doubt, distrust, and deception destroyed their marriage? Dana recalled the sensual glances, the surreptitious caresses, and the endearments her parents had exchanged whenever they thought her attention elsewhere. She'd thought her parents and their marriage perfect.

"Were you home the night your mother died?"

The peace Dana felt fled, strange disquieting memories taking its place with Tyler's query. She inhaled, and then let her breath out slowly. If she planned to become involved with Tyler, then he had a right to know who she was, what she'd become because of a single act of violence.

"Yes, but I'd slept through it."

Her voice was soft, calming, as she told Tyler everything: Alicia and Harry's argument, his decision to divorce his wife, and his threat to seek sole custody of his daughter.

She told him about the fire, which had destroyed all evidence connected with Alicia's murder, Harry's arrest, and the judge's decision to deny bail. Pausing, she related the pain she encountered when her grandmother would not permit her to visit her father while he awaited trial.

Each time she faltered, waiting to regain her composure, Tyler pressed a kiss to the nape of her neck. He made no attempt to interrupt her, and she was grateful for this, because his presence had become more valuable than words of comfort.

She told him everything, leaving nothing out about her forced exile. "After my father took his life by hanging himself in his jail cell, my grandmother took me north to live with her sister. I cried for weeks because I missed my home. I hated my new school, and the students. There were only three black families living the area. Two were childless, and one had two sons. I'd opted not to go to the senior prom because neither of them asked me to be their date. It was in college that I was exposed to black men for the first time. They fascinated me with their regal arrogance and confidence as men. I dated, but refused to commit."

Tyler closed his eyes, enjoying the haunting sound of Dana's voice pulling him into a tightening web of seduction. He was content to lie in bed all day listening to her. She'd revealed her joy, fear, pain, and disappointment, eliciting a desperate need in him to protect her.

A wry smile curved his mouth at the same time he opened his eyes. He was forty-one years old, and for the first time in his life he'd clandestinely assumed responsibility for protecting someone other than himself: Dana Nichols.

Dana sat on the porch, staring at the oak trees shading the backyard. The ban on non-official vehicular traffic was lifted twenty-four hours after it had been imposed, and she was back home.

A letter Georgia Sutton had written to her, but hadn't mailed, dated three years before, lay on her lap. The feeling of security that had lingered with her after she'd shared most of Sunday with Tyler was missing. They'd stayed in bed until late morning, talking while holding hands. She'd found it so easy to talk to him because he listened intently without interrupting her or interjecting what he thought she wanted to hear.

He, in turn, had proudly revealed the professional and personal accomplishments of his mother and sisters. When she'd asked him about his father, he'd said he was a retired businessman.

They finally got up, completed their morning ablutions, she using the bathroom in the master suite, Tyler the one next to it. He slipped into a pair of jeans and a T-shirt, and the stubble of an emerging beard on his lean jaw made his face less perfect—more rugged.

She assisted him preparing breakfast, but neither had much of an appetite because their focus was not on food but on a television screen in a niche in the large kitchen. The news of the destructive tornado had preempted regular programming. The governor had declared Calico and four miles of Washington County a disaster area, requesting federal aid from the president. Repeated footage of the arrival of representatives from FEMA and the Red Cross, and the governor talking directly to the interior secretary, buoyed the sagging spirits of those who had lost everything except their lives and the clothes on their backs.

The dispossessed were put up in school buildings in Hillsboro to wait for trailers, which were to be set up as temporary housing before the rebuilding would begin. The call for clothes, shoes, and money to aid families in the burial of their loved ones brought forth an

outpouring of goodwill and compassion from Missis-
sippians all over the state. Dana had packed up several
cartons containing clothes and shoes her grandmother
had worn, labeling the boxes with their contents.

Eugene Payton had come as promised at ten o'clock
that morning, cradling a leather case with legal documents that would change her and her life—forever. It
had only taken Mr. Payton ten minutes to answer twenty
years of questions—those spoken and unspoken. However, it wasn't the will that had unnerved Dana. It was
the sealed envelope containing the letter from Georgia
that had rendered her mute, unable to move.

She had become the beneficiary of her grandmother's life insurance, home, and its contents. A pro-
vision had indicated she could sell the house a year
following Georgia's death.

Dana unknowingly had also been Harry Nichols's
beneficiary. Her grandmother, as legal guardian, had
used the money to purchase treasury bonds, and at
maturity the result was a modest six-figure sum. The
monthly allotment from the Social Security Admini-
stration for survivor's benefits for Dana had been for-
warded directly to Georgia's sister in New York.

Dana had been orphaned a second time when her
maiden Aunt Fanny died during her college junior
year. She'd considered returning to Hillsboro to complete her studies at Mississippi State, but Georgia forbade her to come back. Adhering to her
grandmother's wishes, she'd earned an undergraduate
degree at Ithaca College.

Picking up the letter, she read it again, analyzing
every word:

> *Hillsboro, Mississippi.*
> *My precious granddaughter,*
> *It is with a heavy heart that I write to you. It is so*

much easier to put everything down in writing that I am unable to say to you in person.

I know you wonder why I do not want you to come back to Hillsboro, but I did what I thought was best for you. What I have tried to do is protect you from the lies and those who would try to hurt you like they hurt your mother.

Alicia was not perfect, far from it, but she had never deliberately hurt anyone. And she did love you. There were times when she did not know how to show it, but I know she did. She would have given up her life rather than let anyone or anything harm you. I cry to this day because she did not deserve to die the way she did.

I know everyone believes Harry killed her. Even a jury said he was guilty, but they were wrong, Dana. All of them were wrong. Harry loved Alicia too much to kill her, no matter what she did.

You are going to have to come back to Hillsboro one of these days, and when you do, I want you to find out who murdered my baby. I will not be here when you uncover the truth, but wherever I am I sure I will be smiling because justice will be served.

I love you, Dana. I have loved you like you were my own child. Do not forget to do good and be generous, for with such sacrifices God is well pleased.

I pray for your happiness, knowing God will give you the desires of your heart.

Love,
Grandma.

Tears filled Dana's eyes, turning them into pools of shimmering gold. From whom did Georgia want to protect her? Who or what? And why hadn't she testified at the trial that she did not believe her son-in-law had fired three bullets into his wife's head as she lay sleeping?

Dana opened her eyes, determination radiating from their moist depths. Twenty-two years was a long time—long enough for her mother's murderer to have passed away or to have left Hillsboro permanently.

Pushing off the cushioned rocker, she climbed the staircase to her bedroom. She had to change her clothes. If she was going to investigate a crime, then she needed to begin with two sources: the Greenville courthouse where her father had been tried for murder, because she would need a copy of the transcript of the trial proceedings. She would also need any newspaper clips covering *The State of Mississippi vs. Harry E. Nichols.*

Fourteen

Dana knocked, and then pushed open the door to the *Hillsboro Herald*. The gold letters on the frosted glass door identified Ryan Vance as publisher and editor in chief.

She stepped into a large pace littered with orderly chaos. Bundles of newspapers were piled high on two long tables, while corkboard walls were covered with paste-up ads. There were two facing desks, both with computers, and a man with thinning red hair sat at one, his fingers skimming over a keyboard. His head came around when she closed the door.

Eyes the color of shiny copper pennies widened as Dana moved closer. "Good afternoon. I'm—"

"Dana Nichols," the red-haired man said, rising to his feet and completing her introduction. "I'd know you anywhere." He had a high-pitched, nasal-sounding voice. He extended a freckled hand. "I'm Ryan Vance, editor of the *Herald*."

She managed a skeptical smile. "You seem to have me at a distinct disadvantage." She shook his hand.

"Please sit down." He waited for Dana to sit down on a chair next to his cluttered desk. "You look exactly like your mother. What I mean is that you look exactly like she *did* before she died."

Dana stared at the newspaperman, who appeared to be in his mid-forties to early fifties. His sedentary ca-

reer was evident by the softness in his slight body under a rumpled white shirt and khakis. His clothes were
clean, although she doubted whether they'd seen an
iron since leaving the factory where they were made.

"What do you know about my mother?"

She listened intently as Ryan revealed he'd been
only twenty-three when he'd covered Dr. Harry
Nichols's murder trial for a Greenville newspaper. His
father, who'd been editor at that time, had come down
with an acute gout attack, and Ryan had temporarily
assumed the responsibility of the running the weekly.
He boasted that the paper's circulation had tripled for
the duration of the celebrated trial.

"Emotions were off the chart, half the populace of
Hillsboro believing in Harry's innocence, and the
other half in his guilt. The beliefs went according to
gender: the men openly condemning Dr. Nichols,
while most women lamented that the handsome doctor
was innocent.

"Alicia Nichols was a very controversial woman,"
Ryan continued. "She was beautiful and extremely flirtatious. Whenever she walked into a room, women
held onto their husbands as if they feared she could
lure one of them away with a single glance."

Dana peered closely at the editor, seeing a flush of
color darken his face. "Did she sleep with other men
beside her husband?" she asked, recalling her parents'
argument the night of the murder.

The color in Vance's face deepened as he shook his
head. "That I don't know. Hillsboro was just beginning
to integrate during that time, so there wasn't too much
mixing socially. The fact that the trial was moved to
Greenville gave me the advantage over the Davises, because I was able to interview blacks and whites without
suspicion. My father was respected for always reporting
the truth."

"And what do you believe was the truth? Was my father guilty of murder?"

Minute lines fanned out around Ryan's eyes as he squinted at a photograph over Dana's shoulder. "I didn't believe he was capable of murder," he said after an interminable silence.

She shifted her eyebrows. "You didn't answer my question, Mr. Vance."

"No, Miss Nichols. I don't believe he killed her."

Her expression softened. "Please call me Dana." He nodded. "I'm going to need your help."

Ryan angled his head, staring at a face that had bewitched him more than thirty years ago. He'd told Dana the truth—during that time segregation had kept the races apart, but that hadn't stopped him or other white men from lusting after Alicia Sutton Nichols. There was something about her most men—young or old—could not resist. And he wondered if Dana, like Alicia, was just as provocative.

He knew Dana Nichols was a journalist. He'd remembered her name in a picture caption under an award-winning syndicated article exposing years of sexual abuse in an upstate New York group home for girls. It hadn't been her name as much as her face, her uncanny resemblance to Alicia Nichols, that had captured his rapt attention.

"How?" he asked.

She smiled, the gesture crinkling her golden eyes. "You covered the trial, so you were familiar with all of the players: prosecutor, defense attorneys, witnesses, and the jurors."

He lifted red-orange eyebrows. "Are you saying you want to talk to them?"

"Yes. And that includes the fire marshal, coroner, crime-scene technicians, and the former sheriff."

"Even if all of them are still alive, do you think they'd be willing to open up to you?" Ryan questioned.

Her smiled faded. "Why shouldn't they?"

"You're a stranger to them, Dana. An outsider. Hillsboro is a strange little town. It has always hid its dirty little secrets well."

Dana stared at the newspaperman, her smooth forehead furrowing. "You live here now?"

Ryan nodded. "I moved here after I brought the *Herald.* I've always liked Hillsboro—even twenty-two years ago when I came here for the first time to talk to your grandmother."

This disclosure forced Dana to sit up straighter. "What did she tell you?"

"Nothing. Georgia Sutton refused to talk to me, the Davises, or her neighbors about her daughter's murder or the trial. The only person I remember her interacting with was her lawyer."

"Eugene Payton," Dana said softly, wondering just how much the elderly man knew. Had Georgia confided in him? She mentally added Mr. Payton's name to her list of interviewees.

A shiver of frustration swept over her. She had four months—less than 120 days to attempt to clear her family's name. "There has to be someone who'd be willing to talk to me about my parents."

"I doubt it," Ryan countered, pulling his lower lip between his teeth. "I happen to know you're a journalist," he countered sheepishly. "I read a syndicated article on the work you did on that residential group home for adolescent girls.

"Come work for the *Herald.* If you want, you can start today with editing copy while you do your investigating. Folks will get used to seeing you around here and connect you with the paper. After a couple of weeks I'll have you cover a story about something of interest. I've begun a column I call *Hillsboro: Then and Now.* I select a date in history, profiling a particular person or event. I also feature a current event or person, which always makes for a lot of excitement because anyone I interview must sign a statement attesting they will not disclose the contents of their interview before that edition of the paper is released. It's a gimmick, but the paper's circulation has doubled since the start of the column."

Dana had to smile. "That's very clever."

Ryan lifted a shoulder under his short-sleeved rumpled white shirt. "It sells copies. The Davises started the *Herald* as a hometown paper, and I plan to continue the tradition."

Dana knew the newspaper editor was right about small towns. It was easier to glean information from intelligence agencies than tight-lipped residents, many of whom would carry secrets to their graves.

She wanted to reject Ryan's offer. She had a job in Carrollton, and she hadn't come to Mississippi to work for a small-town weekly, even if it was only on a temporary basis. However, she was also familiar with people's unwillingness to disclose things to a reporter unless she granted their request for complete anonymity; she'd earned a reputation for never disclosing her sources. She was also aware that if she didn't get the editor's cooperation, then her investigation would be certain to hit a roadblock, if not a dead end.

"I'll accept your offer," she said reluctantly, "but I'm going to need time to go through your morgue. I'd appreciate it if you pull the microfiche on the issues covering everything from the police investigation to the trial. I also plan to visit the courthouse in Greenville to secure a copy of the transcript from my father's trial."

Ryan's eyes danced with excitement. "I can help

with that. I have a cousin who works in court records. I'll call her and tell her to have the copies ready for you. You'll have to fill out a request form and pay a fee for each page. Now, about working here. You can set your own hours as long as you get your assignments completed before each Wednesday. Everything goes to the printer on Wednesday. We drop off the mail subscriptions at the post office Thursday afternoons. Everyone likes to get their *Herald* for the weekend."

Dana nodded. "I'd like to begin tomorrow morning with the microfiche."

"I'll have them ready for you. Meanwhile, I'd like you to set up an interview with one of Hillsboro's newer residents." Ryan stood up and walked over to a table stacked with back issues. Sorting through the dates, he picked up three, handing them to Dana. "He's Dr. Tyler Cole. He's a bachelor and the latest medical director at the Hillsboro Women's Health Clinic. If you read what I've written in these back issues, then you'll glean an idea of what to ask for."

Her expression did not change when Ryan mentioned Tyler's name, despite the rush of heat singing her face. Ryan wanted her to interview the man who'd pursued her with the quiet, determined stalking of a hungry predator. Focused and relentless, he'd temporarily become a part of her life and she his.

She'd slept under his roof, shared his bed, yet he hadn't made an attempt to share her body. She knew he was physically attracted to her, and she marveled at his resolute promise they would not make love with other until the time was right for both of them. She vacillated, wanting to sleep with Tyler, and then changed her mind because of the short time they'd known each other.

What she felt for Tyler, shared with him, she had never experienced with the men whom she'd known

or been involved with. Men who she doubted would
share her bed but not her body. And there was no
doubt Tyler was as virile as any normal male. The obvious difference was that he was in total control of his
mind *and* his body.

She gave Ryan a direct stare. "If Dr. Cole is the column's Now, then who are you profiling for the Then?"

"Your great-grandfather Dr. Silas Nichols."

Dana felt a rush of uneasiness. Had the editor decided to write about one of her ancestors because
she'd returned to Hillsboro? "When did you decide to
profile him?"

Ryan turned back to his desk and picked up several
printed pages. He handed them to Dana, watching intently as she perused the schedule of names and dates
for upcoming issues. A date on the lower left of the
page indicated it had been revised the month before.
The profile on Dr. Silas Nichols was due to run in
three weeks. That meant she had to interview Tyler
and write the column before that time.

"Your return to Hillsboro had nothing to do with
my decision to write about your great-granddaddy,"
Ryan explained. "The fact that he was Hillsboro's first
resident black doctor was a history-making event. And
because there were rumors that he'd saved the life of
a prominent white Hillsboro citizen, that's something
our current citizens should be made aware of. Less
than twenty years after Dr. Nichols purchased his house
from the widow of a former Confederate officer,
Hillsboro had become an all-black town."

Her gaze fused with Ryan's. "How many words?"

"Try to keep it under seven hundred fifty for each
time frame."

She handed him back the schedule. "Give me the
contact data on Dr. Cole, and I'll set up an appointment with him."

What the editor did not know was that she had the numbers to Tyler's home phone, cell phone, and pager. She'd been to the man's house not once but twice. She'd eaten at his table, slept in his bed, and found herself falling in love with him despite her resolve not to get involved.

Pressing a button on his computer, the *Herald*'s editor in chief scrolled through a listing of names, printing out the data he'd collected on Dr. Tyler Cole. He handed her the single sheet of paper.

She picked up a phone on one of the desks, dialing the number to the Hillsboro Women's Health Clinic, asking to speak to Dr. Cole after she'd identified herself as a reporter from the *Hillsboro Herald*. The woman who answered the call identified herself as Ms. Lincoln, informed Dana Dr. Cole was out of the state and wasn't expected to return until the end of the week. Dana left her name and number and a message he call her upon his return.

She schooled her expression not to reveal her uneasiness. When she and Tyler parted the night before, he'd promised to call her after office hours Monday evening. She hoped his absence wasn't the result of a family emergency.

Folding the paper, she put it in her purse, gathered the back issues, thanked Ryan, and walked out of the office. It was only the first day, but she knew she'd made an ally in Ryan Vance. He would be able to confirm or deny most or all of her findings, and she prayed she would uncover the truth before her leave expired.

Fifteen

It was early Tuesday evening when Tyler was finally able to dial the area code and then Dana's telephone number; he sighed in relief when hearing her voice come through the earpiece. He'd left Hillsboro, Mississippi, within two hours of receiving a call from a New Jersey-based pharmaceutical company requesting his presence at an FDA hearing on the approval of a controversial drug deemed safe for pregnant and lactating women.

He'd been waiting for the call for several months, but was told the hearing had been postponed until late summer. Once the call had come through, Imogene Lincoln was given the task of calling patients and rescheduling appointments. A part-time OB-GYN and a physician's assistant were called in to cover Tyler's cases for the week, with a possibility his stay in Washington would be extended an additional week.

"I have a message you called." His soft voice was filled with repressed laughter. "I take it you miss me."

Dana laughed. "I don't think so, Dr. Cole. I didn't know you had such an inflated ego."

It was Tyler's turn to laugh. "Never with you, Miss Nichols."

"Where are you calling from?"

"Georgetown. I'm staying with a cousin. I'm here for a weeklong FDA hearing. Hold on a minute."

Teresa Kirkland toddled across the room, his watch clasped tightly in her chubby little fist. Tyler moved off his chair, picked her up, and eased his watch from her fingers. Teresa shrieked an ear-piercing scream while squirming to free herself from her godfather's firm grip. Holding her under an arm in a football carry, Tyler placed the curly-haired little girl in a playpen filled with stuff animals and soft toys. She stared up at him, electric-green eyes wide with uncertainty. Her lower lip quivered, her eyes filled with tears, but she did not cry. Sighing audibly, she reached for a faded terry-cloth rabbit, pressed it against her coal-black hair, rolled over on her side, and closed her eyes.

It was Tyler's turn to sigh as he returned to his telephone call with Dana. Teresa usually put up quite a commotion when placed in the playpen. Since she'd begun walking on her own she'd exhibited an uncanny sense of independence. She did not want to be held or confined.

"What are you doing, babysitting?" Dana asked when he came back to the phone.

"I told my cousins I'd look after their daughter while they went out to dinner. Jolene warned me not to let Teresa out of her playpen, but I felt sorry for her, so I let her hang out with me. Her mother says Teresa has a habit of flushing things down the toilet. Every bathroom door in the house has to remain closed whenever the toilet bandit is on the loose."

"How old is she?"

"She just celebrated her first birthday. She's incredibly beautiful and very, very bright. I know I sound biased, but she does happen to be my goddaughter."

"If she's all you say, then you have a right to be biased."

He nodded even though she couldn't see him. Interacting with Teresa April Kirkland had evoked a deep yearning for fatherhood. He wanted children. He'd even settle for one child. The desire to father a child was strange, foreign, despite the number of babies he'd delivered since he'd become a doctor. Every child he'd assisted in bringing into the word he deemed a miracle. The entire cycle of conception, confinement, and birth was a miracle.

And he knew who he wanted to carry his babies— Dana Nichols!

"I'm sorry I left without contacting you. I got a call before just before midnight, telling me I was to come to D.C. for a ten A.M. meeting."

"There's nothing worse than a last-minute meeting."

"I agree. These hearings were planned sometime ago, but I hadn't expected them to convene at this time. Are you all right?"

"Why wouldn't I be all right, Tyler?"

"You called my office."

She told him Ryan Vance had hired her on a part-time basis to work for the *Herald,* and that the editor had assigned her to interview him for the *Hillsboro: Then and Now* feature column.

Tyler's smile was dazzling. She had gotten a job with the Hillsboro newspaper. Maybe, just maybe, she would change her mind and remain in Hillsboro permanently.

He'd always shied away from interviews, preferring to let his work speak for him. But Dana was different. He was falling in love—no—he was in love with her. And because he was he would agree to do anything for her.

"How soon would you want to conduct the interview?"

"As soon as possible. Your segment is scheduled to run in three weeks."

"I don't think I'm going to be here more than a

week. However, if I'm not back by the weekend, then I'll call you and give you the interview over the phone."

"Thank you, Tyler."

"No. Thank you, Dana."

There was a pause. "For what?"

"For being you."

"Tyler, don't—"

"Don't what?" he interrupted. "Don't love you? Well, it's a little too late for that because I *do* love you. I *am* in love with you. It's taken two days away from Hillsboro and *you* for me to come to that conclusion. The night we went to Three J's I told you I was a very patient man. Well, I lied, Dana. Right now I don't have a great deal of patience. In fact, I have *nada!*

"The moment I set foot on Hillsboro soil again, I'm coming for you, Dana Nichols. Don't say you haven't been warned, because I intend to court, woo, seduce, entice, pursue, lure, and tempt you in agreeing to sharing my life and our future."

There was a full thirty seconds of silence before Dana's sultry voice came through the wire again. "You're a crazy man, Tyler Cole."

"Yeah, I know," he said, chuckling softly. "Crazy about you."

"Good night."

"Good night, baby."

Tyler ended the call, his heart beating loudly in his chest. He'd opened up to a woman, stripped himself bare emotionally, and she'd called him crazy.

Well, dammit! He was crazy because he was in love, in love for the first time in his life. And whatever he had to go through to get Dana to share his life, he'd do.

Tyler remembered a plaque Martin Cole had hanging on a wall in his office when he was a young boy that read: *I'm going to have a piece of everything I want. Some of if may not work out, but I'm still going to have a piece of it anyway.*

When Tyler asked his father about the inscription, Martin explained that his everything had become his wife—the mother of his children, not the family conglomerate, ColeDiz International, Ltd.

He smiled at Teresa, sleeping peacefully with her head resting on her stuffed toy. He'd thought medicine was his everything until he met Dana. Now she was his *everything.*

Tyler sat with his cousin Michael in a room off the kitchen in the Kirklands' expanded Georgetown home. Renovations were close to completion. A newly installed breezeway connected the house to a two-story guest cottage, and the rear of the house was expanded up and out for three additional bedrooms and two baths.

"I could've saved myself a lot of time and money if I hadn't demolished the house when I first purchased this property," said Michael.

Tyler smiled, his dark gaze fusing with his first cousin's light-green eyes, the color a startling contrast in a rich gold-brown face made even darker by the summer sun. Michael's last name may have been Kirkland, but he was still a Cole. His father, Joshua, was the late Samuel Cole's illegitimate son. Tall, dark, slender, and intellectually gifted, Michael had become an integral component in the most prominent African-American family in the United States.

"You didn't know that you'd end up a married man with children," Tyler said.

Michael nodded. "You're right about that. Living in an expanded twenty-five-hundred-square-foot carriage house suited me just fine. Even with the original three bedrooms, it would've been okay for Jolene and me, but with one baby and another on the way, it was beginning to feel cramped. And every time Emily, Chris, and their three kids, and Salem, Sara, and their three showed up at the same time, this place looked like a love-in with two, sometimes three, in a bed."

Tyler chuckled. "When I heard you grumbling about space, I decided to have a house designed with more space than I actually needed. Thirty acres, four bedrooms, six bathrooms, and a three-suite guest house should more than work for me."

"Damn, *primo,*" Michael swore softly, "What are you expecting? A battalion?"

"Not quite that many. You know for yourself how it is when the entire family gets together. Give the Coles, Kirklands, Lassiters, and the Delgados a few more years and they'll be able to fill a soccer stadium. Aaron told me Clayborne's thinking about proposing marriage to a fellow med student once they graduate."

A slight frown furrowed Michael's forehead. "How old is Clay?"

"He turned twenty-three in May."

Michael shook his head. "You better talk to your godson-nephew, *primo.* Twenty-three is a little young for marriage, especially if they're both faced with residencies and internships. That's a lot of pressure for a young couple to go through without trying to keep a marriage afloat."

Tyler held up his hands. "I'm out of that discussion. Somehow Regina isn't as upset by the news as Aaron. Meanwhile, I thought it would've been the reverse."

Moving from a chair to the love seat where Tyler lay sprawled with his feet resting on a matching ottoman, Michael said quietly in Spanish, "This is off the record. And if I hear my words back, I'm going to plead the Fifth. Jolene said your sister told her that she's looking forward to becoming a grandmother, so she's in favor of Clayborne proposing marriage."

Tyler's jaw dropped. "No!"

"*Sí, primo.*"

"*Por Dios!*" Tyler groaned, crossing himself. "Regina's only going to be fifty-one in July. What's the rush?"

"I don't know the answer to that one and I don't want to know. My father always told me that it's much safer not to try and figure out what makes a woman who she is. You accept her and roll with it. Speaking of rolling, what's up with you? I know you didn't build that mansion to roam around it by yourself."

Averting his head, Tyler stared at the water flowing from a large indoor fountain in a corner of the Japanese tearoom. "I believe I've found someone to share it with me."

Michael's eyes widened until his dark-green irises were visible. "Tell me about her."

Tyler told him everything about Dana, from the time he'd rescued her from mentally disturbed Leon, to treating her burned hand, and to their seeking shelter from the killer tornado, leaving nothing out. He also disclosed her reason for returning to Hillsboro.

"So, she's the one you want to help with her investigation?" Tyler nodded. "I put in a call to Merrick Grayslake, but he hasn't gotten back to me. There are times when he disappears for several months, and then he'll show up at my door without warning. He still frightens the hell out of Jolene, so I've asked that he call before dropping by."

Tyler tried recalling when he'd heard the name before Michael said he would contact him on behalf of Dana. "Didn't he come to your wedding?"

"Yes."

"Tall, thin. Kind of sinister-looking, with gray eyes."

"He's the one."

Tyler remembered there was something both intriguing and menacing about the man who'd had all or most of the single women at the wedding reception flirting with him.

"So . . ." Whatever Michael was going to say was preempted by the soft chiming of the phone on a low table in a corner. Moving quickly, he picked it up before it rang a second time. After dinner, Jolene and Teresa had retired for bed, while he and Tyler cleaned up the kitchen.

"Hello." His laser-green eyes crinkled as he flashed a wide grin. *"Bon soir, ma belle."*

Tyler sat smiling, knowing his cousin was speaking to his sister Arianna. Michael, fluent in at least six languages, always addressed Arianna in French.

"Don't bother to call your brother because he's here," Michael said, switching fluidly to Spanish. "Yes, of course. We'll see you this weekend." He handed the cordless instrument to Tyler. "It's Arianna."

"Welcome home, gypsy, and congratulations on your impending motherhood."

"Thank you, brother," Arianna crooned softly. "It's good to be back. I'm calling because Mom and Dad are putting together a little celebration to welcome Silah and me home, and to make an official announcement about the baby. I'm looking at the schedule Aunt Nancy's Timothy set up for air travel. The New Mexico branch of the family will arrive Thursday afternoon. You were to be picked up Friday afternoon, but since you're already in the Virginia area, then you will come in with Michael and his family Friday morning."

Timothy Cole Thomas, who had assumed the presidency of a company his grandfather had begun more than half a century ago, had continued the air-travel

decree set down by Samuel Claridge Cole. The family
mandate that all who claimed Cole or Kirkland bloodlines were forbidden to fly on commercial airlines
would mean the use of the GIV Gulfstream jet belonging to ColeDiz International, Ltd. The edict was still
in effect after more than forty years, following the ab-
duction of Tyler's sister. Martin Diaz Cole, the family's
reigning patriarch, had stubbornly refused to lift the
ban even though Regina would soon celebrate her fifty-
first birthday.

"Tyler?"

"Yes, gypsy?"

"It's good to be home."

"It's good to have you back."

He hung up, experiencing a gentle peace he hadn't
felt in a very long time. His younger sister was back to
stay, he was to become an uncle for the third time, his
cousin's wife was expecting another child who would
continue their legacy, and he had fallen in love with
a woman whom he would willingly give up everything
he owned to claim.

Sixteen

Tyler, even though surrounded by family members eating, drinking, and laughing, felt alone, isolated. He'd arrived in West Palm Beach with Michael, Jolene, and Teresa early Friday morning to brilliant Florida sunshine and warm ocean breezes. They were picked up at the airport by his uncle and aunt, Joshua and Vanessa Kirkland. Half an hour later, he was reunited with aunts, uncles, and a countless number of cousins who'd had been gathering at the Cole family estate all week.

His younger sister, Arianna Kadir, was stunningly beautiful. She was almost an exact image of their mother. She'd inherited Parris's height, coloring, and eye color. Her eyes were a clear brown with a hint of dark green. Her athletic body was still firm, and although Arianna no longer swam competitively, she still managed to swim laps at a pool at a spa on the outskirts of Paris.

Curving an arm around her ripening waist, Tyler pressed a kiss to her short, professionally coiffed curling hair. "Do you think your husband will adjust to living in the States?"

Arianna smiled up at her brother through the lenses of her sunglasses. "Silah loves it here. Especially Florida."

"If that's the case, then why did it take you so long to come back?"

"Silah wanted to establish his own couture house."

"But he could've done that here," Tyler argued. "You guys have enough money to set up a couple of couture houses if you want."

"That's the problem, Tyler."

"What? Money?"

"The problem is it's my money, not Silah's. He refuses to touch my money. We argued so much about his stubbornness that I threatened to leave him a few times. He says that if he can't make it on his own, then he would give it up."

"That's foolish, Arianna."

"It's not so foolish when you consider his culture is very different from ours. It took a long time for me accept Silah for who he is. That's why I waited so long to marry him."

A label on a garment designed by Moroccan-born, French-speaking Silah Kadir had become as sought after as one from the house of Chanel. His free-flowing colorful designs claimed a definite North African influence.

"What did he say about Mom and Dad giving you guys the house in Ft. Lauderdale?"

Arianna laughed. "Surprisingly enough, he was very accepting because they told him it was a wedding gift." She sobered quickly. "Speaking of weddings, Daddy was royally pissed when I got married without telling him. I think it all stemmed from Regina waiting until after she delivered Clay to marry Aaron. Daddy cursed a blue streak about his daughters not being traditional brides."

"I don't think it has anything to do with Regina and Aaron. I believe it's because Dad had to wait ten years before he was able to marry Mom."

Martin Cole had met Parris Simmons when he'd saved her life from her ex-husband, who'd tried to drown her in a murder/suicide attempt. Parris lived with Martin for several months while she recuperated from a broken jaw. During this time she'd found herself pregnant, and would've married him if not for a threat against her life and that of the child in her womb. They were separated for ten years, and Martin wasn't aware he'd fathered a child until he was reunited with the woman who unknowingly had become his everything. And it wasn't until after they'd married and were expecting a second child that Parris's blackmailer was revealed.

"I know it was because of what Grandpa had tried to do to our mother," Tyler continued. "His emotional break with reality after he'd fathered a child outside of his own marriage had him fixated him with guilt that tortured him to his grave."

Joshua Kirkland, their father's half brother, was the result of Samuel Cole's illicit affair with a young woman who'd worked for him. The enmity between Joshua and his father continued for nearly forty years, until Samuel was felled by a debilitating stroke, which had left him with partial paralysis and slurred speech.

"Enough about the past," Arianna said, waving a hand. "What about you? How's your house coming along?"

Leading his sister out of one of the four gardens on the Cole estate, Tyler told her about his home, its furnishings, and the gardens their sister had designed for him. As they neared the area where tables, chairs, and umbrellas were set up to accommodate five generations, Arianna was hugged and kissed by her many relatives who had come to welcome her back to Florida, back to her home.

Tyler waved to his Uncle Joshua, who cradled his

latest grandchild to his chest. Hands thrust in the pockets of his slacks, Tyler nodded and greeted several youngsters he'd assisted in bringing into the world. Most did not stand still long enough to talk to anyone older than sixteen years of age. They chased one another over the lush lawn, heading for the swimming pool.

"Tyler?"

Stopping at the sound of a familiar husky female voice, he turned and smiled at his mother. Reaching for her hands, he kissed her fingers. "How do you manage to stay so beautiful?"

At seventy-four, Parris Cole was incredibly beautiful. Tall, with a straight trim body, she epitomized grace and elegance. Her short chemically relaxed hair was completely gray, a shocking contrast to her smooth golden-brown skin. The tiny lines fanning out around her mysterious brown eyes added character to her delicate features.

Parris laughed, the sensual sound floating up and lingering in the warm air. "You're definitely your father's child."

Tyler continued to smile, his dimples winking attractively. "Is that a bad thing?"

Parris stared at her son, pride radiating from her eyes. "No, son, that's not a bad thing. In fact, I'm very proud of you. I'm proud of all of my children. But . . ." Her words trailed off when she didn't complete her statement.

Angling his head, Tyler stared down at his mother. "But what, Mom?"

Pulling her hands from his loose grip, Parris wrapped her arms around his waist. "I'm worried about you."

Tyler went completely still in her embrace. "Why me?"

"You appeared lost, confused. Let me finish," she insisted when he opened his mouth to refute her. "I know you have the house you want and the opportunity to work directly with pregnant women, but I sense even that's not enough. You've come back to Florida to welcome your sister home, and I've stood by watching you float in and out of conversations, not stopping long enough to say more than a few words to anyone.

"Even Regina mentioned you seem different, aloof. If you want to tell me I'm being a meddling old woman, then you can. But as your mother, I know what I see and I don't like what I see."

Tyler had to ask himself if he was that transparent. Could his mother see that despite his declaration of love to Dana he was afraid—afraid he would lose her when she left Hillsboro? The realization had come to him that she could possibly leave Hillsboro in less than four months and he wouldn't be able to follow her because of his commitment to the research study.

"I've fallen in love."

Parris's smile was radiant. "That's wonderful, Tyler."

"It is and it isn't." Taking his mother's hand, he led her away from the crowd. "I've fallen in love with a woman who may leave Hillsboro in less than four months. The problem is that I can't follow her. I haven't even completed my first year in the study."

"Does she know you love her?"

"I told her the other day."

"What did she say?"

"She told me I was crazy."

Parris lifted an eyebrow. "At least she didn't tell you to get lost."

"Even if she did that wouldn't matter. I'm not going to lose her, Mother."

Closing her eyes, Parris nodded. Her son looked and sounded so much like his father at forty that she thought she'd stepped back in time. With Martin it had been the gubernatorial election, and with Tyler it was a woman.

Martin Cole had lost the election, and she prayed it would not be the same for her son. It was the first time Tyler had confessed to loving a woman, and she refused to think of Tyler losing a part of himself if he were to lose the woman who'd captured his heart.

Dana climbed into bed, pulling a sheet over her body. Her meticulous perusal of the microfiche coverage of her mother's murder and her father's subsequent trial had yielded a wealth of information.

She'd spent the week taking notes and making copies of the articles, while every once in a while she focused on other articles about Hillsboro during that time. The Davis family had a simple and folksy style of reporting, giving the weekly a definite hometown flavor. Most of the ads were from local businesses, boasting sales and promising special discounts to their longtime customers.

Her tiny notebook listed the names of jurors and their alternates, the prosecutor and assistant D.A., and the witnesses who'd testified on behalf of the State of Mississippi. There was only one witness for the defense—an elderly woman who had given her age as eighty-seven. She'd been called as a character witness for Dr. Harry Nichols. Dana crossed her name off the list when she saw it mentioned in the obituary column six weeks following the conclusion of the trial.

She'd been so caught up with the newspapers articles that she did not think of Tyler until she lay in bed at night, his passionate declaration of love sweeping over her with the force of a raging storm and eliciting a longing that kept her from a restful night's sleep.

Dana lay the darkened room, asking herself if she loved Tyler, could she love him enough to remain in Hillsboro? He'd made it so easy for her to love him, but the fact remained she still had to learn to trust him.

Closing her eyes, she sighed, angled for a more comfortable position, and within minutes she had fallen asleep. Cool air filtered through the screens on the window, bringing with it the scent of pine and blooming flowers. The drought was over with the advent of daily afternoon thunderstorms. Patches of grass sprouted, brooks and streams filled up, and farmers pleaded with bank loan officers for more money for a second early summer planting, with the hope they would have something to harvest in the fall.

Dana heard the ringing, but ignored it. It continued, and at first she thought it was the telephone. Her eyes opened. It couldn't be the telephone because the answering machine was activated to pick up a call after the fourth ring. There were three telephones in the house: one in the bedroom where her grandmother had slept, the second in the kitchen, and another in the living room.

The incessant ringing continued until she realized it was the doorbell. Peering at the luminous dials on the clock radio, she groaned. It was two-ten. She couldn't imagine who would come visiting at that hour.

Sitting up, she reached for the silky cover-up at the foot of the bed. "Hold on, I'm coming," she mumbled, making her way her way down the staircase.

Her bare feet made soft slip-slapping sounds on the bare wood floor. Peering through the security eye, she saw the distorted image of Tyler Cole's face looking back at her.

Unlocking the door, she flung it open. He stood on the other side of the screen door, arms crossed over his chest. The lights on either side of the entrance illuminated his impassive expression. He was casually dressed in a pair of dark slacks and a pale-blue linen shirt he'd left open at the throat.

"What are you doing here?" Her voice was just above a whisper.

"Didn't I tell you that I was coming for you?"

Her eyes widened. "Didn't I tell you that you're crazy?"

His arms came down, and he braced a hand over his head against the door frame. "Open the door, Dana." The command was quiet and lethal.

There was something in Tyler's eyes that made her uneasy. Something made him seem dangerous. She shook her head.

A slight smile softened his mouth. "Either you open the door, or I'm going to wake up your neighbors. I'm certain Miss Janie is already up and peering through her curtains as we speak."

Dana felt her pulse racing uncontrollably as she reached for the latch on the screen door. She'd barely opened it when she was lifted off her feet, her arms going around Tyler's neck to keep her balance.

His head came down, his mouth branding hers with a burning possession that shook her from head to toe. He took a step, pressing her back to the open door. Passion pumped the blood through her heart, chest, and head like the rushing waters from a broken dam.

Holding Dana with one arm, Tyler closed the door, locked it, and headed for the staircase, taking two steps at a time, the heaviness in his groin threatening to erupt at any moment. He'd spent the time during his flight from Florida to Mississippi fantasizing about making love to her until he'd found it almost impossible to sit still. He'd wanted to come to her earlier and take her to his home, but his flight had been delayed taking off because of severe thunderstorms in the Palm Beach area.

He prayed he would remain in control long enough to take her with the tenderness she deserved. He had waited a long time—been celibate a very long time, and he knew the wait would be worth it because he'd waited to fall in love with a woman who made his heart beat a little too quickly, made him want to spend the rest of his life in her perfumed arms, and made him want to experience the joy of fatherhood for the very first time in his life.

Dana had called him crazy, and he was because he'd contemplated deliberately getting her pregnant to make her stay, but dismissed that notion as soon as it entered his head. He wanted an open and honest relationship with her, and her statement that she couldn't trust men was always first and foremost in his mind. She would never trust him if he didn't protect her physically and emotionally. Walking into her bedroom, he placed her gently on the bed, his body following. The sounds of their breathing reverberated in the muted silence.

Dana lay under Tyler, her body aching for his touch. The outline of his hardened flesh burned her through the sheer fabric of her cover-up and nightgown. He had warned her he was coming for her, yet she hadn't believed him until she saw him standing at her door. She moaned softly as he buried his face between her neck and shoulder. The weight of his large body gave her a strange sense of comfort.

"Tyler?"

He raised his head in the darkness, staring down at her. "Yes, darling?"

"It's been a long time for me. A very, very long time."

Running his tongue along the column of her neck, he placed a light kiss at the base of her throat. "That makes two of us."

She gasped. "How long has it been for you?"

"Since before I moved to Hillsboro."

Dana gasped again. "How . . . why?"

He wanted to tell her cold showers and a lot of exercise, but said, "I supposed I wanted to wait for the right woman."

"Did you find the right woman?"

"Oh, yes." Tyler needed to talk, long enough to bring his runaway passions under control. "When I least expected it she appeared before me, the most stunningly beautiful woman I've ever seen, the sexiest female I've ever encountered. A feisty elegant lady who knows what she wants and who's not afraid to speak her mind." His large hand took her face, turning it toward his. "I love you, Dana Nichols."

She felt her eyes filled with hot tears. "I don't want to love you, Tyler."

"Why not, baby? I know we'll be so good together."

"That's what I'm afraid of. I want no regrets when I leave Hillsboro."

"Don't think about leaving—at least not yet. Let us enjoy the time we'll have together. Let's begin with tonight."

Dana nodded rather than answer. At that moment she didn't trust herself enough not to dissolve into a hysterical crying where she wouldn't be able to stop.

"Miss Dana Nichols, may I make love to you?"

Laughing and smiling through her tears, she whispered, "Yes." It was the first time a man had asked permission to share her body.

She lay motionless, enjoying a giddy sense of pleasure as Tyler's hands moved to her shoulders, easing the narrow straps to her nightgown off her shoulders. The harsh uneven rhythm of her breathing increased when his fingers feathered over the slope of her trembling breasts. A tiny flame ignited between her thighs, flaring and sweeping over her until an unrestrained passion incinerated her in the hottest flames possible.

Head thrown back, lips parted, back arched, Dana gloried in Tyler's gentle touch, his healing fingers inching down her breasts, over her flat belly, to find the hot, wet opening at the apex of her thighs.

He inserted a finger, Dana gasping and arching higher from the invasion into her flesh. "Easy, baby," he crooned, gentling her. "I won't hurt you. I promise not to hurt you." He continued to talk to her as he moved his finger in and out of her throbbing flesh.

He changed the motion and rhythm whenever her breathing quickened, tempering her climax until she was mindless with spirals of ecstasy screaming for escape.

Holding her thighs firmly apart, Tyler slid down the length of her body, his mouth replacing his finger. Dana screamed once, then clapped her hands over her mouth to stop the moans, her head thrashing wildly on the pillow.

This was a lovemaking she'd never experienced before. However, she was shocked at her own eager response to his tongue searching between the folds of her femininity as her hips established a rhythm that was untutored, one that could not be taught. She wanted Tyler, all of him, his hardness inside her—now!

She reached out, her fingernails gripping his head, biting into his scalp and holding him fast. "Please," she pleaded desperately. She repeated the entreaty over and over until tears of delight filled her eyes and trailed down her cheeks.

A jolt of hungry desire settled in the area between Tyler's legs as he moved up Dana's body, inhaling her feminine scent in his pursuit to claim all of her—her heart and her body. He wasn't sure how long he would be able to last before exploding.

He kissed her tenderly, his tongue easing between her lips and permitting her to taste herself. His hands were busy as his mouth, undressing her while his tongue simulated making love. He stroked the inside of her mouth with a slow feathery motion that set her nerves on edge.

Dana pulled the hem of his shirt from the waistband of his slacks, her hands sweeping up and over his chest. Her fingers tunneled through the thick mat of chest hair, thumbs sweeping over his flat nipples until they hardened like tiny pebbles.

She charted a deliberate course up and down his broad back, feeling the strong tendons in the back of his neck and the firmness of his buttocks. He had a beautiful male physique: long, hard, and lean.

Tyler took his time exploring Dana's body, glorying in the fullness of her firm breasts, the narrow indentation of her waist above a pair of flared hips perfect for childbearing.

Once her hand moved lower, cradling his straining sex, he knew the extended session of foreplay was over. Reaching into a pocket of his slacks, he placed a condom on the bedside table where he could find it easily. Rising, he took off his belt and shirt, following with his slacks, then his briefs and socks; he opened the little packet on the table, rolling the latex down the length of his throbbing flesh.

Supporting his weight on an elbow, Tyler parted Dana's knees with his, and then positioned his rigid sex at the entrance to the well of her femininity. Slowly, deliberately, he eased himself into her tight body, gritting his teeth against the erotic torture clouding his brain.

Dana's breasts tingled against his hair-roughened chest as she bit down on her lower lip, enduring the burning pain stretching her flesh further than she'd ever thought possible.

Pulling back, Tyler impaled himself in her taut body, shattering the dormant sexuality she'd safeguarded for six years. A flow of moisture bathing the tight walls gripping his sex nearly sent him over the edge. He could feel the heat from Dana's body eddy down the length of his, followed by shivers of delights that left him shaking uncontrollably.

I don't believe it! I can't believe it! The two phrases played over and over in Dana's head as she loathed surrendering to the dizzying passion wrought by the hardness sliding in and out of her body in a powerful thrusting that snatched the oxygen from her laboring lungs.

Her body vibrated liquid fire, the tightness at the base of her spine signaling the beginning of the end. She didn't want it to end, she'd waited too long for the sweet burning pleasure Tyler offered her. The tremors grew stronger and stronger, and when she felt her lover touch her womb she screamed out his name, floating on the hot tides of passion sweeping her up, shattering her into fragments of complete satisfaction.

Tyler gasped, gritting his teeth as Dana's pulsing flesh tightened, then released him over and over as she climaxed, bucking and writhing under him. Cradling her hips in his hands, he raised her hips, lowered his head, and groaned out his release.

Heart pounding painfully in his chest, he struggled for each and every breath. Smiling, he reversed their positions, her silken legs sandwiched between his. It was perfect; she was perfect; the wait had been worth it.

They lay motionless, savoring the lingering vestiges of passion until they left the bed, walked into the bathroom, and shared a shower.

Forty-five minutes later they climbed the winding staircase in the house with a view of the Mississippi River, holding hands. They knew if they wanted to spend the night together, it couldn't be at her house. There was enough gossip about Dana without adding her sleeping with the local doctor to the list.

Tyler had promised himself he would protect her— and he would at all costs, against all odds.

Seventeen

Turning to her right, Dana encountered a solid object. She opened her eyes, meeting the amused gaze of her lover. Ribbons of sunlight peeked under the floor-to-ceiling drapes. Smiling, she moved closer, resting her forehead on his shoulder.

"Hi."

Cradling the back of her head, Tyler massaged her scalp. "Hi, yourself." He buried his face in her hair. It was still damp from their shower earlier that morning. "How do you feel?"

She giggled like a little girl. "Wonderful."

"Are you experiencing any pain?"

It came to her he wasn't asking about her state of mind, but her body. "I'm a little sore."

Pulling back, Tyler stared down at Dana, admiring the length of lashes touching the curve of her high cheekbones. "I'm sorry I hurt you. I promise I won't touch you again until you're completely healed."

Peering up at him through her lashes, she flashed a sensual smile. "I love making love with you, Tyler." Her cheeks flooded with heat as she revealed what lay in her heart.

He smiled. "And I you, darling."

She moved closer to his side. "How were your hearings with the FDA?"

Tyler shifted her effortlessly until she lay over his

chest, her legs cradled between his. "Just a lot of talk, but nothing conclusive."

"Are you in favor of approving the drug?"

"I'm still undecided." The truth was he wasn't in favor of approving the drug, not without more tests. "How's the job at the *Herald*?" He'd deftly changed the topic. His findings and statements were off the record, because he'd taken an oath not to discuss them with anyone.

"Good. I did a lot of research on my great-grandfather. I think I have enough information to write a brief but in-depth piece on him. What makes writing the piece so exciting is that I found a large tin canister in my grandmother's closet filled with photographs of deceased relatives on both sides. My father had to have given Grandma the photographs of his family, because how else would she have gotten them?"

When she'd opened the canister, she'd sat for hours poring over letters, newspaper articles, flyers announcing fund-raisers and dinner dances. She also found engraved invitations to weddings, birth announcements, and death certificates.

She'd wondered how her grandmother had come to have possession of the Nichols family archives. Had Alicia given them to her, or had Harry for safekeeping? And if Harry had given them to his mother-in-law, was it because he wanted to save the records preserving his family's history before he torched his home, destroying the evidence, which could possibly link him to his wife's murder?

"I discovered several well-preserved photographs of my paternal great-grandparents on their wedding day. There is one of Silas Nichols. He was dressed in a high-collared shirt and black suit and tie. Tall, with a dark, clean-shaven face, his dark eyes literally dance with pride and excitement. I turned the photo over and the inscription read: *Dr. Silas J. Nichols—Graduation Day—Meherry Medical College, Nashville, Tennessee—May 1902*. I took that photograph and several others to a professional photographer in Greenville to have them restored."

Tyler trailed his fingertips up and down Dana's straight spine. "It's admirable that your father followed in his grandfather's steps by becoming a doctor."

She shook her head. "My father, grandfather, and great-grandfather were doctors. They all lived in Hillsboro, where they'd set up their family practice, tending the sick and caring for their people during a time when white doctors refused to treat people of color."

Tyler snorted. "Whatever happened to *do no harm?*"

Lifting her head, Dana stared up at Tyler peering down at her. She didn't know why, but she found him sexiest in the morning. His eyelids, heavy from sleep, and shadowed jaw afforded him a sense of virility she found impossible to ignore.

Tiny dots appeared between her eyes as she frowned. "Racism and bigotry is not only an illness but a sin." Her frown vanished, replaced by an enigmatic smile. "Speaking of sin—I attended Mt. Nebo Baptist Church yesterday. I got there early and took a seat in a pew that my family had literally paid for when the members of the building fund were soliciting money to renovate the church twenty-five years ago.

"Everyone who came in saw me, stopped, and stared as if dumbstruck before moving on to their seats. The current pastor, who had been a deacon when I left Hillsboro, nearly fainted when he stepped up to the pulpit. I look exactly like my mother did, except for this." She touched the tiny beauty mark on her right cheekbone.

Tyler laughed, displaying his straight white teeth. "He probably forgot his sermon."

"He fumbled and stammered so much everyone started whispering and laughing behind their hand-held fans. There was so much cardboard snapping that it sounded like rushing wind. I'd sat alone until the Wilsons came. It was apparent they'd claimed the pew for themselves since my grandmother had stopped coming to church after my mother died. Mr. Wilson looked as if he was about to have a stroke, while his wife started shaking so hard her son had to escort her downstairs. I stayed until Reverend Wingate gave his sermon, then left."

"What was the topic of his sermon?"

She closed her eyes, took a deep breath, and then said, "The adulterous woman who Jesus saved from stoning by the Scribes and Pharisees. Every head in the church turned in my direction when the pastor said, 'Let the one among you who is guiltless be the first to throw a stone at her.' I'm certain that had to be the quietest church service in Mt. Nebo's ninety-eight-year history."

"Lord, deliver us from hypocrites," Tyler intoned in a grave tone.

"Amen."

They lay in bed for another quarter of an hour, Dana outlining what she'd uncovered in the articles she'd read about Alicia's murder and Harry's trial. She also told him about the list of names she'd compiled and those she hoped to interview.

Tyler left the bed before Dana to shave and prepare himself for the day. She followed him ten minutes later, brushed her teeth, and then joined him in the over-sized shower stall. They splashed each other like children after soaping each other's bodies, the session ending with Tyler licking Dana from the top of her head to the soles of her feet. It ended with a passionate kiss and a promise of more—much more.

After a light breakfast of fruit, juice, coffee, and toast, Tyler dropped Dana off at her house before heading to the clinic. She offered to cook dinner later that evening when he promised to let her interview him for her column.

Dana completed a handwritten draft of her article on Dr. Silas Nichols, editing it over and over until it her prose was lean, spare. She knew she could've accomplished the task in half the time it had taken her if she had a computer. She'd left her laptop in Carrollton. She knew she could always use the computers at the *Herald*, but that would not prove convenient if she wanted to work on something in the middle of the night.

Glancing at the first name on her list, she decided to stop to see if she could glean some information from ex-sheriff Philip Newcomb, but first she would call Ryan to see if he had a laptop computer to loan her. If not, then she would purchase one. There was no doubt it prove invaluable during her short stay.

Dana maneuvered into an area set aside for parking at the Crescent Moon Trailer Park. Her telephone call to the *Herald* answered two questions: Ryan did not have a laptop, but he did have Philip Newcomb's latest address. Mr. and Mrs. Newcomb had sold their home, bought a double-wide, and had settled in a nearby trailer park.

Following the directions given her by a skinny barefoot boy, she made her way to a new trailer under a copse of pine trees. A mailbox with the name NEW-

COMB stenciled on the side identified the residence as the one owned by the ex-sheriff.

Stepping up on a large cinder block, Dana knocked on the door. Within seconds it opened, and a petite woman with a mass of jet-black hair teased and styled in a beehive hairdo glared at her. The hairstyle, doe-eyed liner on her lids, and the pale mouth harkened back to a time when miniskirts, Edwardian jackets, and love beads were in vogue.

Dana flashed a friendly smile. "Mrs. Newcomb, I'm Dana Nichols and I'd like to know if I could have a word with your husband."

Mrs. Newcomb's face flushed a deep red, making her mouth look even paler. "He doesn't want to talk to you. He doesn't want to have anything to do with you."

Venom radiated from the woman, and Dana was tempted to turn and go back to her car. But she didn't, deciding to stand her ground. She needed answers—answers she knew the ex-sheriff could give her.

"Your husband doesn't even know that I'm here. Why don't you ask him whether he'll see me?"

Folding her hands on her hips, Mrs. Newcomb shook her head from side to side. "No! Now you git the hell out of here and go back where you came from." Stepping back, she slammed the door in Dana's face.

Dana stood motionless, staring at the closed door. If she hadn't been so shocked, she would've laughed at how she'd been dismissed. At least the angry woman could've warned her that she was going to slam the door in her face.

Stepping down off the cinder block that doubled as a step, she made her way back to her car. She'd struck out with the first name on her list, and wondered how

many more doors would be slammed in her face before
it was time for her to return to New York.

If Philip Newcomb refused to help her, then perhaps
the current sheriff would. She would call Lily, asking
for her husband's assistance. After all, William, a former special agent with the F.B.I. and now the current
sheriff, had married her best friend. She doubted
whether he would refuse to help her.

The sheriff's office was located in a brick structure
behind Hillsboro's town hall. Parking in a municipal
lot, she walked the short distance to the sheriff's office.
Pushing open the door, she stepped into a cool space
with several desks and an area set aside for a state-of-
the art computer system, office machines, and a large
display case with colorful arm patches from police de-
partments all over the country. There were several
rooms in the rear of the building, one a holding cell
for prisoners.

William Clark hadn't changed much in twenty years,
except to bulk up. His starched tan uniform fit his
muscular body like a second skin. His sandy-brown hair
was cropped close to his head, while his clear brown
eyes sparkled in his burnished gold face. Rising slowly
to his feet, he stared at her as if she were an apparition.

"Lily told me you were back."

Dana smiled. Even his voice was the same—deep
and soulful. Everyone said he should've become a radio disc jockey, but Billy preferred law enforcement.

He returned her smile, extending his arms, and she
walked into his embrace. "Welcome home, Dana," he
said, pressing his mustached mouth to her cheek.

She pressed her lips to his smooth cheek. "Thank
you, Billy. Lily came to see me last week, then I saw

her and your mother at church yesterday, but I didn't stay to talk to her."

"My mama told me about everybody's reaction to seeing you." A slight frown marred his forehead. "The only argument Lily and I ever have is about my not going to church. I keeping telling her that I have no intention of sitting down with a bunch of Bible-thumping, psalm-singing vipers who grin in your face from eleven to one on Sundays, then cuss you, your mama, and your firstborn the other six days of the week. She calls me a heathen, but this heathen would rather spend his Sundays driving to Three J's, where I can put my feet up, down half a bushel of blue crabs, suck on a couple of long-neck beers, while listening to a jukebox filled with the best music in the whole damn state."

Dana had to smile. It was apparent Tyler wasn't the only one who liked patronizing Three J's. Pulling out of Billy's loose embrace, she told him what she needed from him. She also told him about Mrs. Newcomb's refusal to let her talk to her husband. Billy listened, not interrupting until she was finished.

"I'm certain I can retrieve Newcomb's records, but it may take me a while. When would you need them?"

"Anytime before the end of September."

"I should have them to you next week."

She offered him a bright smile. "Thank you, Billy."

"Think nothing of it. Expect a call from Lily. We usually throw a little something every July Fourth. We'd love for you to come. We bought the place where the Bowdens used to live."

"Thanks for the invitation. I wouldn't miss it." Moving closer, she kissed him again. "Your daughter is beautiful."

Beaming, he nodded. "Along with her mother, she's the love of my life."

Turning on her heel, Dana walked out of the sheriff's office to where she'd parked her car, a satisfied smile on her face; she was batting .500. Billy Clark would give her what she hadn't been able to secure from Philip Newcomb.

It was later that afternoon, as she stood in the kitchen washing a whole chicken for a dinner she planned to cook and share with Tyler, when Dana recalled Billy Clark's statement: *Along with her mother, she's the love of my life.*

Lily had taken a chance on love and married her childhood crush. Why, then, was it so difficult for her to trust Tyler enough to accept what he was offering her? The whys attacked her relentlessly as she forced herself to concentrate on preparing a special meal for a man she'd not only given her body to, but also her heart.

Eighteen

Dana set the table on the back porch with her grandmother's best china, silver, and stemware. Lighted candles flickered in the lengthening shadows, creating a surreal look. Smoothing down the bodice of her dress over her flat middle, she surveyed her handiwork, pleased. The music coming from the speakers of a radio set the mood that screamed romantic.

Tyler had called her at six-twenty, informing her he was leaving the clinic to return home to shower and to expect him at her place around seven-thirty. The chiming of the doorbell echoed throughout the house. Glancing at the watch on her wrist, Dana had to smile. It was exactly seven-twenty-eight. Taking a deep breath, she walked back into the house.

Tyler skirted a few puddles left over from an earlier thunderstorm, hoping to avoid Janie Stewart. The elderly woman sat on her front porch rocking and protecting the block from foreign invaders.

"Dana feeling poorly again, Dr. Cole?"

Forcing a smile, Tyler nodded to her. "No, Miss Janie."

"Why you bringing her flowers then? They are for her, ain't they?"

Stopping, he gave her a long stare. "Yes, these flowers are for Dana. I'm giving them to her because she and I are keeping company."

He knew if he hadn't told Janie Stewart the truth about his visits to Dana's house, then she was certain to make up her own version as to why he'd come so often. He couldn't stop people from gossiping, but he'd try to shield Dana from lies and untruths by being open about his relationship with her.

His explanation seemed to please Miss Janie. "That's so nice, Dr. Cole. Your mama must be so proud of you. She sure raised you nice and proper. I thought my daddy, God rest his soul, was the last gentleman in Hillsboro. Tell Dana I said she's a lucky girl. I just hope she doesn't make the same mistake her mama did with her daddy."

Ignoring the woman's parting remark, he stared at Dana, waiting for her to unlatch the screen door. "Save me," he groaned under his breath.

She smiled at him. "Miss Janie?"

"Yes," he said between his teeth.

"Hurry up and come in."

Tyler stepped into the entryway, closing and locking the door behind him. He loomed over Dana, dwarfing her with his height, although she wore a pair of high-heeled sling-strap sandals. "She asked me about coming to see you, and I told her we were keeping company."

Dana shrugged a bare satiny shoulder under a silk dress with a squared neckline. Each time she inhaled, a soft swell of breasts rose above the revealing décolletage, drawing Tyler's heated gaze to the spot.

"Telling Miss Janie our business is akin to free advertising."

Leaning down, he brushed his mouth over hers. "It doesn't bother you that she'll announce it to everyone who'll stand still long enough to listen to her?"

Wrapping her arms around his slim waist, Dana smiled up at Tyler. "No, it doesn't, because when I walked out of Mt. Nebo Baptist Church yesterday, I took Reverend Wingate's sermon with me. 'Let the first one among you who is guiltless be the first to throw a stone, at her.' Words, stones, or stares can't hurt me. Right now I will not permit anything or anyone to hurt me."

An inexplicable look of withdrawal came over Tyler's face as he noted the stubborn set of Dana's delicate jaw. She'd offered him her body, but continued to withhold her heart. He successfully hid his disappointment when he forced a smile he did not feel.

Extending his right hand, he handed her the flowers. "These are for you."

She took the cellophane-wrapped bouquet of white foxgloves and snow-white calla lilies amid a profusion of pale creamy roses. Delight fired her sun-lit eyes. "They're beautiful." Smiling, she glanced up him through her lashes. "Thank you."

Curving an arm around her waist, Tyler pressed a kiss to her hair. She had pinned it up off her neck in an elaborate twist. Curbing the urge to kiss the nape of her neck, he asked, "What's for dinner?"

Angling her head, Dana bit down on her lower lip. "Come and see." She led him to the back porch. "I've decided we'll eat here because it's cooler than the kitchen. I had the oven going for a couple of hours."

Tyler stared at the inviting space, smiling. Dark-green and white tapers in clear chimneys flickered in the waning daylight. Wisps of sweet peas spilled over the sides of a crystal vase that had a pattern that matched the water goblets and wine glasses. Dana set a beautiful table. She would become the perfect hostess.

Unwrapping the bouquet, Dana rearranged the flowers in the same vase with the sweet pea, the overall effect romantic and ethereal. Taking a step back, she admired her handiwork, smiling.

"Perfect."

Tyler wanted to tell her she was perfect—perfect in and out of bed. They returned to the kitchen, and he washed his hands in the small bathroom while Dana busied herself taking a platter with a golden roasted chicken to the porch. He carried several covered serving dishes and a basket covered with a white towel from which came the most tantalizing smell of fresh bread. A pitcher of homemade lemonade, a carafe of chilled Chardonnay, and a bottle of sparkling water completed the beverage selections.

Tyler seated Dana, and then rounded the table to sit down opposite her. Bowing her head, Dana blessed her food. Then Tyler said his own prayer of thanks before making the sign of the cross over his chest.

Dana stared, momentarily shocked. "You're Catholic." The question came out like a statement.

He looked at her intently, unblinking. "Yes."

"There're generally not too many Catholics in the Bible Belt."

"I'm Catholic because of my grandmother. She was born in Cuba."

Dana's eyes widened with this disclosure. There was so much she didn't know about the man she'd fallen in love with. "Do you speak Spanish?"

He lifted an eyebrow. "Not as often as I'd like, but yes, I do."

"That's wonderful."

"You think so?"

"Of course, Tyler. I've always wanted to speak more than one language. Will you teach me?"

He placed his hands, palms down, on the linen tablecloth. "Why should I, Dana, when you're going to leave in four months?"

She stared at Tyler staring back at her, his expression a mask of stone. He was so still he could've been carved out of granite. Dropping her gaze, she picked up her napkin, placing it on her lap.

"You're right, Tyler. Forgive me for asking."

"There's nothing to forgive."

Dana registered the sharpness in his retort. "I didn't invite you here to argue."

His eyes widened. "I'm not arguing, Dana. I merely stated a fact."

"A fact I'm very much aware of . . ."

"A fact you manage to remind me of every damned day of the week," he retorted angrily, interrupting her.

"How dare you bark at me! Just what is it you want from me?" She'd raised her voice above its normal soothing tone.

"You know what I want."

"You can't have what you want, Tyler Cole. Just once in your life you have to face the fact that you can't have everything you want."

Pushing back her chair, she stood up and threw her napkin on the table, leaving him to stare at her retreating back. The emotions of frustration and rage singed the edges of her brain when she realized she'd made a mistake becoming involved with Tyler. She'd outlined in advance the terms of their relationship, yet he wanted what he couldn't have.

Dana stood in the middle of the kitchen, arms around her body, attempting to force her warring emotions into order. There was no way she could give Tyler what he wanted without turning her own world upside down. What about her career, her reputation with the *Chronicle?* Why, she asked herself as she closed her eyes, did men expect women to do all of the giving up, the sacrificing? Whatever happened to compromise?

She detected the scent of his aftershave first, then

the warmth of his large body as he pulled her to his length. He'd come after her.

Tyler tightened his grip on her body. "I'm sorry, Dana."

She opened her eyes, staring up at him. "Are you really? Or are just saying what you think I want to hear?"

He smiled a smile that did not reach his dark eyes. "I am sorry. I know no other way to say it unless you want me to tell you in Spanish." Lowering his head, he brushed his mouth over hers, tasting her with light nibbling kisses. He murmured in Spanish, ribald phrases he would never translate for her.

Curving her arms under his shoulders, Dana held onto him like someone drowning in the middle of the ocean. She returned his kisses, her tongue dueling with his. Her anger fled, her thoughts spun, her passion escalated as she was transported to another universe, one in which there could possibly be a happily-ever-after.

Tyler's mouth was everywhere: her jaw, throat, breasts, and shoulders. Shifting, he nipped the tender skin on the nape of her neck. Her knees buckled and if he hadn't held her, she would've collapsed to the floor.

His lovemaking was frantic and restrained at the same time. His tongue and teeth were as busy as his hands. His fingers plunged into the neckline of her dress, gently massaging her breasts, before they searched under the hem, moving up her thighs. Dana felt his heartbeat pounding against her ear when she collapsed on his chest, moaning as if in pain.

Dana's moans fired Tyler's banked passion. He opened his eyes, peering through a haze of red. He blinked to clear his vision, realizing it was Dana's dress. His hand moved higher and higher, fingers slipping between her legs and finding her wet, hot, and throbbing with a need that matched the excruciating pulsing between his own thighs.

His hand grazed her tender flesh, Dana pulling away, gasping. He went completely still, his eyes filling with understanding. Resting his forehead on hers, he kissed her parted lips.

"I'm sorry, baby. I forgot you're still sore there."

Cradling his face between her hands, Dana pressed her lips over his eyelids. "I know you would never deliberately hurt me," she whispered.

They held each other until their pulses slowed to a normal rate. Then, on cue, they retreated to bathroom to wash their hands before returning to the porch to eat.

Tyler finished off his second slice of apple pie, rubbing both hands over his belly. "I cook a little," he said in falsetto, mimicking Dana.

"I do cook a little."

Lowering his chin, he smiled, shaking his head in astonishment. "Perhaps you don't cook very often, but you definitely can cook."

He'd had two servings of everything: roast chicken, candied sweet potatoes, collard greens, homemade rolls, and deep-dish apple pie for dessert.

Their former confrontation forgotten, he told Dana everything about himself—everything except his family's business enterprises and his own personal worth. Other than family members, only his close friends from medical school were aware that the moment he drew breath for the first time, it was documented that he'd come into a five-million-dollar trust fund on the day he celebrated his twenty-fifth birthday.

"You haven't written anything down," he said as she rested her chin in one hand, listening to him talk.

"I usually don't have to. I'll remember the important facts."

"Do you have a photographic memory?"

She shook her head. "No, just excellent concentration."

The sun had set, night had fallen, and nocturnal sounds were magnified in the velvety darkness. Some of the candles had burned out, while others sputtered and hissed behind the glass chimneys. Closing her eyes, Dana hummed along with a song playing on the radio from a station that featured oldies from the past four decades.

"Please dance with me," he said.

She opened her eyes to find Tyler standing beside her. She hadn't heard him get up. Placing her hand in his outstretched one, she permitted him to pull her to her feet. Walking over to an open space on the porch, she folded against his body in a gentle embrace.

Rocking gently, he sang in her ear. She smiled against his cheek. He had a wonderful singing voice. He was halfway through the song when she decided to listen to the lyrics. It was Aretha Franklin's "Ain't No Way." Tyler sang with such passion and conviction that she felt his pain as surely as if it were her own.

He loved her! The man truly loved her, while she'd balked at finding happiness because of a career—a job! She could find a position with any paper she chose because of her credentials and prior experience. After all, she had been a part of an award-winning Pulitzer team.

Pressing closer, she tightened her hold on his neck. She couldn't disguise the shudder that shook her from to toe. "Tyler?"

"What is it, baby?"

She shuddered again as his warm breath swept over an ear. "What do you really want from me?"

"You know what I want."

"Say it!"

He shook his head. "No."

"This is no time to be mule-headed. You better tell me now, Tyler Cole, before I lose my nerve."

He cradled her face between his large hands, staring down at the moisture filling her eyes. "I want you to love me, Dana. Love me as much I love you. I want you live with me, marry me, and bear my children. And I want you to trust me enough to protect you and the children we hope to bring into this world. I know I'm asking a lot, but that's what I want from you."

Dana smiled, her tears overflowing and wetting his fingers. "It's not too much to ask. I'm going to give you everything you've asked for and then some."

Tyler looked at Dana, utter disbelief freezing his features. Dana had just agreed to everything he'd wanted and felt since meeting her for the time, and he was just standing there staring at her like a stunned mute. She rested her head on his chest, breaking the spell.

Bending slightly, he picked her up, cradling her to his chest. "I'll make certain you'll never regret this moment." Feeling a sense of bottomless peace and satisfaction, he swung her around and around until she pleaded with him to stop. Waiting until the spinning subsided, he set her on her feet. She was still clinging to him like a frightened child.

Laughing, she buried her face against his shoulder. "You know you're crazy."

"Oh, yeah! Crazy about you, baby."

Dana held onto Tyler, feeling his elation, his joy. "I'm crazy, too. I've known you exactly two weeks and I here I am accepting your proposal of marriage."

"I guess I changed your mind, didn't I?"

"About what?"

"Love at first sight."

"You don't have to be so smug about it," she teased.

He laughed softly, the warm sounds rumbling in his chest. "When do you want to go look at rings?"

A shock flew through her when she realized the import of his question. A ring symbolized commitment, announcing to the world that she had pledged her future to Dr. Tyler Cole.

You are just like your mother! The taunting inner voice screamed at her. She was repeating her mother's life because like Alicia, she would also marry a doctor—a doctor who practiced medicine in Hillsboro, Mississippi.

"It doesn't matter when we go," she said.

Tyler was too euphoric to register Dana's flat response. "I'll check out some jewelers in Jackson, then we can drive down and look at a few stones and settings."

"I'd like that," she said as if in a trance.

"I want you to meet my family."

"I'd like to wait a while before I meet them. Things are moving so fast that I find it hard to think straight."

He gave her long, penetrating look, his heart turning over when he saw the apprehension in her eyes. He knew he come on strong, but he did not want to lose her.

"Of course, darling."

The Four Tops' "Baby, I Need Your Loving" came through the speakers, and Tyler spun her around, and then threw her out before bringing her up close to his chest, their hips rocking in perfect rhythm.

Dana pulled out of his loose grasp, snapping her fingers and gyrating in front of him. He stood completely still, watching her lush body as she seduced him. Leaning over, she displayed a generous amount of breasts, then turned and wiggled her hips. Tyler thought he was going to lose it completely when she eased the hem of her dress up her thighs and over her hips, flaunting her firm buttocks and a red-lace thong to his shocked gaze. She continued her exhibition, kicking off her sling-strap sandals before unzipping her dress and shimmying out of it.

She stood before him naked, except for the tiny triangle of red lace that revealed more than it covered. Closing his eyes, Tyler swayed, moaning like a wounded animal. Even with his eyes closed, he still could see the lushness of her golden breasts with their large nut-brown nipples perched high above her narrow waist.

He finally opened his eyes, passion glittering in their depths like bits of coal. Who or what had he planned to marry?

Dana Nichols was a tease. A beautiful, provocative tease he'd love until his last breath. Taking two steps, he bent down and picked up her dress, holding it over her breasts.

"Count yourself lucky, Miss Nichols, that I'm a doctor, because if I wasn't I'd take you right here—standing or reclining. Now, if you'll excuse me for a few minutes, I have to take care of myself."

Dana's jaw dropped when she realized what he was about to do. Clapping a hand over her mouth, she struggled not to laugh as he shot her a murderous look.

"It's not funny, Dana." This time she did laugh until tears rolled down her face. His fingers snaked around her arm, pulling her up close. "There's an expression about payback," he growled against her moist face.

"I . . . I know," she said, hiccupping.

Mumbling curses under his breath in Spanish, Tyler retreated to the house, hoping he would be able to ease the bulge in his slacks without resorting to an act he hadn't had to perform since adolescence.

Dana blotted her cheeks with a cloth napkin before she put her dress back on. She did not know what had possessed her to strip for Tyler, but she had enjoyed the freedom she felt taking her clothes off for him; she knew she'd shocked him, but more than that, she knew she felt comfortable enough with him to become an exhibitionist.

A dazzling smile curved her lips. She'd been able to do it because she'd trusted him to accept her—anything and everything about her.

Nineteen

Dana did not get the opportunity to strip again for Tyler because by the time her tender fleshed healed from their initial lovemaking, her menstrual cycle had begun. The first night she lay beside him, he tossed and turned all night, keeping her awake. She slept in her own bed the following night, promising to return when they were able to make love again.

She'd spent several hours at the *Herald* printing out a copy of her column. She handed gave it to Ryan, pleased with the results of the research she'd done on her great-grandfather.

Dr. Silas Jeremiah Nichols had moved to a little town outside Hillsboro, Mississippi, from his native Tennessee, where he worked at a local Colored Soldiers Hospital. He'd lived in a boardinghouse until he purchased a large imposing mansion from the widow of a Confederate Civil War officer. The woman had put the property up for sale because of back taxes. Silas paid the asking price, taking up residence two weeks after the widow and her unmarried daughter vacated the premises. He lived alone until at the age of forty-two, he married a pretty young nurse, twenty years his junior, who'd come to work at the hospital. She bore him one child—a son whom they named Jeremiah.

An article in the *Herald's* archives hinted that Silas had saved the lives of a wealthy white couple *who had been set upon by a trio of Coloreds roaming the countryside bent on robbery.* During that time in the South, it was illegal for a black doctor to treat white people, a white woman in particular, so the rumor remained just that—a rumor.

Jeremiah Harry Nichols followed in his father's footsteps when he also attended and graduated from Meherry Medical College in Tennessee. He returned to Hillsboro and the house he'd eventually inherit. It was Jeremiah who had taken to calling the property Raven's Crest—the original name listed on an 1805 land grant. By this time Hillsboro had become an all-Negro town. Dr. Jeremiah Nichols also married later in life: forty-six. His wife was a pretty light-skinned woman from a well-to-do family from Baltimore, Maryland. Rebecca Nichols miscarried three times before she gave her husband his first and only child—a son whom they named Harry.

Her column on Tyler wasn't as colorful as the one on her great-grandfather, but his accomplishments in medical research were outstanding. She concentrated more on Dr. Cole than Tyler Cole, and when she read him the final edit, he was quite pleased with what she'd written.

Dana sat in Eugene Payton's parlor, waiting for an answer to her question. "Did my grandmother ever discuss my mother's murder with you?" she repeated, thinking he hadn't heard her the first time.

Running a bony hand over the thinning, straight silver hair brushed off a high forehead, Eugene stared at Dana with a pair of intelligent gray-green eyes.

"I heard you the first time, child," he said in a soft drawling voice.

She flushed under his perusal. "Forgive me, Mr. Payton."

He smiled. "Nothing to forgive. I still marvel at how much you look like Alicia. It's as if Harry Nichols had nothing to do with conceiving you."

Dana froze, her eyes narrowing. "Are you saying Harry wasn't my father?"

"I did not say that, child."

"What are you saying, Mr. Payton?"

"I haven't said anything yet, have I?"

She wanted to shake the man. He was playing word games with her. She'd come to him because she suspected her grandmother might have confided in him. After all, he had been her attorney and her friend.

Crossing one knee over the other, Eugene fingered the sharp crease in his tan slacks with the thumb and forefinger of his left hand. "Georgia and I talked about a lot of things." His head came up and he gave Dana a direct stare. "And with Georgia the topic of Alicia was off-limits—to everyone, including me. After my wife died, she'd invite me over for dinner and we'd talk." He shrugged a narrow shoulder. "We'd talk about the weather, baseball, the little wars going on all over the world, and we'd talk about you."

"Me?"

Eugene affected a sad smile. "Yes, you. Georgia adored you. There were times when she said you should've been her daughter instead of Alicia's. She always left explicit instructions for me whenever she left to spend the summers with you. I had to come twice a week to water her plants, pay the yard man, and check to make certain the water was running and the electricity was on. The thing she was most concerned about was her grandfather clock. It had to be wound once a week very, very slowly until the spring tightened just a little. She claimed the clock had never stopped in all the years it had been in her family."

Nodding, Dana said, "I remember her always talking about that clock. She taught me how to wind it the year I turned six. We made a game of counting the number of revolutions whenever I turned the key."

She wanted to tell Mr. Payton that Georgia was not only concerned about her clock, but also about every piece of furniture in her house, which was filled with pieces that had been passed down to Georgia after her marriage to Daniel Sutton. Dana did not think of them as antiques, but as family heirlooms.

Her maternal great-grandfather, a talented cabinet-maker, had crafted all of the tables, chairs, stools, headboards, and footboards by hand. The distinctive design of a soaring eagle with several spears in his beak had been carved into every piece he'd created during his lifetime.

The story handed down over several generations was that Moses Sutton symbolized his ancestors as spear-carrying eagles prepared to smite any proponent of racism. Whether the tale had any merit, Dana had to decide what she was going to do with the furniture. Each piece was heavy and constructed of solid oak or mahogany. The furnishings in the modest two-story house were a part of her legacy—a legacy she did not want to sell or give away.

"What can you tell me about my father?" She refused to leave without getting some answers to her questions.

"What is there to say about Harry? He was Dr. Nichols: healer, comforter, and the consummate gentleman. We once had an influenza epidemic, and I watched Harry go from house to house tending the sick without stopping to eat or sleep for more than twenty-four hours. It was a miracle he didn't come down with the virus.

"You ask me about your father, and I can tell you the man was a saint. He would've given up his own life to save someone else's." He held up a hand. "And before you ask me—the answer is an emphatic *NO!* Dr. Harry Nichols did not kill Alicia Sutton Nichols because he'd taken an oath to preserve life, not take it."

"But there are doctors who do take lives."

"That may be true, but not Harry Nichols."

Closing her eyes, Dana rested the back of her head on the cushion of the rocker, trying to bring her fragile emotions under control. She felt as if she'd asked a hundred questions and not one had been answered.

She opened her eyes, staring directly at Eugene Payton. "Why weren't you a material witness at my father's trial?"

"I'd asked to be one, but the defense attorney refused my request."

Sitting up straighter, she shook her head. "Why?"

Eugene did not drop his gaze. "I don't know."

"Why didn't you defend Harry Nichols?"

"I couldn't because he'd turned down my offer in favor of Ross Wilson's cousin, a hotshot attorney from Jackson who'd earned a reputation of never losing a case after he'd sued an insurance company and won because they reneged on paying blacks death benefits they were entitled to. I told Harry that he was going to be tried before small-town folks who would resent him hiring a big-town lawyer. He wouldn't listen, and in the end his plan backfired."

"I'm going up to the Greenville courthouse tomorrow to pick up a transcript of the trial. I would like your assistance when I go over it."

Eugene shook his head. "Save your time and your money, Dana."

She sat up straighter. It was the first time the elderly attorney had called her by her given name. "Why, Mr. Payton?"

"Because it will yield absolutely nothing. I have some notebooks I'm going to lend you which should answer some of your unanswered questions. I attended every session of Harry's legal proceedings, from the grand jury hearing to the actual trial and finally his sentencing. Not only did I want to support a friend, but I also wanted to see firsthand what Sylvester Wilson had planned for Harry's defense, because if the jury had come back with a guilty verdict, I was preparing myself for Harry's appeal. None of that mattered after Harry hung himself." Placing his hands on the arms of his chair, he pushed to his feet. "Let me go and get the notebooks for you."

Dana picked up a glass of sweet tea, taking a sip, realizing she'd been away from the South too long to appreciate the preferred beverage of most Southerners. She took another sip, finding the brew too strong and too bitter for her taste, despite the sugar settling in the bottom of the glass.

Eugene returned, his arms filled with a stack of leather-bound notebooks. He placed them on a table. "I have to get the rest."

Dana picked up one, thumbing through it. The writing was small, neat, and precise. Eugene Payton's notations were more detailed than a court transcript. Each day was noted with date, time, and weather. On each day he'd describe all the jurors, their clothing and attitudes—whether they were alert or lethargic. Her pulse quickened. Mr. Payton's notebooks would give her what no official court transcript could—an instant replay of her father's trial.

* * *

An hour later, Dana completed setting up her office-in-the home on the back porch. She'd picked up her laptop computer, installed several programs that were not factory-installed, called to activate her newly purchased cellular telephone, unwrapped a package of legal pads, sharpened a dozen of the half gross of pencils she'd decided to buy at the last moment along with an electric pencil sharpener.

When she had changed out of her dress and into a pair of shorts, tank top, and a pair of leather thongs, she noted the chipped nail polish on one of her big toes. Dialing the number to Hot Chocolate, an upscale salon in downtown Hillsboro, she set up an appointment for Friday morning for a wash, set, manicure, and pedicure. She and Tyler planned to celebrate their recent engagement over dinner at a trendy restaurant near Greenville.

Sitting down on the glider, she opened the first page of the first notebook she'd put in chronological order, shivering when she read the opening line: *I received a telephone call at 10:11 this morning that Dr. Harry Nichols is being held and questioned about a fire which destroyed Raven's Crest less than two hours after Alicia Nichols was found dead in her bedroom. Alicia had been shot three times in the head, at close range. Dana, the couple's only child, is reported to be staying with her grandmother.*

Tyler massaged the back of his neck with one hand, and then rolled his head from side to side. He had both the Connellys on the phone, trying to convince them to have their premature son transferred to a hospital in the capital that specialized in low-birth-weight babies.

"Your son cannot get the care he needs here that he can get in Jackson."

"But I don't want to be away from my baby," Miranda wailed into the receiver." She went to the hospital every day to look at her tiny son.

"Don't cry, Mandy. We'll work something out," Charles crooned on an extension. "Dr. Cole, I'd like to say yes, but there's no way Mandy can travel to Jackson every day to see Chuck, Jr. And I we don't have any relatives in Jackson who she can stay with."

"I think I can help you out," Tyler said before he could censor himself.

"How?" Miranda and her husband had spoken in unison.

Thinking quickly, Tyler said, "There's a fund set up for a situation just like the one you're facing. I'll call you tomorrow with details."

"What kind of fund?" Charles asked. "We're proud people, you know. We ain't asking for no handouts."

"This is not going to be a handout, Mr. Connelly. The money will come from a foundation."

"What's the name of this foundation?"

Tyler cursed under his breath. Why didn't the man just accept his offer? "The SCC Foundation for Medical Research," he said quickly.

"Okay. We'll wait for your call. Won't we, Mandy?"

"Yes, Chuck."

"Good night, Mr. and Mrs. Connelly."

Tyler hung up quickly before he'd be forced to tell another lie. There was no SCC Foundation for Medical Research, but that didn't mean there wouldn't be in the near future.

Glancing at his watch, he noted the time. It was almost nine-thirty, and he had yet to prepare to go home. It was Thursday, the clinic's late night. Rising from his chair, he walked over to a shelf and picked up a telephone book. Thumbing through the business section, he found a listing of hotels.

After ten, he turned off the lights, set the alarm, and walked out of the Hillsboro Women's Health Clinic to where he'd parked his truck. He'd made a reservation for Miranda Connelly to stay at a hotel near the hospital where her son would be transferred until he received medical clearance to come home. Tyler had given the clerk at the reservation desk his credit-card number with explicit instructions the hotel not disclose his name. The clerk reassured him his personal data would remain privileged information. Chuck Connelly may be a proud man, but he wasn't a proud fool.

Dr. Tyler Cole had come to Hillsboro to lower the infant-mortality rate, and even if he had to use his own money to make the project a success, he would.

He started up his truck and backed out of the lot. He waited until he was on the road before he activated the hands-free phone in his vehicle. Tiny lines fanned out around his eyes when he heard the break in the connection followed by Dana's husky greeting.

"Hi, darling," he said.

"Hi yourself, lover."

"Are we still on for tomorrow night?"

"Are you calling to cancel, Tyler Cole?"

"No."

"Good."

"How was your day?"

"Quite eventful. I'll tell you everything when I see you."

"Tell me now." Tyler wanted, needed to hear her voice. It had been four days since he last saw her.

"It's a long story."

"I have nothing but time, sweetheart."

"Where are you?"

"I'm in my truck on my way home. I just thought of something."

"What?"

"What if I swing by and pick you up? You can spend the night and hang out until I come home tomorrow afternoon."

"That sounds wonderful, but . . ."

"But what?"

"I have an eleven o'clock appointment at Hot Chocolate for my hair and nails."

"I'll drop you off and pick you up. Do you think you'll be finished by two-thirty?"

"I don't know."

"If you're not, then I'll wait. Maybe I'll get a haircut and manicure while I'm there if you're not finished." There was a prolonged pause and Tyler turned the wheel to right, executing a tight U-turn.

"What was that?" Dana asked.

"My tires making skid marks on the asphalt. Pack a bag, Dana. I'll be there in five minutes."

"But I'm in bed!"

"Then don't get up."

Pressing a button, he ended the call, his white teeth gleaming in his brown face.

Twenty

Tyler didn't know how she readied herself so quickly, but Dana was waiting for him, bag in hand, when he pulled into the driveway behind her car. Not waiting for him to get out to help her up, she opened the passenger-side door and slid in beside him.

Grinning at him, she ordered, "Let's get this party started."

Tyler shifted into reverse, and then slammed on the brakes when she reached over and placed her hand on his groin, squeezing him gently.

Eyes bugging, Tyler collapsed over the steering wheel, gasping painfully. "Whoa, Dana! What are you trying to do to me?"

She flashed a demure smile. "I just wanted to see if you're as ready for me as I am for you."

Biting down on his lower lip, he gave her a sidelong glance. "We can do it here. Right now. In the backseat." Each word came out in a slow measured cadence.

Dana looked out the side window. "No, thanks. I can wait."

Easing his foot off the brake and onto the gas pedal, Tyler did know whether to laugh or call the teasing minx's bluff. It would serve her right if he parked somewhere near the woods and took her in the backseat. The risk of being discovered would probably bring her teasing to an abrupt halt.

The heat between his legs increased with the speedometer inching above the speed limit. Having sampled Dana body's once had not been enough. She was a drug he'd become hooked on from the first encounter.

The ten-minute drive from her house to his was accomplished in five as he pulled into the garage. His right hand moved quickly as he placed his hand over her breasts, massaging them until the nipples sprang into prominence.

"Don't you dare move," he said.

Dana sat motionless, waiting for Tyler to come around and help her out. She had barely had time to catch her breath or grab her small overnight bag when he lifted her into his arms and carried her toward the house.

She knew by the set of his jaw he was angry, but that did not bother her. If they were to marry, then there would many times when they would not agree with each other, leaving them to try and work out their problems or disagreements. She was also aware that she probably would not come to know who Tyler Cole actually was until after she married and lived with him.

Tyler carried Dana up the staircase as if she were a small child. Eight steps. She counted them. It had taken eight long steps for him to cross his bedroom and place her on the bed. As he stood over her, his hands went to his waist, unbuckling his belt. She waited until he had shed his shirt and slacks before she moved off the silken quilt.

"No, Dana," he drawled, capturing her arm. His voice was so low it resembled a growl. "No more teasing."

First she was standing, and seconds later she was on her back with Tyler straddling her, her top pushed up to her neck and his mouth on her breasts. He suckled one, then the other, until she thought she was going to lose her mind. Raising his hips, he undid the button on her shorts. She gasped loudly when it was his turn to cup her warm musky heat.

"Are you ready for me?" he rasped in her ear. "Tell me, baby."

"No!"

He laughed deep in his throat. "Oh, yes, you are. The love is pouring out of you."

"Ty—" His mouth covered hers, cutting off all speech and sound. Dana felt as if she'd been submerged in molten lava as waves swept over her.

Her arms circled his neck, bringing him closer. She opened her mouth, her tongue meeting his. Their kisses grew stronger, more passionate, as their passions escalated.

Tyler ground his hips into hers, wanted to melt into her. He wanted her moaning, writhing, and pulsing under him. Fastening his hands in the straps of her tank top, he pulled it off her shoulders, the fabric parting where he'd ripped it in half.

The sight of her full breasts rising and falling above her tiny waist in the dimly lit room was his undoing. He undressed her, then himself, throwing each discarded garment on the floor. Curving an arm around her waist, he lifted her and stripped the bed of the quilt in one sweeping motion.

Dana felt the coolness of the sheet against her naked back. She gasped once before moaning in an exquisite ecstasy when Tyler's hardness pushed into her quivering wet body in one sure thrust of his hips and she took all of him into her up to the root of his rigid sex.

Closing his eyes, Tyler struggled not to climax. "Don't make a sound," he whispered.

Dana kissed his shoulder, tasting salt and inhaling

the sensual fragrance of his cologne. "I think asking me not to breathe would be an easier task." Her husky voice was warm and smooth as velvet.

Tyler's hips rocked in an up-and-down motion, setting a rhythm Dana could follow easily. "Don't do that either. I'll breathe for the both of us."

That said, he led her on a journey of sexual pleasure she'd only glimpse before. Just when she felt herself going over the precipice, he pulled her back, changing positions. He tasted her, she him. He took her as she knelt, holding onto the headboard for support. She reciprocated when she straddled him, establishing a rhythm that left both of them moaning and gasping for their next breath.

It all ended when Tyler turned her over and loved her as if it would become their last time together. Anchoring her legs over his shoulders, he stared at the passion tightening her features, and then he did what he had promised—he released her legs, covered her mouth, and breathed for both of them as he melted into her.

The pleasure lingered, long after their breathing resumed a normal rate. It was still there when Dana lay against damp chest, his arms around her. It lasted throughout the night until the pinpoints of light found their way under the drawn drapes.

Dana's eyelids fluttered several times before she came awake. She eased away from Tyler, not wanting to wake him. A sensual smile curved her lips when she recalled what they'd shared the night before. Tyler had made love to her like a man possessed, and she'd accepted everything he offered.

Straightening a leg, she turned on her side, but never completed the motion. A flicker of apprehension coursed through her as her fingers touched the sticky substance on her inner thigh. Her eyes widened with realization. They'd made love without protection.

Turning over, she pounded on Tyler's shoulder. "Wake up!"

He came awake immediately. "What is it?"

Dana sat up, pulling the edge of the sheet to her breasts. "Do you know what we did last night?"

He flashed a lecherous grin. "Oh, yeah. Do you want an instant replay?"

She slapped his hard shoulder. "Be serious, Tyler."

His expression changed, sobering. "What the matter, Dana?"

"You didn't protect me, Tyler. We made love without using anything."

He placed a hand along the side her head. "I know it sounds lame, but I meant to protect you, darling. Things just got out of hand."

Crossing her arms under her breasts, she glared up at him, her lashes fluttering as she struggled to form her words. "That is a juvenile excuse."

Going to his knees, Tyler held her shoulders in a firm grip, pulling her up with him. "It wasn't my intention to make love to you without using a condom. It happened, Dana, and nothing we can say or do will change that."

"What if I'm pregnant?"

A tender smile softened his face. "There are worse things than having a husband who's an obstetrician. I'll deliver the baby."

"Be serious, Tyler."

"I am." He pulled her into a protective embrace, one hand moving up and down her back. "We can marry now. That way no one will begin counting their fingers once the baby's born."

"What if I'm not pregnant?" she said close to his ear.

"Then that will just give us another month to try again. I've always heard from my patients that baby-making is incredible."

She smiled, curving her arms around his strong neck. "Last night was incredible."

"It was mind-blowing, sweetheart."

"When do you want to get married?"

"How about this weekend?"

Pulling back, she stared at him as if he'd taken leave of his senses. "This weekend?"

"We can fly to Florida."

"Are you serious, Tyler?"

He lifted an eyebrow. "Didn't you tell me to be serious?"

"Okay," she said, shrugging a bare shoulder.

"Okay, what?"

Her smile was dazzling, the gesture lighting up her golden eyes. "Let's do it."

Tyler moved off the bed, pulling her with him and spinning her around and around. He finally stopped, swaying slightly. "I have to make a few phone calls. I need to reserve a jet for later today."

Dana stood in the middle of the bedroom dazed as Tyler picked up a cordless phone and began dialing numbers. His first call was to Florida.

A sleepy Martin Cole answered the telephone. "Yes."

"Hi, Dad. I need you to do a favor for me."

"Do you know what time it is, son?"

"Yes. It's one hour later where you are than here."

"What do you want?"

Tyler ignored his father's coolly disapproving tone. "I need you to call one of your legal associates to secure a marriage license for me and a Dana Nichols. Then need you to contact Timothy about flying me and Dana into West Palm tonight."

"Marriage? Who is *Dana?*"

"She's the woman I plan to marry this weekend."

"Who's getting married?" Parris Cole's voice came through the earpiece. It was apparent she'd picked up the extension.

"I am," Tyler announced proudly. "Hey, Mom, you win the bet."

"What bet! Will someone please tell me what the hell is going on here!" Martin shouted.

"There's not much to tell. I'm coming in tonight, and plan to marry Saturday, then fly back to Mississippi on Sunday."

"Sweet heaven," Parris moaned, "my children are going to put me in my grave before my time. Why didn't you say something when you were here two weeks ago?"

"I hadn't proposed two weeks ago."

Parris sighed heavily. "I have to contact everyone to come back to Florida."

"No, you don't," Tyler countered. "Dana and I can go to Vegas."

"Oh, hell, no," Martin shouted again. "I'm not going to have my only son get married and not witness it. What the hell kind of kids did we raise, Parris? One lives in the Amazon jungle, the other shacks up with a man for ten years before she decides he's good enough for her, and now our son . . . no, *your* son . . . wants to marry some girl in a gambling juke joint."

"Hang up the phone, Martin."

"Parris."

"I said to hang it up." There was a distinctive click, followed by Tyler's mother voice. "You're going to have to excuse your father. He's getting old and cranky."

"Who the hell is old?" shouted Martin in the background.

"He's become his father," Parris whispered softly.

"Are you finished, Mother?"

"Don't you dare call me Mother."

Tyler ignored her protest. "I need a marriage license, a judge, and a jet. Not necessarily in that order."

"Is she pregnant?"

Tyler turned and stared at Dana for the first time since dialing the telephone. He didn't know if she was pregnant, didn't want to know—at least not until after they'd exchanged vows.

"No."

"Are you sure?"

"I am a doctor, and I think I'd know if she was."

"I still get to name your firstborn."

He chuckled softly. "And knowing you, you've probably already selected the names."

"Of course. Martin if it's a boy, and Simone if it's a girl. That's only if your wife doesn't object."

"You can talk to her about it once you meet her. Hold on a minute, Mom. I'm going need your help with something else."

He moved over to Dana, curving an arm around her waist. "What size is your finger, and what cut of diamond do you like?"

She stared at Tyler as if he'd taken leave of his senses. He was making wedding plans like someone compiling a weekly shopping list.

"I think I'm a five."

"What cut of stone?"

"Emerald." It was the first thing that came to her mind.

Tyler kissed the top of her head. "Mom. I need you to select a ring for Dana. She's a five and she prefers an emerald cut."

"Would you like baguettes?" Parris questioned.

"Yes."

"White or yellow gold?" she asked, continuing her questioning.

"Platinum. The band can be plain or with baguettes. If Dana doesn't like it I can always buy her another one."

"What about you, Tyler? Do you want to wear a ring?" Parris asked.

"Yes, please order a band for me."

"How about a gift for your bride?"

"Pick out something nice for her. You have exquisite taste."

"How about her family? When are they getting in?"

Tyler hesitated, staring at the woman he loved staring up at him. She was barefoot, naked, her face so open and trusting. She stood by silently, permitting him to plan her future. And for the first since meeting Dana Nichols, he was suddenly cognizant that she was totally alone. Her parents were gone, as was her grandmother, and as an only child she was unprotected. But she wasn't alone because she had him. She had his family, who would become her family.

"They're not. We'll become her family."

"I hope she won't mind if I assume the responsibility of becoming mother of the bride. If she doesn't have a dress, I'll take her shopping early Saturday morning."

"Mom, we'll talk again."

"Tyler?"

"Yes?"

"I love you."

"I love you, too." Depressing a button, he ended the call.

Dana rested her head against Tyler's shoulder. "Was that your mother?"

Lowering his head, he kissed the end of her pert nose. "No, darling. That was *our* mother."

Moving closer, Dana melted into his strength. She

clung to Tyler until he swept her up in his arms and carried her back to the bed, where they had demonstrated a love so strong and profound that there was a possibility a new life might have begun in her womb.

Twenty-one

Tyler extended a hand to one of the pilots flying the Gulfstream IV jet, shaking his hand. "Good afternoon, Captain Gonzalez."

The pilot inclined his head. "Dr. Cole."

The fingers of Tyler's left hand tightened around Dana's waist. "Dana, this Captain Gonzalez, our copilot for this flight. Captain, I'd like to present my fiancée, Dana Nichols."

Smiling broadly, Captain Gonzalez removed his cap, tucking it under his arm. "My pleasure, Miss Nichols. I'd like to offer my congratulations on your upcoming marriage."

Dana found it impossible not to return the handsome pilot's disarming smile. "Thank you very much."

"Are you ready?" Tyler whispered close to her ear.

"Yes," she replied breathlessly. And she was ready, ready to become Mrs. Tyler Cole and ready to share her life and future with him.

She followed Tyler up the stairs and into the sleek jet, her eyes widening in shock as she surveyed a forty-foot cabin that was configured for eleven to thirteen passengers, with sofas that folded out into beds. There was also a full galley and two rest rooms.

Captain Gonzalez entered the aircraft, pulled up the steps, then closed and locked the cabin door. He walked to the cockpit and took his seat next to the pilot, where they awaited the signal from the tower to take off.

Tyler belted Dana in, before he sat beside her and repeated the action for himself. Holding her hand, he stared at her looking out the large oval window. She'd had no way of knowing when she'd made an appointment to have her hair styled that it was because she was going to a wedding—her own. The pale rose-pink color on her nails and toes was soft and complementary to her tanned golden coloring. Her chemically straightened hair, set, blown out, the blunt-cut ends turned under with a large curling iron, swayed above her shoulder each time she moved her head. The hot summer sun had bleached the light brown strands until they shimmered like liquid gold.

"Who owns this jet?" she asked, her attention focused on the activity outside the aircraft.

"A cousin."

Turning her head, she stared at Tyler. "Your cousin in Georgetown?"

He shook his head, knowing it was time he revealed his family connections. "No. The cousin is the eldest son of one of my aunts. Timothy Cole Thomas is the CEO of ColeDiz International, Ltd. ColeDiz is family-owned, operated, and controlled."

Dana's mouth formed a perfect O when realization dawned as to whom she would marry. "You're one of those *Coles?*" Closing his eyes, Tyler nodded slowly. "Why didn't you tell me who you were?"

He opened his eyes and smiled. "Would it have made a difference, Dana? Would you not have consented to marry me if you'd known that I was one of those *Coles?*"

"I don't know," she answered truthfully. "To be completely honest, I never considered marrying anyone."

"Why not?"

"I guess it was because of my parents. Their marriage seemed perfect for so many years, but toward the end they argued every day about every little thing. After a while I didn't want them to stay together because of the constant bickering. And it was always the same thing, my dad accusing my mother of running around with other men."

"Could he prove she was seeing other men?"

"I don't think he could at first."

A slight frown marred Tyler's smooth forehead. "He did later?"

"Yes. At least that's what he said the night she was murdered. I don't know why, I can recall every word of their argument that night. He said, 'How can you still do it now that I have proof? Don't you have any shame?'"

"Do you know what proof he was talking about?"

She shook her head. "No, but he did call her a tramp."

Turning in his seat, Tyler caught her delicate chin, forcing Dana to directly look at him. "Did you ever think that maybe your mother was pregnant and that the child in her womb wasn't your father's?"

"I don't think so. There was no mention of a baby."

"Please fasten your seat belts. We're cleared for take-off." The pilot's voice came through the speakers positioned throughout the cabin, and the conversation about Harry and Alicia Nichols was dropped.

The jet eased forward, taxiing down the runway before picking up speed. Closing her eyes and pressing her head against the back of the seat, Dana felt the power of the jet as it lifted off, climbing steadily before leveling off above the clouds.

She sat, Tyler's hand cradling hers protectively in his stronger grasp, willing her mind blank. Dr. Tyler

Cole was a ColeDiz Cole! The enormity of the life she would be thrust into was too unbelievable to fathom.

Her soon-to-be husband was a member of the wealthiest African-American family in the country, though the Coles had never disclosed the extent of their vast wealth. He'd talked about looking over loose diamonds the way a farmer would discuss his antici-pated yield from a corn or soybeans crop.

You're just like your mother, her inner voice nagged at her again.

Alicia had wanted to marry up, live in a grand house, and flaunt her status as the wife of Dr. Harry Nichols.

Dana wanted to shout to the world that she wasn't Alicia Nichols because when she married Tyler she would remain faithful to him.

She loved him!

"I love you."

Tyler went completely still, his whole face spreading into a smile. She'd finally said it!

Reaching over, he unbuckled her belt, lifting her effortlessly onto his lap. "Say it again," he whispered in her ear. "Please." At that moment he didn't care how desperate he sounded.

Holding his head to her breasts, Dana pressed her lips to his close-cropped salt-and-pepper hair. "I love you, Tyler Cole."

Rocking her gently, he kissed her mouth. "You are my everything. My life. My all."

The time passed in a blur for Dana from the mo-ment a limousine met them on a private airfield at the West Palm Beach airport for the drive to the Cole fam-ily estate.

She stared out the window at a large house designed

in Spanish and Italian Revival styles with barrel-tiled red roofs, a stucco façade, and balconies shrouded in lush bougainvillea and sweeping French doors that opened onto broad expanses of terraces with spectacular panoramic water views. The magnificent structure was surrounded by tropical foliage, exotic gardens, and the reflection of light off sparkling lake waters.

"No, I didn't grow up here," Tyler said, reading her mind. "My father did. But he lives here now because of my *abuela.*"

"I take it *abuela* is grandmother?"

"Sí, senorita."

She cast her eyes downward, blushing. "I suppose I'll be around for more than four months, so now you can teach me to speak Spanish."

"I intend to have your around for a long, long time, Mrs. Cole."

She placed her fingertips over his mouth. "You can't call me that for another twenty-four hours." Their wedding ceremony was planned for seven Saturday evening.

"I'm just practicing. You'll become one of only three other Mrs. Coles. There's my mother, my uncle David's wife Serena, and of course my grandmother."

"There are no other Cole men?"

"Uncle David has two sons, Gabriel and Jason, but everyone's given up on any of his children marrying."

The driver stopped the car, shifting into park. Just as he exited the limousine to open the back door for his passengers, the front door to the opulent structure opened. A knowing smile touched Dana's mouth when she saw a tall, silver-haired man descend the steps. She knew this man was Tyler's father and her soon-to-be father-in-law.

She stepped out, reaching for Tyler's hand, but he was already striding toward his father, arms outstretched. Watching, she saw them embrace warmly before Tyler kissed his father on both cheeks.

Shifting, Tyler held out his hand to her. She took it, moving closer to his side. "Dad, I'd like you to meet Dana Nichols. Dana, this is Martin Diaz Cole—my father."

Martin stared at the delicate woman standing beside his son through half-lowered lids, his mind taking him back fifty years to when he first saw a young woman walk into the private room at a Palm Beach restaurant for an engagement party for a mutual friend. Dana Nichols wasn't as tall as Parris, but her coloring and jewel-like eyes were similar. And it was like father, like son. He'd fallen in love with Parris Simmons on sight, and it was apparently the same with Tyler and Dana Nichols.

Martin pulled Dana to his chest, lowered his head, and kissed her tenderly on the lips. "I welcome you on behalf of the entire family. I hope you think of me as your father, because as of now you are my daughter."

She felt the power in the solid body pressed to hers. Martin Cole had celebrated his eighty-first birthday in January, but could easily pass for a man ten years younger. His silver hair lay against his scalp in layered precision, while a network of lines around his large dark eyes were more from squinting in the hot sun than age. And like fine wine, he'd aged beautifully.

"Everyone's out back waiting to meet you," Martin said in a soft drawling voice that reminded Dana of Tyler's.

Tyler winked at her. "Are you ready?"

She flashed a tight smile. "I think I am."

Martin instructed the driver to leave Tyler and Dana's luggage in the foyer while he led the way along a flagstone path to the rear of the house.

Dana would've bolted and run if Tyler hadn't tightened his grip on her fingers. There appeared to be hundreds of people sitting and standing around a grassy area large enough for two football fields. Moving closer to her fiancé's side, she affected what she hoped was a smile.

Leaning down from his superior height, Tyler whispered, "Each one is going to come to meet you and I'll introduce them to you. We'll begin with my *abuela.*"

Tyler led her over to a frail white-haired woman sitting in a wheelchair. The beauty that had been so obvious in her youth had not faded completely with age.

Hunkering down, Tyler held Marguerite Josefina Diaz-Cole's hand in a gentle grip. *"Abuela,* I'd like you to meet the woman who's going to become mine tomorrow." He'd spoken in Spanish because M.J., as everyone called her, had decided she didn't want to speak English anymore.

M.J. raised her head, staring up at Dana for a long moment. She smiled, and twin dimples creased her paper-thin cheeks. "She's lovely," she remarked in Spanish. "She will give you beautiful children."

Tyler translated his grandmother's remarks for Dana, who blushed furiously. "Tell her thank you."

"Tell her yourself. All you have to say is, *gracias, abuela.*"

Bending slightly, Dana kissed M.J. on the cheek, repeating the Spanish. *"Gracias, abuela.*"

"De nada, nieta."

"She said, 'Thank you, granddaughter,' " Tyler explained, translating the Spanish again.

"Why didn't you tell me I needed a crash course in Spanish?" she whispered to Tyler.

"You're safe now. Everyone else speaks English." He led her over to his mother, flashing a wide grin. "This beautiful lady is my mother, Parris. Mom, Dana."

Parris flashed her son a thumbs-up sign before she

hugged Dana. "If you call me Parris I'll disown you. I want you to call me Mom."

Dana stared at the tall woman with the mysterious brown-green eyes. "Thank you."

Holding her at arm's length, Parris smiled. "No. Thank *you*. I can see that you've made my son very happy."

"That's because he makes me deliriously happy."

Tyler led her over to another couple. There was no doubt the tall woman leading against a man with silver-gray hair and a neatly barbered gray mustache was Tyler's sister.

"This very beautiful woman is my older sister, Regina. The gentleman with her is her husband and my brother-in-law. Aaron and Regina live half the year in Bahia, Brazil, and divide the other half between Mexico and Florida. Aaron can take all of the credit for helping me to decide to go into medical research."

Regina moved forward, hugging Dana while kissing her cheek. "Welcome to the family."

Dana was surprised to hear Regina's low throaty voice. Tall and elegant, she was definitely her parents' child. She'd even inherited the trademark Cole dimples.

Tyler walked over to another woman, who sat on a cushion chair while a man stood behind her, one hand resting possessively on her shoulder.

Hunkering down, he held Arianna's hands. Her fingers were cool, clammy. Vertical lines formed between his eyes. "What's the matter?"

She rested her forehead on her brother's shoulder. "I feel like I'm going to lose the contents of my stomach."

Rising to his feet, he motioned to Silah. "Get her back in the house. She needs to lie down. Put a cool cloth on her forehead. And if she asks for something to drink, give her water with ice. Don't let her gulp it. Small sips. If she wants food, then tell my mother to get some dry crackers for her. Understand?"

Silah Kadir nodded. *"Oui."*

Silah did not hesitate as he eased Arianna to her feet. Everyone stared silently as she held her belly and permitted her husband to lead her back to the house.

Tyler watched his sister until she disappeared before he returned his attention to Dana. "That's my younger sister, Arianna. As you can probably guess, she's pregnant."

"Is it her first child?"

"Yes. My parents are overjoyed because it's been a long time since they've had a grandbaby to spoil. You've met my siblings. Now it's time for aunts, uncles, and cousins."

Dana lost track of the names as she met Tyler's two aunts and two uncles. Josephine and Nancy were both great-grandmothers, while their half-brother Joshua Kirkland proudly boasted about his four, and soon-to-be-five, grandchildren. His son Michael, daughter Emily, grandson Alejandro, and granddaughters Esperanza and Teresa had all inherited his green eyes. But it was six-year-old Alejandro who had also claimed his silver-blond hair.

Tyler kept up a running commentary each time he introduced her to another family member. Emily's husband, former New Mexico Governor Christopher Delgado, was now a federal district judge. The Delgados had celebrated the birth of their third child six months ago. Mateo Arroyo Delgado already showed signs of being spoiled by his older siblings Alejandro and three-year-old Esperanza, who regarded her new baby brother as one of her dolls.

Dana knew she was impolite, but she couldn't help staring at Salem Lassiter. Salem was married to Christopher's sister Sara. The silky ponytail flowing down his back was liberally streaked with gray, which made him very sexy. Even the small silver hoops in his pierced lobes made him more attractive—as if he needed to be.

Sara and Salem, like Emily and Chris, lived in Las Cruces, New Mexico, and had three children: a son and twin daughters. Isaiah was as strikingly handsome as his father, while Nona and Eve had their mother's beautiful gold-green eyes.

Her head spinning with faces and names she was certain she'd never remember, Dana came face-to-face with someone she did know and recognize.

Standing in front of her with arms crossed over his chest, perfect white teeth gleaming his sun-browned olive face, was Gabriel Cole. The rays of the setting sun glinted off the twin gold hoops in his pierced lobes and the coal-black, wavy long hair he'd secured on the nape of his neck.

She affected a similar pose, grinning at him. "Fancy meeting you here," she teased.

"And I you," Gabriel shot back.

Tyler stared at his cousin, then his fiancée. "You two know each other?"

"Only superficially," Dana said.

"Yeah, superficially," Gabriel confirmed, pulling Dana to his body. Lowering his head, he kissed her passionately on the mouth. "That's payback for writing that article about me and defaming my character."

Not knowing why, Tyler felt an uneasiness he could only identify as jealousy. He was jealous of his cousin's familiarity with the woman he would exchange vows with in less than twenty-four hours.

"What's up with you mauling my woman, *primo*?" he rattled off in Spanish.

"I owe your *mujer* because she almost destroyed my

career. I'd performed in a fund-raising event in upstate New York, and she covered the concert for that tacky little rag she calls a newspaper. Her article was so scathing about my performance that I had to lay low for a couple of months to recover my pride."

"Don't you mean your arrogance?" said Dana. "You were terrible, Gabriel."

"I was ill, Miss Nichols. I went on stage even though I running a fever of one-oh-two."

"You could've canceled. You sounded like a choking frog that night."

"You never printed a retraction when I came back the following month to perform for free, did you?"

"I was on vacation at the time."

"How convenient," Gabriel drawled. He shook his head, his ponytail sweeping back and forth over his broad shoulders. "I can't believe you're going to become my cousin."

"Believe it, Mr. Cole."

"I'm afraid I'm going to have to, Mrs. Cole. I suppose I can call you that although your wedding is still a day away. What song do you want me to play for your wedding?"

Dana gave Tyler a sidelong glance. " 'Baby, I Need Your Loving.' "

Gabriel lifted an eyebrow. "The old Four Tops hit?"

"I think we'd better pick another song," Tyler stated firmly. It was the song that had prompted Dana to strip for him.

Wrinkling her nose, she said, "I think you're right, darling."

"I know I'm right, baby."

Gabriel clutched his stomach. "I think I'm going to be sick. Darling! Baby!" He stumbled, pointing his finger in his mouth. "Help, I need a doctor."

Martin and Parris preempted further introductions

when the caterers arrived and began setting the many tables on the lawn. Twilight settled on the Cole estate as everyone sat down to eat, drink, and prepare to witness a wedding. It was the second time within two weeks the Coles, Kirklands, Delgados, and Lassiters had come from places far and near to celebrate one of their own. The first was to welcome Arianna and Silah home, and the second was to bear witness to Tyler Cole exchanging vows with Miss Dana Nichols.

Everyone knew Tyler would one day replace his father Martin as patriarch of the family, but they weren't certain whether Dana was aware of her role in the Cole hierarchy.

Parris stared at Dana, a knowing smile softening her lush mouth. She knew she had to talk with the lovely young woman, but she would wait—until *after* the wedding.

Twenty-two

Dana closed her eyes briefly as Martin Cole led her down the flower-strewn path in the formal English garden to where Tyler stood, with his nephew/godson/best man Clayborne Spencer, waiting to make her his wife. She forced her feet, shod in a pair of Stuart Weitzman off-white peau de soie evening sandals, to move—one foot in front of the other. The hand resting on the sleeve of Martin's startling white dinner jacket appeared even more delicate because of the flawless two-carat emerald-cut diamond ring on her third finger. The matching platinum bangle banded all around with a double row of princess-set diamonds gracing her wrist was Tyler's wedding gift to her.

Parris had come to the bedroom she'd shared with Regina Spencer's daughter Eden and Kim Cheung, Clayborne's girlfriend, whispering it was time for her to get up.

She'd protested, mumbling that she'd just gone to bed, but jumped up like a jack-in-the box once Parris reminded her it was her wedding day. It had taken her twenty minutes to brush her teeth, shower, and dress. Clad in a pair of faded jeans, an oversized T-shirt, and running shoes, she had shared breakfast with Parris on the loggia as the brilliant Florida sun rose above the horizon.

Dana had listened quietly as Parris explained that if

Martin Cole passed away, then Tyler was expected to become the family's patriarch. Parris's words were branded on her brain: *Martin was Samuel Cole's eldest son. Therefore, the line is passed along through firstborn sons. If you and Tyler have a son, then he is next in line.*

Nodding numbly, Dana could do nothing but stare, wondering what she was marrying into. It was apparent the Coles regarded themselves not only as privileged, but also as African-American royalty. And like in the fairy tales, she had come to the ball and captured the heart of the prince. Tyler Simmons Cole was her prince and black knight—one who would pledge to love, honor, and protect her until they parted in death.

She and Parris drove to Palm Beach to shop. Four hours later they returned with her wedding rings, a platinum band edged with narrower bands of eighteen-carat yellow gold for Tyler, the diamond bracelet, and a Giorgio Armani short-sleeve lace-bodice gown with an ivory organza skirt and shoes. Dana lingered in the jewelry store long enough to purchase a gold key fob with the insignia of a caduceus for Tyler as her wedding gift to him.

Gabriel Cole, who had threatened to sing Billy Idol's "White Wedding," sat at a keyboard, crooning Jon Secada's "Angel." His beautiful voice was clear as bell as he sang the words, which seemed to come from his heart. Several members of his band had come to lend their musical talent, and a drummer and guitarist accompanied him with the moving rendition.

Martin winked at his son, placed Dana's hand on Tyler's, then stepped back to sit beside Parris. Holding her hand tightly, Martin recalled the night he'd exchanged vows with Parris on the very property they now owned.

Dana lifted her gaze to meet Tyler's glittering obsidian one, smiling. Parris's personal stylist had pinned her hair up off her neck in a twist, then pinned a circlet of baby's breath and fresh orange blossoms in her sun-streaked hair.

Vanessa Kirkland had suggested orange blossoms, saying they signified a long and happy married life. Joshua's wife had shooed everyone out of the bedroom, helping Dana dress for her special day. She'd confessed in a quiet voice that her daughter had eloped, and that she hadn't been afforded the privilege of helping Emily dress for her wedding.

It had taken less than a day, but Dana felt as if she'd known the Coles all of her life. They had warmly embraced her as one of their own, and she'd felt like family even before her name was changed from Nichols to Cole.

An elderly judge smiled at the young couple, waiting. Tyler nodded, and the judge began the ritual that would make them husband and wife. Dana's gaze never left Tyler's as they repeated their vows, exchanged rings, and then sealed their promises with a passionate kiss.

Turning to face the assembled, the judge said in a commanding voice, "Ladies and gentlemen, Mr. and Mrs. Tyler Cole."

There came a thundering round of applause, followed by whistles and hooting from the younger members of the family. Tyler curved an arm around Dana's waist, spinning her around when Gabriel launched into "Baby, I Need Your Loving."

Pulling her close, he whispered close to her ear, "I dare you to strip here."

She showed him her teeth, wrinkling her nose. "I'll strip for you later."

Throwing back his head, he laughed loudly. "I can't wait."

Parris, exquisitely attired in a peach-colored silk suit,

tapped her son on the shoulder. She kissed him, then his bride. "Darling, you and Dana must meet your guests. You can dance later."

Holding his arms above his head, Tyler snapped his fingers and gyrated to the Latin rhythms pulsing through the powerful sound system in the garden as Gabriel sang the Marc Anthony hit, *"Te Conozco Bien."*

Parris lifted her shoulders and looked at her husband. "I suppose this is not going to be a traditional wedding."

Martin reached for Parris, pulling her close to his chest. "Since when have we ever been traditional? I would like a little conventionality, but I suppose that's not much fun, is it?"

"No," she whispered, pressing her mouth to his.

"What do you say we go back to the house and fool around?"

Parris stopped short, staring at the man she'd loved for more than fifty years of her life. "Why, you dirty old man."

"I'll admit to being dirty, but I'm certainly *that* old. At least not so old I don't want to make love to my wife."

"Martin, you're eighty-one."

"So? And you're seventy-four."

A flush suffused Parris's face. "Do you really want to . . ."

"Yes," Martin rasped in her ear.

She stared him, seeing a look of determination in his large dark eyes. "Okay. Do you have any condoms with you?"

Martin bit down on his lower lip to keep from laughing. "No, but I'll ask Clayborne for one."

Parris arched an eyebrow. "Only one?"

"Don't push your luck, Mrs. Cole."

She tugged on his hand. "Let's go, Martin. It's time

for you to put up or shut up." She clapped a hand over her mouth when she realized the pun.

Holding hands, Martin and Parris did not retreat to the house, but further into the garden, where they could talk without being overheard. Now that their last child had married, it was time for Martin to change his will.

Dana danced every dance, fast and slow. She found herself in David Cole's arms for a slow number. The diamond studs in his pierced lobes twinkled like stars.

He smiled at her, flashing the trademark dimples he'd passed along to all of his children. "My nephew has chosen well." His soft baritone voice rumbled over her, a voice so much like Gabriel's.

She offered him a demure smile. *"Gracias, Tío David."*

Throwing back his head, he laughed loudly. *"Perfecto.* Do you have a girlfriend you can introduce to one of my sons?" he whispered conspiratorially. "Serena nags me constantly that she doesn't want to wait until she's seventy to become a grandmother."

Dana gave him a look that mirrored skepticism. "I heard your brother say it's you who wants grandchildren, not your wife."

David scowled. "You don't have to tell which brother said that. One of these days I'm going to forget that Joshua is my brother and call him out."

"It wasn't Joshua."

David's chiseled jaw dropped. "Martin? Don't tell me it was Martin!"

"Are you going to call him out, too?"

David looked as if he was deep in thought, and then shook his head. "Nope. At least not until the next wedding."

Angling her head, Dana smiled up at his incredibly handsome face. "Maybe the next wedding will be for one of your sons or daughters."

He grinned, exhibiting a set of straight white teeth. "Maybe."

Dana slept during the return flight to Mississippi, despite the constant chatter from the Delgado and Lassiter children. Emily, Christopher, Sara, and Salem had elected to fly back to New Mexico on Sunday with Tyler and Dana. Judge Christopher Delgado was scheduled to hear a case involving a law firm that had been charged with siphoning millions from the estates of their deceased clients.

The jet landed in Greenville at mid-afternoon, and Tyler and Dana bade good-bye to everyone, promising to get together at Thanksgiving at Michael and Jolene's Georgetown residence.

Jolene Kirkland hadn't joined much in the festivities because, like Arianna, she was faced with throwing up when she least expected it. She'd run from the table Saturday night moaning that she was probably carrying a boy this time because she hadn't thrown up once when she was pregnant with her daughter.

Dana stood in the middle of the master bedroom in what was now her and Tyler's bedroom, staring up at him. The imported ivory-white silk nightgown, trimmed with gold thread, a wedding gift from Arianna and Silah, felt cool against her fevered flesh. Tyler, wearing a black silk caftan-styled gown bearing Silah's label, smiled the sexy smile she'd come to look for and love.

His fingers trailed along the curve of her cheekbone, down her throat, and over the fullness of her breasts. She closed her eyes, trembling slightly with anticipation. This was to become the first time she and Tyler would make love under this roof as husband and wife.

Lowering his head, Tyler pressed his mouth to her ear. "I love you, Mrs. Cole."

Her hands went to the middle of his chest, feeling the heat of his body through the delicate fabric. The diamonds on her left hand gave off blue-white sparks under recessed lights in the ceiling.

A mysterious smile curved her lips as she moved closer, her breasts grazing his chest. "Not as much as I love you, Mr. Cole."

Curving an arm around her waist, he pulled her against his middle, permitting her to feel his rising desire. "Would you like to make a wager?"

"Yes, I would, Mr. Cole."

"What are you prepared to put up?"

"A lifetime of happily-ever-after."

He smiled, nodding. "I'll accept it wholeheartedly."

Bending slightly, he picked her up and carried her to the bed. They took their time undressing each other, savoring the taste and texture of perfumed flesh as they began a journey of exploration and discovery. This was no frantic coupling because they had the rest of their lives to laugh and love together.

Dana moaned softly when she felt her husband enter her body. Raising her legs, she wound them around his waist, permitting him deeper penetration. He loved her a long time, whispering endearments in Spanish. She didn't understand the words, yet Tyler had managed to communicate his love as he buried his face between her scented neck and shoulder and groaned out his passion.

Dana's own release followed his, overlapping and

merging as she surrendered to the ecstasy taking her beyond herself and reality. She lay motionless, eyes closed, savoring the lingering pulsing of her flesh squeezing the thick, heavy organ nestled inside her hot, wet body.

They'd made love again without using protection. They hadn't talked about not having a child, which translated into wanting a child. And she did want children—Tyler's children. He'd had asked for one child, but she wanted more than one, because she'd been an only child.

Tyler rolled off Dana's slight body, reversing their positions. He held her protectively as she fell asleep atop him, and minutes later he joined her.

Twenty-three

The news of Dr. Tyler Cole's marriage to Dana Nichols spread throughout Hillsboro like a wildfire sweeping across a bone-dry wheat field.

They decided to breakfast at Smithy's, walking in together amid a round of applause. Tyler accepted handshakes, slaps on the back, and good wishes from all while Dana stood by watching. Most everyone stood a distance away from her, nodding and referring to her as Mrs. Cole.

How ironic, she mused. Tyler was the newcomer, while her family's roots were planted deep in Hillsboro's soil for the past one hundred years.

She remembered Billy Clark talking about deceitful people. She'd come home, and she wondered long she would have to pay for the sins of her mother.

Tyler dropped her off at her grandmother's house, where she told him she had some documents to research. She told him that the house and its contents now belonged to her, yet she was undecided what she wanted to do with it, only because she had to wait a year before she could sell it. He told her to take her time, and if she needed investment advice he would refer her to Vanessa Blanchard Kirkland, the family's financial guru.

Dana walked into the entryway, looking at the space as if seeing it for the first time. The house seemed so much smaller after living in Tyler's house. She mentally corrected herself. It was no longer Tyler's house, but *their* house.

Heading for the kitchen, she put up a pot of coffee, waited for it to brew, then retreated to the porch and the notebooks filled with Eugene Payton's detailed notes.

She'd filled both sides of a legal pad when the tiny cellular telephone on the desk rang. Recognizing the number on the display, she picked up the phone, pressing the TALK button. She took a quick glance at her watch. It was after three. She'd been working nonstop all morning and most of the afternoon.

"Hello, darling," she said.

"Dana, I can't talk. I'm on my way to the hospital. They just brought someone in who's hemorrhaging. I'm not sure whether I'll be home in time to have dinner with you."

Before Dana could say another word, the line went dead. "O—kay."

It'd come out as two words. She'd gotten up early to defrost and marinate meat she planned to cook on the outdoor grill along with ears of corn and skewered vegetables, but it looked as if she'd have to scrap her plan.

She left a strip of paper in the notebook to mark her place, and closed it. Resting her left hand over the leather cover, she stared at the precious stones on her finger. The rings reminded her she was now Mrs. Tyler Cole, the wife of Dr. Tyler Cole.

Closing her eyes, she recalled times when the telephone rang minutes after Dr. Harry Nichols sat down to dinner with his family. Dana always watched her mother's face when her husband apologized, then

walked out to see a patient. Dana had become accus-
tomed to the routine: if Harry was called before he
sat down to the table, then Alicia would put his plate
on the warmer for him to eat upon his return. But if
he'd taken a single forkful, then she would empty the
plate in the garbage, clean up the kitchen, drive Dana
to Georgia's, leave her, and disappear for hours. Georgia always rebuked for her actions, saying she shouldn't
have married a doctor if she hadn't been willing to
share him with his patients.

Pushing back her chair, Dana stood up rotating her
stiff shoulders. She'd been sitting for hours. The
phone call had shattered her concentration, so she decided to call it a day.

She lingered at the house for another half hour,
watering the plants, winding the clock, and wiping
away a layer of dust on tables and mirrors. It was exactly four-o'clock when she parked her car in an empty
space in the garage, deactivated the alarm, and walked
into the cool interiors of the house she shared with
her husband.

Her steps were slow as she mounted the staircase
and walked into the bathroom to shower. At the last
moment she decided on a leisurely bath; she stepped
into the large sunken tub, turned on the pulsing jets,
and sat in the swirling waters until she felt herself falling asleep. Stepping out, she dried her body, applied
a moisturizer, and walked back into the bedroom to
an area Tyler had set up as dressing room. Shelves in
the large walk-in closet were filled with laundered
shirts and sweaters, the built-in racks crowded with
slacks, jackets, suits, and ties. She counted more than
thirty pairs of shoes. There was no doubt her husband
was a clotheshorse.

Tyler had given her half the closet, and she stared
at her meager garments. It went without saying that

she had to go shopping for clothes. Pulling on a loose-fitting smock dress, she went downstairs to the kitchen. A rumbling in her belly verified she hadn't eaten anything since her breakfast at Smithy's.

Dana prepared a Caesar salad, adding strips of grilled chicken and tossing hers with garlic-flavored vinaigrette. She put aside a portion for Tyler, covering the bowl with a plastic wrap and placing it on a lower shelf in the refrigerator. Scribbling a note indicating his dinner was in the fridge, she stuck it to the door with a magnet advertising the services of the Hillsboro Women's Health Clinic.

She ate her salad and cleaned up the kitchen, filled a water bottle with ice water from the dispenser on the refrigerator door, and left the house. The sun had shifted behind a copse of pine trees in the distance, leaving the garden and the orchard measurably cooler. She walked around to the pool area, peering at the plastic covering spread over the hole in the ground. The workmen had begun placing the blue tiles along the floor of the pool.

She continued her leisurely stroll into the garden, stopping to smell the flowers as a riot of color greeted her. Following a narrow path, she stopped suddenly when she spied a large pond filled with lilies floating on its placid surface. Covering her eyes, she saw an outcropping of trees and shrubs on the opposite bank. Large boulders created a natural barrier from which a steady stream of water poured into the pond. The skeletal remains of one tree resting in the water created a natural effect—a collaboration between Mother Nature and Father Time.

How beautiful, she mused. Everything was peaceful, beautiful, the perfect place to raise a family. She circled the pond, coming out in a cleared area that sloped down a steep cliff. Lying on her belly, she looked over the precipice, shrieking when she felt herself propelled back in a savage jerk that snapped her teeth so hard her jaw ached.

The hot breath on her neck sent a shiver of fear racing down her spine. Her hand formed a fist as she turned around, ready to protect herself against whoever it was that held her captive.

"What do you think you're doing?"

Her eyes widened in shock when she looked into the stormy gaze belonging to her husband. "Let me go, Tyler."

"Not yet," he snapped, literally dragging her away from the cliff. Rage had darkened his face under his deep tan. "Are you crazy? Don't you know you could've fallen off?" The fabric of her dress was bunched in his fist.

She stared him down. "Please, let me go, Tyler." He released the back of her dress. Going on tiptoe, she went close to his face, their noses inches apart. "For you information, I had no intention of falling off. I just wanted see over the side."

"You could've lost your life just wanting to see what's on the other side of this cliff. The ground we're standing on has a sandy and spongy base. After a heavy rainfall it will give way and end up in the gorge."

"Is this part of your property?"

He gave her long, intense look. "Yes, Dana. *We* own this property."

Heat stole into her cheeks. He'd just reminded her of what would take her some time to get used to.

"I decided to go for a walk."

He lifted his eyebrows. "And I'm glad I decided to come home when I did." His expression softened. "I didn't marry you to lose you, Dana."

"And you won't lose me, Tyler. Not for a long, long time."

He raised his arms. "Let me hold you, baby."

She took a step, curving her arms under his shoulders, holding him to her heart. Summer bloomed around them as butterflies flitted from flower to flower, bees buzzed noisily, frogs who'd made the pond their home called to their mates, and high above their head a hawk circled lazily, searching for his dinner before he settled in for the night.

"I left dinner in the refrigerator for you," Dana said quietly after a pregnant silence.

"I grabbed a sandwich at the hospital cafeteria."

"You're not hungry?"

Tyler chuckled against her hair. "I'm very, very hungry, but not for food."

Easing back, Dana saw the hunger in his eyes—his hunger for her. "Come here," she said in a mysterious voice, pulling him away the cliff.

"Where are you taking me?" Tyler called after her as they skirted the lily pond.

"Over here." They stood under the sweeping branches of several fruit trees. Floating down to a carpet of green, Dana patted the grass beside her. "Please sit down, Tyler." He sat down, pulling her into his arms. Slowly, deliberately he eased her back to the grass.

Staring up at him through half-lowered lids, she smiled. "Just this once I want you to pretend that I'm Eve and you're Adam seeing me for the first time."

Hovering over Dana, Tyler smiled. There was so much about her that was a little girl and so much a woman. Whenever he looked for the girl, he found the woman.

His hands went to the front of her dress, deftly undoing the buttons. "There's no need to pretend, because you are the woman of my dreams and my heart."

Tyler unbuttoned her dress, his gaze lingering on a lacy white bra. His body reacted violently as he stared at the dark nipples showing through the delicate fabric. He unsnapped her bra, parting it in slow motion.

The waning rays of the setting sun filtered through the leaves of overhead trees, throwing light and dark shadows over the lovers as they stared into each other's eyes while articles of clothing were laid aside, until they lay as naked as the human race's first husband and wife in their own private Garden of Eden.

Dana wanted to look away, but couldn't. She didn't think she would ever get used to the perfection of the body poised above her, visually caressing the broad chest covered with thick black curling hair, which tapered to a thin line before it disappeared into an inverted triangle from which throbbed a long, thick length of dark-brown flesh nestled between strong muscled thighs. He came closer and she closed her eyes, enjoying the heat and weight of the body against her own.

Every muscle in Tyler's body screamed and vibrated as he pushed into the moist heat of his wife's body. The smell of her perfume on her skin and hair rose sharply in his nostrils, wiping away the scent of the antiseptic soap he'd scrubbed with before going into surgery. The smell had lingered even after he'd stripped off his scrubs and showered.

"I think it's time we get to know each other in every way possible," he said, breathing heavily in her ear.

Dana thought she knew all there was to know about Tyler—at least in bed. But he proved her wrong when he loved her like a man possessed; both of them were insatiable.

Under the emerging quarter moon, the twinkling

stars, the heavens, and the infinite beauty of the Creator, they acknowledged his command to go forth, be fruitful, and multiply.

Twenty-four

Dana and Tyler's first social event as a married couple was the Clarks' July Fourth celebration. The aroma of barbecue wafted in the air as they made their way to the backyard where large umbrellas were erected to keep the harmful rays of the summer sun at bay.

Lily let out a little shriek of joy when she spotted her childhood friend heading toward her carrying a box. Dr. Tyler Cole followed, carrying a larger box. Blue and white sparks glinted off the square-cut stone on Dana's left hand.

"I baked a few pies and jelly-roll cake. Tyler brought a couple of watermelons and beer." Dana thrust the box at Lily, who motioned to her husband to come and take the boxes. Billy took both boxes, anchoring the smaller one under his arm.

"You know you didn't have to bring anything," Lily admonished in a soft tone.

"And you *know* we were raised never to come empty-handed or we'd never stop getting screamed on."

Lily bobbed her head up and down. "Go figure that one. Now tell me, girlfriend, how did you hook the most eligible brother to have set foot in Hillsboro in twenty years in just two weeks?"

Raising her shoulders, Dana threw up her hands. "You're going to have to ask Tyler. I tried *everything*, and I do mean everything, to send him packing, but he just wouldn't take no."

"How did he get you to change your mind?"

"He wore me down."

Lily sucked her teeth. "That's what I call a persistent brother."

"Who's persistent?"

Dana and Lily turned to find Billy and Tyler standing less than three feet away. "My mother," Lily lied smoothly. "I was just telling Dana that my mother is very persistent once she sets her mind to so something."

Billy cut his eyes at his mother-in-law, who'd taken over manning the grill. "She's more than persistent. She has the tenacity of a pit bull, a Doberman, and a rottweiler all rolled into one little nasty Jack Russell terrier."

Lily folded her hands on her hips. "William Clark, I know you're not calling my mama a dog."

Billy held up his hands in a gesture of surrender. "Of course not, baby. You know I love your mama. She just won't let me get to *my* grill," he added through clenched teeth. "A man can't feel like a man in his *own* house unless he can tend to his *own* grill."

"Just give her a few minutes, then I'll tell her you want to take over for a while," Lily crooned, kissing her husband's cheek. Shifting, she smiled sweetly at Tyler. "Look at you, Dr. Cole. You up and married my best friend." She patted his arm. "You're a smart man to have snapped her up as quickly as you did, because there are a few guys we went to school with that were talking about hitting on her if she hadn't married you."

Curving an arm around Dana's waist, Tyler affected a wry smile. Lily couldn't see the hardness in his eyes behind the lenses of his sunglasses. He had no intention of sharing Dana—especially with other men.

"I suppose I was born under a lucky star," he said.

"I'd say you're lucky and smart," Lily told him, looping her arm through Dana's. "I'm going to steal your wife for a few minutes. I want to introduce her to a few guys she hasn't seen in years."

Tyler stood, arms crossed over his chest, watching Lily lead Dana toward a quartet of men standing under a tree, talking and laughing with one another.

His eyes narrowed as he stared at three of the men, who shook her hand politely. However, the last one hugged her. He recognized the man as Ross Wilson. R.W., as he was called to distinguish him from his father, Ross Wilson, Sr., lowered his head and kissed her cheek. Tyler saw Dana stiffen in R.W.'s embrace, knowing it was time he rescued his wife.

Taking long, measured strides, he approached the group, a polite smile curving his mouth. "Good afternoon, gentlemen."

Two he recognized as employees at a local bank, and R.W.—who most considered a business wizard because he'd initiated the deal that brought a car-manufacturing plant to Hillsboro, but not the fourth man.

All extended their hands, acknowledging him. The last one held back. "Tyler Cole," he said, introducing himself.

"James Curtis."

There was something about Mr. Curtis Tyler disliked, something he could not place. And that wasn't like him, because he made it a point never to prejudge anyone. The man's smile was too wide, his casual attire was too perfect, and his hands were too soft for a man. Everyone who'd come to the Clark cookout wore colorful shirts, tank tops, shorts, T-shirts, cutoffs, and sandals, while James Curtis was decked out in wheat-colored linen gabardine slacks, a matching raw silk shirt, and a pair of shoes that cost enough to buy a Hillsboro family of four enough groceries to last a week.

R.W. ran his fingertips over the thick mustache framing his upper lip. "Curtis is a political analyst. His specialty is campaign strategy."

Quietly, smoothly, Tyler threaded his fingers through Dana's, easing her to his side, his polite smile still in place. "Are we to assume you're serious about entering the mayoralty race?"

"Quite serious," R.W. said, showing all of his bought-and-paid for thirty-two porcelains. "Can I count on your vote, Dr. Cole?"

"I'm not ready to commit to any candidate without hearing the issues."

R.W. turned his attention to Dana. "What about your lovely wife?"

Tyler's smile faded. "You'll have to ask herself yourself. I do not presume to speak for her."

R.W. affected an expression that used to send chills up and down Dana's spine while making her stomach muscles contract. He'd lowered his eyelids and stared at her as if she were a piece of food to be devoured in one bite. What she'd once thought sexy was now lecherous.

He lifted one eyebrow. "Dana?"

"I, too, can't commit. I haven't been back long enough to qualify as a legal resident of this county. I'm certain when the election comes around, I'll definitely be a registered voter." Shifting slightly, she rested a hand in the middle of Tyler's chest. "Darling, will you please get me something to drink?" Her hand went from his chest to her throat. "I find myself so parched." Her drawl was so authentically Mississippi, one would've never thought she'd been away twenty-two years.

"Why don't we go and get something together, sweetheart?" Tyler's voice was soft as sterile cotton.

Dana fluttered her eyes. "I'd love that."

The four men watched, mouths gaping, as Tyler led Dana over to a tent that was set aside for refreshments. Four pairs of admiring male gazes lingered on the perfection of her legs in a pair of white walking shorts.

"Damn!" moaned the loan officer from Southern Trust. "Now, that's what I call a *real* woman. A woman like Dana will always let a man feel like a man, unlike that hoochie mama I had to cut loose last week. She claims she's so independent, but because I work in a bank, she thought I could go and take money out of the vault like I have my own private stash. She's taken begging to a level that is truly phenomenal. She asked for money to get her hair and nails done, and then turned around and said her mama and sisters needed theirs done, but the straw that broke the camel's hump was when she wanted me to buy Pampers for her baby. Because she wasn't talking to her baby's daddy, she didn't want to ask him for money."

"Walter, you know you're talking smack," R.W. drawled sarcastically. "I told you before that you can't get rid of that woman because she put a root on you. Did your mama tell you about eating from women?"

"She ain't got no root on me," Walter grumbled, pushing out his lower lip.

The three laughed at his expression, and the more they laughed the more Walter pushed out his lip.

Dana was finally able to get Billy alone to ask him about Sheriff Newcomb's notes. "What have you discovered?"

Billy shook his head. "Not much, Dana. It appears as if Philip Newcomb wasn't much for writing. But I did place a call to the police in Greenville. I was told they had jurisdiction in all murder cases in the county at that time. Twenty or thirty years ago small-town sheriffs had little or no actual police training.

"But that all changed, because everything's now high-tech. I have a computer in my office that will match up fingerprints and give me a rap sheet on a defendant in less than three minutes. I have the most up-to-date crime-scene equipment on the market today. You can't blame Philip Newcomb, because he's a dinosaur. He wouldn't know the first thing about turning on a computer, collecting hair samples for DNA testing, or how to use a rape kit." He patted her hand in a comforting gesture. "I'm sorry."

She smiled despite the disappointing news. "It's all right. I plan to go to Greenville to check out the coroner's and fire marshal's reports."

"If I can help you in any way, please let me know. For the more technical pieces I can hook you up with a few of old friends from the Bureau."

She kissed his cheek. "Thanks again. For everything."

Tyler listened to the incessant ringing in his ear, swearing softly under his breath. Why couldn't he connect with anyone in his family? He'd called Palm Beach, hoping to talk to his Aunt Vanessa, but the Kirklands had deactivated their answering machine. His next call was to Las Cruces, New Mexico, hoping Emily would be able to give him the information needed to contact her mother, but again he heard the persistent ringing.

His last resort was to call Michael. Someone had to be home at the Georgetown residence. Michael, as a teacher, didn't work the summer months, and Jolene, the mother of a one-year-old, was four months pregnant.

He sighed audibly when he heard the break in the connection. "Hey, *primo.*"

"How's married life, Tyler?"

"Excellent, Michael. I'm calling because I'm trying to locate your mother. I called Chris, and Emily, but there's no answer there, too."

"Everyone's in Ocho Rios for a month. Mom and Dad went down last week, and Emily, Chris, and the kids left yesterday. I told them to use the house, because it looks as if Jolene and I won't get down there this year."

"How's she feeling?"

"She had a couple of weeks of morning, afternoon, and evening sickness, then it stopped. She's eating a lot of little meals to try to put on the five pounds she lost during that time. This pregnancy is so different from her first one. I can't wait until it's over. She won't let me look at her. And if I try to touch her, it's ten times worse than the Tet Offensive, the Battle of Gettysburg, and the Battle of Hastings combined. I'd rather face a napalm assault than have her in my face. *Primo,* the woman hates me."

"Your wife is pregnant, Michael. You should get some literature and read about the changes in her body."

Tyler held the phone away from his ear when he heard his cousin cursing about what he could do with his literature. "Why don't you take her away?" Tyler asked. "Maybe you guys should go to Ocho Rios. After all, you own the property now." Michael's parents had given him and Jolene the house and five miles of private beach for a wedding gift.

"Right now it's too hot for Jolene. All she complains about is the heat."

"I'd have you guys come here, but I'm still waiting for furniture for the bedrooms. In fact, half the rooms are still empty."

"Thanks for the offer, *primo*. I guess it's not as bad as I'm making it out to be. I'm glad you called because I got a postcard from Gray a couple of days ago. He's touring Europe this summer. He wrote he should back right after Labor Day. I'm sorry about that. I guess it comes down to bad timing. By the way, how's Dana?"

"She's good. If you hear from your mother, have her call me. I need her help in setting up a philanthropic foundation."

"I'll call her and tell her to call you."

"Thanks, Michael."

"No problem, *primo*."

Tyler hung up, his anxiety dissipating quickly. He'd received his credit-card statement with the hotel charges for the Connellys. Writing a check, he paid the charges, his mind working overtime when he realized he had to set up a foundation for medical research in Hillsboro. The nearest county hospital was several miles outside Calico, too far for Hillsboro residents. He'd told the Connellys the foundation was the SCC Foundation for Medical Research—the initials SCC for Samuel Claridge Cole—his grandfather.

Samuel Cole had been a businessman, not a medical practitioner. If Tyler was going to give away his wealth, then maybe the name of the foundation should honor a medical professional.

His forehead furrowed slightly as he scribbled names on a pad that was advertising a new drug. He wrote down his grandfather's name with a money sign next to it. After all, the money he planned to donate he'd inherited following Samuel Cole's death.

The newspaper on a corner of his desk caught his eye. It was the edition of the *Herald* with the column

Dana had written. Reaching for the paper, he flipped pages until he saw her byline. He read the column, smiling. His wife was a very talented journalist. Her portrayal of Dr. Silas Nichols was not only vivid, but also informative.

He picked up the pen and wrote: *Dr. Silas Nichols— SCC Foundation for Medical Research.* As soon as the letters formed themselves, he knew that would become the name of his foundation. Nowhere would anyone connect the C to Cole. One thing he was certain of, and that was that the new medical facility would have a modern neonatal unit.

Tyler pulled Dana closer to his body, pressing a kiss on the nape of her neck. He'd found the back of her neck as sexy as her lush mouth. "Why do you go to your grandmother's house to work on your notes when you can use the library here?"

Dana heard the censure in his voice. "If I worked here, then it wouldn't feel as if I'm working."

"Come again?"

"If I worked here, then I wouldn't get up early. I'd lie in bed, wasting precious time. I'd probably laze around, hang out in the garden, or perhaps even stop and watch the contractors putting in the pool or the ball court. Meanwhile, if I go to my grandmother's on the days I don't go to the *Herald,* at least I know have to get up, shower, and get dressed just like I was going into an office. I'm much more productive over there."

"Have you decided what you're going to do with the property?"

"You know I can't sell until next June."

"You might not be able to sell it, but you can rent it."

She shook her head in the dimly lit bedroom. "No, Tyler. I can't do that."

"Why not?"

Turning over, she tried to make out his features. "I'm not ready to let it go. I used to love going to Grandma's. Everything good from my childhood came from that house."

Tyler kissed her forehead. "You're going to have to let it go sometime."

"I know. But not now."

"How are you coming with your research?"

"Good."

"Just good?"

"Good is good, Tyler."

There was a swollen silence, then his soft drawling voice. "Have you told your editor that you're not coming back?"

"No."

"What are you waiting for?"

"This is only the beginning of August. I have until the end of September before my leave expires."

"Our marriage is not a trial run, Dana."

"I know that, Tyler."

"Then why do I feel as if at the end of September it's going to end?"

His voice was void of emotion, and that bothered Dana more than if he'd barked at her. "I can't help how you feel."

"Do you even care how I feel?"

"Of course I care, Tyler."

"Do you really care?"

"Yes, I do!"

"I don't believe you, Dana!"

She moved away to the edge of the mattress. "It sounds as if you have a personal problem, Dr. Cole." Sitting up, she swung her legs over the side of the bed.

Moving quickly, Tyler snaked an arm around her waist, pulling her back into the middle of the bed. "My problem is I've spoiled you."

Turning, she pounced on him with the speed of a cat. "And you're delusional," she breathed out against his mouth.

He went completely still, staring up at her, her hair falling over her forehead. At that moment she reminded him of a cat. There was enough light coming from a tiny lamp on a table in the sitting room to make out her eyes shining like polished amber.

"I do spoil you, Dana." He brushed his mouth over hers, nibbling on her lower lip. "The only thing I can't do for you is breathe," he crooned deep in his throat.

"You don't spoil me," she retorted, refusing to acknowledge his declaration. "It's I who spoil you. I keep house for you—"

"A house you don't have to clean," he said, cutting her off, "because someone comes in and cleans twice a week."

"I cook your meals."

He nodded. "Granted you do prepare dinner."

"And I warm your bed."

He chuckled. "That you do. Don't forget the garden."

Her face burned when she recalled their passionate encounter in the garden. "Don't forget that I strip for you, too."

"How can I forget your striptease?"

"I did promise to strip for you again, didn't I?"

"Yes, you did. I'm still waiting, Mrs. Cole."

Wrinkling her nose, she kissed the side of his strong neck. "You're going to have to wait a little longer." Tyler groaned in her ear, his teeth catching her lobe and nibbling it.

She longed to tell him what she'd expected for several days. Her period was late—five days late.

Sliding gracefully off her husband's body, she lay on her side, her splayed fingers resting on her flat belly. Although her leave of absence was no longer an issue, she knew carrying a child would impact greatly on her efforts to clear her family's name.

Each legal pad was filled with notes from a corresponding notebook, and the notes she'd gleaned from the notebooks would be entered into a database she'd created to analyze Eugene Payton's observations. She wasn't certain how he'd done it, but the attorney had used a cryptogram, using the alphabet, to record direct testimony. It had taken her two days before she was able to decode his secret language.

It wasn't what was said during the trial as much as what hadn't been said or asked. There were instances during testimony and cross-examination when she found it difficult to differentiate between the prosecutors and her father's defense attorney.

Two names jumped out at her over and over: the defense attorney, Sylvester Wilson, and Peter Gillespie, the medical examiner from the coroner's office.

Tyler's moist breath swept over her shoulders. "Are you feeling okay?"

"Yes."

And she was. She wasn't sick; in fact, she felt wonderful. What she wanted to tell her husband was there was more than a fifty-percent probability he was going to become a father.

Twenty-five

Dana left the house minutes after Tyler, stopping to fill up her car before heading for Jackson, Mississippi. She'd called Sylvester Wilson, identifying herself. He'd hesitated for several seconds, then asked if he could help her. She'd told him that she wanted to talk to him about Harry Nichols's trial. The soft-spoken attorney had agreed to meet with her following morning at ten-thirty. He'd insisted she not be late because he had a lunch meeting with the governor.

She maneuvered into a parking space in the back of a modern two-story brick building. The number of luxury cars in the lot indicated the lawyer either had a very lucrative practice or well-heeled clients.

A legal assistant showed her to an office filled with exquisite reproductions, informing her Mr. Wilson would meet her as soon as he completed a telephone call.

When Sylvester Wilson walked into the small conference room, Dana felt a cold chill race over her before she was given the opportunity to view his face. Extending his hand, he offered her his professional grin, one that usually disarmed people immediately.

She rose slowly from the plush armchair and shook the proffered hand. His glossy dark eyes roamed over her body before settling on her face.

"It's a pleasure to meet you, Miss Nichols. It is Miss

Nichols, isn't it?" he asked, glancing at the rings on her left hand.

"Actually it's Mrs. Dana Cole. I thought if I'd identified myself as Mrs. Cole you wouldn't have granted me an audience so easily."

She studied the face of the man who'd been charged with the responsibility for keeping her father out of jail, for proving him innocent beyond a shadow of a doubt. Sylvester Wilson was medium height, probably five-ten, and slightly built. His custom-made suit was cut to fit his slender body. She estimated him to be in his mid-to-late fifties. His coarse hair was close-cropped and sprinkled with silver. His accessories were impeccable, silk tie, handkerchief, and gold monogrammed cufflinks.

"Please sit down, Dana. May I call you Dana?"

She retook her seat, smiling. "Yes, you may."

Sylvester took a seat opposite her, clasping his hands together on the highly polished surface of the rosewood table. He had to admit that he'd thought Dana Nichols Cole was Alicia Nichols come back to life when he first walked into the room. Her face, hair, body, and voice were the same as the murdered woman. In his family, the girls usually favored their fathers, but with Dana it was the opposite. Dana was Alicia's clone.

"How can I help you?"

Dana decided to be direct. "I've been studying the details of the case you handled on behalf of Harry Nichols, and I have a few questions to ask you."

He waved a manicured hand. "Ask."

"Why did you only call one material witness on my father's behalf? Why did you turn down Eugene Payton's request to be called as a witness? Why wasn't Georgia Sutton asked to testify? And why on earth didn't you permit my father to testify in his own behalf?"

Leaning back on his chair, Sylvester gave Dana a long, penetrating stare. "Mrs. Cole—"

"Dana," she insisted with a cold smile.

"I'm sorry. Dana, what you don't understand was the sentiment at the time. Everyone was calling for Dr. Harry Nichols's head. They were grumbling about how the act was not only heinous, but also cowardice because he'd waited until she was asleep to kill her. A few said it was a crime of passion because he'd blown off her face in a jealous rage. Rumors were circulating that he couldn't stand other men looking at his wife."

She gave the lawyer a narrowed glare. "The gossip was coming from people in Hillsboro. Wasn't the trial held in Greenville?"

He nodded once. "Yes."

"I'm certain most Greenville residents knew nothing about Dr. Harry Nichols or his wife Alicia. Weren't all of the jurors from Greenville?"

"Yes."

"I'm not buying your argument, Mr. Wilson. You did my father great injustice. You accepted his case, knowing you couldn't win it. Your specialty is litigation, not criminal law. In other words, you handed him the rope he needed to hang himself.

"Did you take the case for the money or for the notoriety? Which one was it? Whether my father was found guilty or innocent, you still got your money."

Muscles in his jaw throbbed noticeably under his smooth dark-brown skin. "What are you implying, Mrs. Cole?"

Her eyes darkened with rage. "I'm not implying anything. I telling you outright that you were incompetent."

Sylvester rose gracefully to his feet. "I believe this conversation has come to an end."

Dana stood up. "You're right, Mr. Wilson. My father

might not be alive, but I'm going to reopen his case and if it takes every penny that I have, I'm going to make certain you lose your right to practice law in the State of Mississippi." She offered him a sensual smile. "You can send me a bill for your time."

Turning on her heel, she walked out of the conference room, leaving Sylvester staring at her straight back. He waited several minutes, and then picked up one of several phones on a side table. He dialed a number, drumming his fingers on the table.

"Guess who came to see me," he said when he heard a familiar voice. "Dana Nichols. She says she's now Dana Cole." A feral smile crossed his face. "Ain't that nothing?" he remarked, lapsing into dialect. "Now, ain't she just like her momma. They must have a thing for doctors. She's planning to open her old man's case. Hell, yeah, she can request it. There's no statute of limitation for murder. I suggest you take care of her before she opens a barrel of snakes. The one that escapes just might be poisonous." He held the receiver to his ear, nodding. "I'll ask her if she's willing to do it. If she's anything like her momma, she'll probably say yes. I'll ask her, then get back to you. I know. We don't have much time. "

Without a parting greeting, Sylvester Wilson hung up. Something had told him twenty-two years ago not to accept the Nichols case, but he had needed the money. He'd had an underage pregnant girlfriend at the time who was threatening to tell his wife about their extramarital affair. The grubby little whore didn't want the baby, but money. Money he didn't have. He'd accepted Harry Nichols's fee, given his girlfriend money for an abortion, and a thousand dollars for her to forget she ever knew him.

However, it was years later that he found out that Thelma hadn't had the abortion. She'd taken his money, moved to Chicago, and given birth to a baby girl. One who, she wrote to tell him, looked exactly like him. Thelma lived in Chicago for twenty-two years before she decided to come back to Mississippi.

She came to see him, and he was shocked at how good she still looked. And he had to admit his daughter was quite an eyeful, too. Twana looked like him, but she was her mother's child. Both of them had hustling in the marrow of their bones.

Tyler sat on a stool at the end of the examining table, adjusting a gooseneck lamp. The young woman was a new patient who'd told the social worker her mother had kicked her out of the house because she couldn't keep a job. She was twenty-one, a high school dropout, had just gotten out of an abusive relationship, and Tyler would now have to tell her the results from her latest urine sample—she was pregnant!

"Miss Singleton, please move a little toward me, and relax your knees."

She scooted closer to the edge of the table. Tearing open a prepackaged vaginal speculum, Tyler inserted the instrument, dilating her vaginal canal. He examined her vaginal walls and cervix. His nurse handed him a cotton-tipped applicator, and he gathered a culture for a routine Pap smear. He handed the nurse the applicator and she prepared the slide, which would be sent to an outside lab for testing.

He removed the speculum, applied a lubricating jelly on the examining glove, gently inserting a finger into her vagina. With his other hand, he pressed along the lower portion of her abdomen as Twana moaned softly.

"I'm trying not to hurt you," Tyler said, offering her a comforting smile. "It's almost over." He felt her

ovaries. "One more and we're done, Miss Singleton.
Now I want you to take a deep breath, and then let it
out slowly." Her chest rose and fell under an examining gown at the same time he inserted his middle finger into her rectum and his index finer into her
vagina.

"Do you really have to do that, Dr. Cole?"

"Yes, because I need to get a better feel of the back
wall of your uterus. I can also check for hemorrhoids
and other growths known as polyps." He extracted his
fingers, removing his gloves. "You're done." Rounding
the table, Tyler patted her shoulder. "The nurse will
help you to get dressed, then I'll see you in my office."

He was still entering notes in Twana Singleton's
chart when she walked into his office. She was petite
and very pretty. A soft curling natural hairstyle was flattering to her perfectly rounded face. Her large brown
eyes gave her the appearance of being perpetually surprised. Her attire was totally inappropriate for daytime
wear. A skintight skirt, which showed a lot of thigh,
and an equally tight tank top were better suited for
the clubs many young people favored.

Rising to his feet, he came around his desk. "Please
sit down, Miss Singleton." She took the chair he indicated, crossing her shapely legs.

Tyler sat down opposite Twana, his expression impassive. He'd stopped counting the number of patients
who believed they were flirting with him. The fact that
he now wore a wedding band apparently was not a
deterrent.

"Are you certain you had a period last month, Miss
Singleton?"

Her eyes shifted upward as she appeared deep in
thought. "I think so."

"Are you very sure?"

Her tongue darted out, and she ran it over her lower lip in a seductive gesture. "I think so," she repeated.

"I'm asking you about your period because the results of a urine test indicate you're pregnant."

Twana shook her head. "That can't be true, Dr. Cole."

"Our test detected the presence of HCG, human chorionic gonadotropin, a hormone found in early pregnancy."

Twana leaned forward, displaying her large breasts. "Don't you understand I can't be pregnant, Dr. Cole? I don't want to be pregnant." She jumped up, heading for the door. "I can't talk about this."

Tyler was right behind her as she ran down the corridor toward the exit. He caught up with her in the crowded waiting room. "Miss Singleton, please come back."

Turning, she pointed an airbrushed finger at him, her face contorted in rage. "You stay away from me! I want nothing to do with you!" She spun around on her heel, opened the door, and walked out, slamming the door, so hard the glass rattled.

There was complete silence in the waiting area as all eyes were focused on the tall man with the white lab coat. Tyler looked at his patients, seeing shock and uncertainty in their gazes. It was a full thirty seconds before he turned on his heel and retreated to an examining room.

He saw eight patients that day, but only one stuck in his head—Twana Singleton. He'd had women deny their pregnancies almost up to the time they were ready to deliver. It was apparent Twana would become one of those women.

Twenty-six

Dana couldn't pull her gaze away from the typed report prepared by a medical examiner twenty-two years ago. He listed the cause of death as two bullet fragments lodged in the frontal lobe and one in the neck, which had severed an artery.

One entry in particular got her complete attention. Alicia Nichols was pregnant at the time of her death—estimated gestation period: twelve weeks.

Tyler had guessed correctly. Alicia was pregnant when she was murdered.

Burying her face in her hands, she tried bringing her fragile emotions under control. Harry Nichols's strident voice invaded her thoughts: *How can you still do it now that I have proof?*

Now Dana knew what the proof was. Her father had found out his wife was pregnant—by another man.

If it wasn't Harry's baby she was carrying at the time—then whose was it? She read the report over and over until she'd memorized every typed word.

Lowering her hands, Dana sat on the slider, staring out into nothingness with unseeing eyes. The sun had passed over, indicating it was late afternoon. It was time she went home. And it was also time she told Tyler of her suspicions. Her period was more than ten days late. What surprised her was that Tyler seemed oblivious to her physical condition.

A slight frown appeared between her eyes. They hadn't made love in more a week. She was usually in bed and asleep when he slipped in beside her, and when she woke up the space beside her was empty.

She stood up at the same time the tiny phone in her purse rang. Retrieving it, she answered the call, her heart racing uncontrollably when she heard Tyler's voice.

"Come home, Dana."

"What's the matter, Tyler?"

"Now!" His voice reverberated in her ear.

Her temper exploded. "Don't yell at me!" The words were forced from between her teeth.

He cursed. Words she couldn't understand—violent curses in Spanish.

"Tyler, talk to me—in English!"

"Dana, baby. Please come home."

She nodded even though he couldn't see her. "Okay. I'm on my way."

Her heart was pumping so fast she felt light-headed as she locked up her grandmother's house and walked to her car. Her hands shook, and it took several attempts before she was able to turn the key in the ignition.

It was Thursday, his late night at the clinic. Why was he home? The whys followed her as she tried to stay under the speed limit. The last thing she needed was to be stopped for speeding.

She turned off onto the private road leading to her home. The word slapped at her. *Home.* The large house overlooking the Mississippi was her home, yet she spent more time at her grandmother's house than in her own house. She only stayed when there was a delivery of another piece of furniture; other than that, she stayed away.

She hadn't notified her boss that she wouldn't be

returning to her position at the *Chronicle*, or her land-lady that she would come and clean out her apartment. All of her energies were focused on clearing her family's name. And if she did prove Harry Nichols hadn't murdered her mother, what would it change? It wouldn't bring him or her mother back.

She'd come back to Hillsboro to bury her last sur-viving relative, and had fallen in love with a sexy, pas-sionate, patient man, marrying him within two weeks of their meeting.

Now, she was certain she carried his child beneath her heart—a child who would carry on the bloodlines of generations of Nicholses and Suttons. The spirits of Harry, Alicia, and Georgia were still alive in her and in her baby yet to be born.

Tyler was waiting for her when she pulled into the garage. One look at his face told her something was wrong. She got out of the car, quickening her pace until they were face-to-face. Lines she'd never seen be-fore were etched in his forehead and alongside the length of his thin nose.

"What is it?"

He stared at her for a full minute. "Come in and I'll show you." She followed Tyler into the house and into the library. "Sit down. Please."

She sat on the love seat facing the flat-screen tele-vision mounted on the wall. Her gaze followed his fluid stride as he walked over to his desk and picked up a white business-size envelope. He returned to where she was sitting, handing it to her.

"I found this pushed through the slot in the door after someone called me at the clinic telling me I should go home and pick up a package that should be of great interest to me."

Dana stared at the envelope. There was nothing writ-ten on it. "What's in it?"

Tyler drew his lips back over his teeth. "Open it and find out."

Staring at the envelope, she turned it over and pulled out a single sheet of paper. Her eyes widened when she read the cut-out letters glued haphazardly on the paper: *DOC—TELL YOUR WIFE TO STOP SNOOPING OR YOU WILL END UP LIKE NICHOLS.*

Dana stood up, the paper falling to the floor. "What's going on, Tyler?"

His eyes widened until she could see their raven depths. "You tell me, Mrs. Cole."

Her fingers curled into tight fists, her nails biting into the tender flesh of her palms. "You think I have something to do with that piece of garbage?"

Closing his eyes, Tyler breathed in and out through his mouth, struggling valiantly not to lose his temper. He opened his eyes, staring through her. "I don't know what to think right now. I wanted to show it to you before I call Billy Clark. I wanted to give you the opportunity to open up to me before the law gets involved."

Her mind refused to register the significance of his statement until he picked up the telephone, asking the operator to connect him to the sheriff's office.

Picking up the tiny purse she'd left on a side table, she threw it at his head, missing him by inches, the contents spilling over the floor. "How dare you!" she screamed uncontrollably.

Taking two long strides, Tyler caught her wrists, tightening his grip when she attempted to free herself. "I dare, Dana, because I don't want anything to happen to you."

She tried pounding his chest. "Nothing's going to happen to me."

"Didn't you read it? Really read it? It's not an invitation to a formal dinner party. It's a death threat."

Her brow creased in worry. "Death threat?"

"Yes, baby. It says *you will end up like Nichols.* It's not specifying which Nichols—Harry or Alicia."

Tyler led her back to the love seat, sitting and pulling her down beside him. "I need you to tell me what you've uncovered about your mother and father before Billy gets here."

"Not much."

"You say not much, but someone else probably thinks you're close to uncovering the truth. Which means Harry did not kill your mother, and that the murderer is alive and living in Hillsboro."

"You were right," she began. "My mother was pregnant when she died. She . . ." Her words died on her tongue when the phone rang.

Tyler got up to answer it. The natural color drained from his face, leaving it a sickly yellow under his tan. Dana rose as if in a trance.

"What is it?" she asked as he ended the call.

"Billy says he has a warrant for my arrest. He says one of my patients claims I raped her."

Dana felt the room spinning, but she didn't faint. She refused to faint. Reaching for Tyler's hand, she held it in both of hers.

"No, no, no." She didn't recognize her own voice. She held him until the doorbell rang. It was then she stood up and walked with her husband to the door to meet Billy Clark.

The news of Tyler's arrest had everyone shaking their heads. People stood around in small and large groups, discussing what they believed was the truth: Twana Singleton had come to the clinic late one night, complaining of pains in her abdomen. Even though Dr. Cole said it was after hours, he agreed to see her.

He waited for her to undress, and then he forced himself on her. She only came back a few days ago because she suspected she was pregnant. He pretended he didn't know her because his nurse was present. But then he confirmed that she was pregnant. He told her because he was married she had to get rid of the baby. Twana broke down, crying pitifully because although she'd been raped, she didn't believe in abortion. There were at least five people in the clinic's waiting room who overheard Twana tell Dr. Cole to stay away from her, that she didn't want to have anything to do with him.

Dana longed to tell the ignorant gossipers that Tyler would never agree to see a patient without a nurse present, that he would never rape a woman.

Billy Clark had apologized profusely when he had to read Tyler his rights. But he'd spared him the humiliation of handcuffing him. Dana had called Eugene Payton even before Tyler was in the police cruiser, asking him to represent her husband. Eugene had instructed her to meet him at the Greenville Court, and to make certain she brought her checkbook.

It took less than four hours, but after being arraigned, Tyler was released after Dana posted a fifty-thousand-dollar bond. She'd written a check from the account she'd set up with the proceeds of her inheritance.

Tyler was home, but he hadn't returned to the clinic. The judge had ordered him not to return until after a grand jury heard the charges against him.

She and Tyler were married, living under the same roof, but they could've been strangers. Tyler moved out of the bedroom, preferring instead to sleep in his library. She waited for him to finish in the kitchen before she entered to prepare her own meals. Whenever their gazes met, Dana felt his enmity radiating from the depths of his coal-black eyes.

After three days cooped up in the house, she felt as if she were the one under house arrest. Swinging her legs over the side of the bed, she headed for the lower level. The fish she'd prepared the night before had triggered an uncommon thirst.

Walking into the kitchen, she didn't see Tyler until she heard his sudden intake of breath. He was sitting in the dark in the breakfast room. Rising slowly to his feet, he glared at her. There was something so menacing about him standing there in his bare feet, his chest bare and the three-day stubble darkening his cheeks. A pair of drawstring sweat pants rode low on his narrow hips. It was apparent he'd lost weight.

"When were you going to tell me, Dana?"

She stared at him as if he were a stranger. "What?"

He moved closer, literally stalking her, but she refused to move. Tyler Cole had to know he couldn't intimidate her.

Reaching out, he placed his hand over her belly. She looked at his hand before tilting her chin. "How did you know?"

A half smile lifted one corner of his mouth. "I'm a doctor, and I'm your husband. I happen to know your body." His hand moved up over the lace on her nightgown to cradle a breast—one that was fuller, heavier.

He quickly calculated the last time Dana had had a menstrual flow. "You should give birth before the end of March."

She placed her hands over his. "I wanted to tell you, Tyler, when I realized I hadn't gotten my period, but it was never the right time."

Vertical lines appeared between his eyes. "What do you mean about the right time? Despite what's going on in our lives at this very moment, it is the right time." Closing her eyes, she smiled the most beautiful he'd ever seen.

"I knew if I told you, you probably would've tried to stop me from continuing my project."

"You've got that right."

She opened her eyes. "That's why I didn't tell you."

"You're very close to uncovering the truth, baby. Very, very close, or someone wouldn't be working so hard to destroy my career and my reputation. The only way they can hurt you is through me."

She touched his mouth with her fingertips. Seconds later her mouth replaced her fingers. "I came down here because I want a glass of water," she said.

"Sit down. I'll get it for you."

She moved to chair and sat down at the same time a loud popping sound exploded in the air. One moment she was sitting. Then she sprawled facedown on the floor, Tyler's weight bearing down on her.

"Tyler!"

"Don't move, baby."

"What was that?"

"Someone just shot at us through the window."

"No!"

"Don't panic. I'm going to try to get to the telephone to call the police. I don't want you to move."

She squirmed under him. "Tyler!"

"Don't move!"

"Whoever it is will see you."

"No, they won't. I'm going to crawl into the bathroom."

"What the hell do you want to do that for? There's no phone in the bathroom!"

"Yes, there is. I left one of the cordless in there."

Raising her head slightly, she tried to see his face.

"What were you doing with a telephone in the bathroom?"

"Don't ask, Dana."

She lay motionless while Tyler eased off her body and slithered along the floor in the direction of the bathroom. A small scream escaped her parted lip with the sound of breaking glass.

Dana lost track of time as she lay on the cool tiles. Without warning, the track lights over the sink went dark. "Tyler! Where are you?" She'd whispered, but her voice sounded unusually loud in the stillness.

"I'm here. The police are coming." His hands roved her over body, searching for her hand. "I'm going to get you upstairs where it's safer."

"No, Tyler. I'm not going to leave you here alone."

"I'm going to be all right."

"Don't lie to me."

"I have a gun in the library."

"What are you doing with a gun?"

"I'm going to get it and pop whoever the hell it is that's shooting at us. I'm going to count to three, then I'm going to pick you up and sprint for the staircase."

Dana hesitated. She didn't want to leave Tyler, didn't want him to leave her. But she had to trust him, enough to believe he would protect her, keep her safe. "Okay."

Tyler breathed out a sigh before he began counting. He hadn't expected Dana to cooperate. "One . . . two . . . three."

Gathering her in his arms, he adjusted her weight, and then moved quickly across the kitchen. A barrage of bullets smashed windows, slivers of glass spraying walls and floors like confetti.

Tyler sprinted up the staircase, breathing heavily. It wasn't the added weight of carrying Dana that made it hard for him to catch his breath, but fear. Someone wanted to kill him and Dana. Her probing into a long-ago murder trial had spooked a murderer—someone who had actually gotten away with murder until now.

Billy Clark had sent the pasted-up threat to a crime lab for fingerprints. The result had been negative. Whoever had composed the threat had taken great care to wear gloves. The cut-up letters were from a variety of printed matter: magazines, newspapers, books.

Tyler had had Eugene Payton present the letter to the judge as evidence that someone wanted to threaten, blackmail, or possibly harm Dana or himself. The letter and the fact that he'd never been arrested had become the deciding factors for the judge's decision to set bail.

Tyler made it up the staircase to temporary safety. Dana's labored breathing echoed his as he left her in the landing at the top of the narrow stairs off the sitting room.

"Stay here, baby. I don't want you to come down until I come back for you."

Reaching out for him with trembling hands, Dana sank her nails into the flesh covering his broad shoulders. "You better come back, Tyler. I'm not going to raise this baby without you."

"And you won't," he promised. He gave her a hard kiss, then was gone, melting like a specter into the darkness.

She sat on the floor, the coolness of the wood seeping through the delicate fabric of her nightgown. A light from a full moon poured through the tiny window above her. She'd always loved full moons, but tonight it had become a natural beacon for whoever was firing at her house. The person could see in, while making it impossible for Tyler to see out.

Time and events had reversed themselves. Twenty-two years ago, she lay in her bedroom praying her parents would stop fighting, withdraw their threats, while now she sat on a wood floor, praying that the father of the child in her womb would not forfeit his life to a crazed lunatic who'd murdered before and had no qualms about murdering again.

Pulling her knees to her chest, Dana wondered who it could have been who hated Alicia that much to take her life, the life of the tiny one in her womb, and in the end cause Harry to end his life so tragically. She sat in the same position so long, her legs began to cramp.

What seemed like hours later, when in reality it was only ten minutes later, she heard movement and footsteps below her. Pushing to her feet, she stood, waiting for whatever it was that awaited her.

Pulling her shoulders back, she raised her chin and stared at the space at the top of the stairs. She held her breath, her lungs laboring, until she spied the head of the man who'd captured her heart with a single glance, her black knight.

"Tyler." His name slipped out unbidden as she launched herself against his chest.

Gathering her to his chest, he rubbed her back in a comforting gesture. "It's over, baby. Twenty-two years of deceit, disgrace, and duplicity ended tonight."

Suddenly, the burning need to discover who'd murdered Alicia Sutton no longer mattered as Dana clung to her husband. Clearing her family name no longer mattered. None of it mattered because she was home.

Tyler Simmons Cole was home.

He was the family she needed to sustain her until she was reunited with her ancestors in the next life.

Epilogue

A year later . . .

Dana sat in her garden, her son cradled to her full breasts. Closing her eyes, she smiled, enjoying the pull of his tiny mouth on her flesh as he drank greedily.

The madness and mayhem threatening his life had ended the night his father became aware that he lay beneath her heart. Billy Clark had arrived at the house, along with several law officers from a neighboring town, to find a gunman shooting at the house belonging to Dr. Tyler and Mrs. Dana Cole.

The gunman had surrendered without a struggle. He'd been more than willing to tell who'd hired him to kill the local doctor and his wife. After being read his Miranda rights, the man shocked the law officials when he revealed he'd been hired by Mrs. Ross Wilson, Sr., to kill Dana.

A warrant was sworn out for the arrest of Lucinda Wilson, who on advice of counsel, confessed to a secret she'd harbored for more than thirty years: Her husband, not Harry Nichols, had fathered Dana Alicia Nichols.

Married and the father of a young son, Ross had not been able to resist the flirtatious Alicia Sutton. However, when the beautiful teenager found herself pregnant, Ross turned his back on her. She, needing a father for the child growing rapidly in her womb, turned her attention to Dr. Harry Nichols. Harry, unable to father a child because he'd contracted mumps during puberty, accepted Alicia as his wife and the child she carried as his.

Alicia and Harry's marriage was perfect until Ross decided he wanted Alicia again. His own marriage floundering, when Alicia came to Ross for the second time with the news she was pregnant with his child, Ross asked Lucinda for a divorce.

However, Mrs. Lucinda Wilson refused to give up her status in a town where she'd become a social grande dame. It was Lucinda who'd walked into Harry's house and shot Alicia as she lay sleeping. It was she who'd paid someone to torch Raven's Crest. It was she who'd paid the then-deputy sheriff to hang Harry Nichols in his cell, making it look like a suicide.

Lucinda accepted a plea bargain rather than face the humiliation of a trial. She was sentenced a life sentence in a state prison in a remote part of the state.

Ross Wilson, Sr., was given five years probation for paying an illegitimate niece to accuse Dr. Tyler Cole of rape.

Twana Singleton served six months in a local jail for perjury.

And R.W., Ross Wilson, Jr., abandoned his plan to seek political office. He waited until his mother was transported to prison, then left Hillsboro, declaring passionately he would never return.

Dana had several years before she had to decide whether to tell her son that his grandfather was not Dr. Harry Nichols, but Ross Wilson, Sr.

Running a fingertip over his black curly hair, she smiled at the peaceful expression on her son's face. Martin Diaz Cole II had decided to compromise—he'd

inherited his father's hair color and dimples, and his
mother's brilliant jewel-like golden eyes.

A shadow fell across her, and she glanced up to find
Tyler standing several feet away, smiling. He was close
to completing his second year in his medical study to
lower the infant-mortality rates in Hillsboro. So far, he
hadn't lost a baby.

He'd spent most of his inheritance building a hospital in Hillsboro. The anticipated date for completing
the building of the Dr. Silas Nichols—SCC Hospital
was the end of the year.

The Coles had come through as anonymous donors
when they pledged a hundred million dollars to honor
the memory of Samuel Claridge Cole.

Returning her husband's smile, Dana nodded. "I'm
ready." She and Tyler were going to West Palm Beach,
Florida, to introduce a future patriarch to his family.

This family gathering was to become an exception-
ally joyous occasion because of three new babies. Mi-
chael and Jolene had welcomed a son, Joshua Michael
Kirkland; Silah and Arianna a daughter: Marguerite
Selima Kadir; and then there was their own Martin
Diaz Cole II.

Dana handed Tyler his son, covered her breasts, and
then grasped his free hand as he pulled her to her
feet. Hand in hand, they walked to the car parked in
the driveway, where a driver waited to take them to
the airport.

Dana glanced at the detached guest house, smiling.
The furniture that had been in Georgia Sutton's house
now filled the rooms. Her grandmother's beloved
clock graced the entryway of the main house, chiming
the hour and half hour as it had done for more than
a century. The little house on the dead-end street had
been sold.

Dana hadn't known her return to Hillsboro would

change her life—for the better. She slipped into the backseat of the limousine, holding out her arms for her son. Tyler handed her Martin, slipping in beside her. The driver closed the door, took his seat behind the wheel, and drove away from Nichols Landing.

After the birth of his son Tyler had changed his mind, deciding to name his property. After all, Hillsboro was his home for the present. He knew one day he and Dana would relocate to West Palm Beach, but he hoped that day would not come for a long time—a very, very long time.

Dropping an arm over her shoulders, he lowered his head, kissing her tenderly.

His life was perfect because he'd become his father's son. *I'm going to have a piece of everything I want. Some of it may not work out, but I'm still going to have a piece of it anyway.*

His everything was Dana Alicia Nichols Cole.

Dear Reader:

Tyler and Dana have joined the others in their generation as they continue the legacy of sophisticated men and women who dare risk everything for love.

The final book in the HIDEAWAY Legacy Series will debut June 2003. In RENEGADE, Gabriel Cole, an artist-in-residence at a suburban Boston high school takes one glance at Summer "Renegade" Montgomery and loses his heart and his head to a woman living a double life. Danger and deception threaten a red-hot passion and a future generation of Coles as Gabriel and Summer embark on a race against time to defeat a powerful enemy.

RENEGADE will reunite everyone from HIDEAWAY to HOMECOMING for a family reunion of love that promises forever.

Peace and Blessings,

Rochelle Alers
Post Office Box 690
Freeport, NY 11520-0690
roclers@aol.com

COMING IN DECEMBER 2002 FROM
ARABESQUE ROMANCES

__THROUGH THE STORM
by Leslie Esdaile   1-58314-288-6 $6.99US/$9.99CAN
Journalist Lynette Graves has always had a way with words, but the
sight of Foster Scott Hamilton, Jr., leaves her speechless. After the recent breakup of her marriage—and seeing everything she owned
washed away by a hurricane—romance is the last thing on her mind.
Will fate allow them to create a future of fair weather?

__TRUE DEVOTION
by Kim Louise   1-58314-284-3 $6.99US/$9.99CAN
Marti Allgood is a gifted artist who paints for healing, not profit. But
art collector Kenyon Williams believes Marti may be the next great
African American woman artist—and he means to prove it. As Marti's
career blossoms, so does a romance with Kenyon. Soon, she discov-
ers she is pregnant. But for Kenyon, the news is a painful reminder that
his wealth stems from a shameful family secret . . .

__HAUNTED HEART
by Francine Craft   1-58314-301-7 $5.99US/$7.99CAN
Annice Steele lost the love of her life the day Lucas Jones walked out
and never looked back. Determined to move on, the budding psy-
chologist has accepted a job on scenic Paradise Island, helping
troubled kids. When she arrives, she is stunned to discover that Luke
is now running the school.

__JUST FOR YOU
by Doreen Rainey   1-58314-329-7 $5.99US/$7.99CAN
Alexis Shaw's company, Just For You, plans everything—except weddings. The policy hasn't hurt her any—she's even named
Businesswoman of the Year by *Image Magazine*. To celebrate, Alexis
goes out to dinner with her best friend. All's well, until an admirer
sends over a bottle of champagne—and won't take no for an answer.

More Sizzling Romances From
Gwynne Forster

More Sizzling Romance From
Doris Johnson